Home in a Hundred Places

Also by Sarah Dayan Mueller

Greater than the Still

Home in a Hundred Places

Sarah Dayan Mueller

Cover photo by Wil Stewart on Unsplash

Printed in the United States of America

First Printing, 2021

IBSN: 978-0-578-87029-8

They called him Raymond. I call him dad.

One

Port-au-Prince, Haiti, 1934

They called him Raymond.

The echo of his name found a soft landing in the rustle of banana leaves like it always did. They only ever said it in French, and he never questioned why. The last few letters drifted off into the air as if they had other places to be. He bore the name the way his mother wished he would, like it was his own. They called him Raymond, and even though it was just a nickname, it would always be the way he defined himself to the world.

That day, it was Adele who called for him. He knew her voice by how it traveled like the sound of rain. The only reason she ever called for him was when he was needed inside. The sun started to duck behind the Earth like she was done for the day, and he knew it must have been time for dinner.

He promised Adele and Rose that he would bring home enough mangos and oranges to last the week. The half-empty basket attached to the front of his bicycle suggested otherwise. Albert's basket wasn't full either. The cousins had gotten a late start after school let out, and the other classmates had taken the best fruit.

"Was that your sister?" Albert asked. He scooped up an oversized mango and placed it into his basket.

"It was." Raymond looked towards the trail of her voice.

"Just stay out for ten more minutes," Albert pleaded. "What's another ten minutes?" Charisma traced the edges of his upturned smile and round eyes. Albert would always have an undeniable influence on him.

The ripe surfaces of mangos and oranges poked through blades of grass and downed palms. The off-white plantation shutters of his house stood behind him; the windows were a reminder of home. Adele waited on the porch, beckoning for him to return.

1

Raymond continued to gather all the fruit that could fit in his arms, not because he wanted to ignore his sister but because he wanted to give her something special. His cousin followed suit until they both had enough mangos to last until the next hurricane season.

The recipe for a hurricane is simple; crank up the heat in the Caribbean; make sure the ocean is warm; ensure there is enough moisture in the air to make the clouds thick enough that walls will question their own existence. Then add some wind, some rain, and hope for the best.

The last storm was a strong one. The oceans swirled under the watchful eye of the hurricane. It up-earthed trees from their roots and cracked them in half like matchsticks. In a matter of one day, the storm dumped what seemed like a year's worth of rain onto the roofs of Port-au-Prince homes. It battered and bruised the only island Raymond ever knew, just as it had done every year. It always unnerved his father for more reasons than a seven-year-old boy could understand. It made his mother hold on to the children tightly when the wind whistled by.

Raymond also knew what waited for him once the hurricane ended.

Mangos, oranges, soursops, and lemons rained down from the trees like candy from the sky. Raymond looked forward to the storms, but he never dared to tell his father that. When the eye moved on to the rest of the Caribbean and the sun found its place in the sky once again, Raymond and Albert picked the misplaced fruit from the ground as if they were harvesting pearls.

A stream of beaded sweat ran down Raymond's spine. Even though the sun wasn't at its strongest, it was still hot. There was a different kind of heat in the tropics, but its warmth comforted Raymond. It was a dependable kind of heat, and he breathed in its humidity like it was the only air that could give him life. It melted off the coconut trees and hung low with the weight of a thousand suns. He was born into it in the same way stars are born from midnight. It was home, and even ninety years after he came into this world, Haiti was still the only place that could ever make him feel carefree.

It was hard to find a day when the heat wasn't almost relentless, but it was also hard to find a day that wasn't beautiful. The heat pinched Raymond's skin and deepened his naturally light complexion into an olive tone. His favorite part of the day was the afternoon which he spent just outside of his house. He was far enough away to feel a small sense of independence but still close enough to be in earshot of his mother and sisters.

Only when his basket overflowed with fruit did he decide it was time to head back. He gripped the handlebars and walked his bicycle home. Raymond's palms sweat of childhood adventures. It was the first bicycle he ever owned, the one that taught him to explore. He never truly lost his sense of adventure, even long after Haiti and when his body wouldn't allow it anymore.

Decades later, a tattered photo of him on his bicycle stood framed in his Brooklyn apartment. It was the only photo he had from Haiti, and even though he couldn't remember why mango was his favorite fruit, he still held on tightly to the memories on his bicycle, as if he still had a grip on its handlebars.

"Raymond!" his sister yelled again for him from their front porch. "Raymond!"

A warm gust of island air sifted through the coconut trees. The rustle of the leaves masked the sound of his sister's footsteps moving toward him.

"Mama wants you inside," Adele said as she walked down the steps of the porch. She eyed the basket of fruit, and Raymond immediately knew it had won his older sister's approval.

Raymond plucked the shiniest mango from his basket and handed it to her. "I got this one for you."

Adele smoothed the palm of her hand over the skin of the mango. "Thank you, Raymond."

Raymond's sister looked away, but not before he caught the corners of her smile and a moment of her happiness. All he ever wanted was to make her smile.

"Should I bring in all of this fruit now?" Raymond asked.

"Later," she said. "Mama and Papa want us inside. Leave the fruit where it is."

Raymond hesitated to leave his basket out in the open. His classmates were picking fruit that evening as well, and he worried they'd find his treasures. Adele stretched out her hand, and Raymond took it reluctantly. They would always find a sense of comfort in each other's palms.

3

Their bare feet tap-danced their way up the front steps of the porch, almost in unison. He ran ahead of his older sister to hold open the door for her. Even though their house was in Port-au-Prince, the aromas from within were from Egypt. The kitchen was laced with cumin and licorice-scented anise. Fresh pita bread warmed in the oven, and the sizzling of hot oil promised Raymond the tastes of crunchy *kobeba.*

For the majority of Haiti, dinner that evening meant plates of *griot* or *lambi guisado*, but Raymond and his family were part of the minority on the island. For them, dinner was a celebration with prayers and family, of hope and prosperity. As the sun set in the Caribbean, Raymond's father prepared to recite prayers in Hebrew. It was Rosh Hashanah. The country was predominantly Catholic, but in his Sephardic Jewish home, it was the New Year.

"*Mon chéri,*" his mother said as she snuck a kiss on his forehead when their paths crossed. The walls of their kitchen hadn't seen a fresh coat of paint in more than ten years, and the cupboards were worn, but that never stopped the kitchen from being the heartbeat of the home.

"Yes, Mama."

"Go have a seat at the table." Her voice carried softly and was Raymond's greatest teacher of patience. "All the girls are already there."

"Where is Papa?" Wherever his father was, Raymond always wished to be too.

"He will be there in a moment, *chéri.*"

Raymond found his place at the dinner table, amongst his five sisters. The table was set for the occasion, with plates they only used for Rosh Hashanah and Passover. The silverware sparkled as if they were made from diamonds and the glasses twinkled as if they were made from stars. Raymond's mother spent the last couple of days shining and polishing all the family's most elegant dinnerware, just for that evening.

"Did you find enough mangos?" Sylvia asked. She was the oldest, but age never got in the way of Raymond's lifelong instinct to protect her.

"They were everywhere," Raymond said, unable to hide his excitement.

"Do you have your yarmulke?" Rose asked. Her voice was always gentle, even when the world proved itself to be the opposite.

Raymond looked between the place settings and behind a decanter of wine for the yarmulke but came up empty-handed.

"I have it here." Raymond's father walked to the head of the table and gave the traditional head covering to his son.

"Thank you, Papa," Raymond said. He placed the midnight blue, velvet yarmulke on his head and waited for his father to begin the prayers.

Raymond's father covered his thick head of hair with his own yarmulke and pulled out a wooden chair from underneath their dining table. The walnut table was in the house when they moved in. He considered it theirs but never thought about where it came from.

If the kitchen was the heart of the house, the dining table was its steady beat. It was at the walnut table where Raymond spoke with his sisters in French and Creole and picked up a few words of Arabic from his mother. It was where Raymond and his sisters finished their homework and made artwork. It was the epicenter of his childhood, where the worries of the world couldn't penetrate.

Raymond's father often invited colleagues from his textile business to their house, and they always congregated at the dining table for strong Turkish coffee and homemade baklava. All of them were originally from the Middle East, one way or another, and each bite reminded them of that.

Raymond's father placed his weathered elbows on the walnut wood and leaned towards all the people in his life for whom he was ultimately responsible.

"Let's begin," his father said.

Raymond's father lit candles right before the sun fully set, marking the beginning of the Jewish New Year. His sisters' chatter fell to a hushed silence as their father recited prayers in Hebrew. The prayers wished for abundance and happiness, along with a sweet new year to come. Raymond was learning to speak and read Hebrew himself. One day, it would be his responsibility to lead the prayers of the Jewish high holidays. But he was still nearly fifty years from truly understanding what it meant to be a father at the head of his own family.

When the prayers were finished, they ate. Raymond and his family dipped apples in honey. They ate sticky dates and ruby pomegranate seeds, all for a sweet new year. Raymond didn't always understand the symbolism in the traditions but still looked forward to licking the sugars off his fingers.

The main course was Egyptian and was accompanied by conversations in Creole. The Middle Eastern dishes were garnished with herbs grown in the Caribbean. The family was a world away from where they originated from but found ways to carve their own identity in a land that wasn't their own. It was all Raymond ever knew. He was as much Egyptian as he was Haitian, even though, in the long run, neither country would ever recognize him as one of their own.

Raymond's parents didn't always live in Haiti. They had a life in New York City, in a Brooklyn neighborhood full of other Sephardic Jews. They had a community and a sense of belonging, but Raymond's father also had an opportunity he couldn't pass up. He had the chance to become an importing merchant in a textile business. That business just happened to be in Haiti.

He wasn't the only Egyptian Jew from New York who had the same idea. A few hundred people from their community, mostly Egyptians, Syrians, and Lebanese, plucked their families from their New York homes and traveled south by boat until they reached Port-au-Prince. Their community was small, but it was tight-knit and found its way into the history of Haiti's minorities.

Business was good for years. They weren't rich, but they lived comfortably. Raymond attended a good school, and his sisters wore well-made dresses. Their bellies were always full. Raymond never questioned what life had been like for his parents in New York because Haiti was home.

They ate sweets to commemorate the beginning of a prosperous New Year, but the prosperity wasn't in Haiti anymore. It wasn't what his father had set out to accomplish. It wasn't what he had in mind more than ten years prior.

The evening was supposed to be a celebration, and for the most part, it was. Raymond's sisters chatted about school and their friends. His older sisters checked in to make sure he had found enough fruit for all of them. They teased him for always wandering off on his bicycle. They found it to be a childish thing to do, but Raymond found independence in it.

Raymond's father indicated the meal was at an end when he placed his silverware on his plate and leaned back in his chair. Raymond's mother hushed all the girls. She already knew what was about to happen.

"Girls, a minute, please," Raymond's father said. He took a handkerchief out of his pocket and dabbed the corners of his mouth. When Raymond got older, he'd always have a handkerchief in his pocket too. "Raymond," he said, reaching for his son's hand and giving it a squeeze.

All eyes were on his father, as his stern voice always commanded the room.

"We will be moving on to our next adventure," Raymond's father said as if it was a game they would all enjoy together.

"Our next adventure?" Rachel asked.

"Yes, *Rohey*," he answered in Arabic. The nickname meant "my soul," and he used it to describe all his children.

"We will be moving back to Egypt," he said with finality.

"To Egypt?" Olga asked in a hurry. She was the youngest and didn't know what Egypt was.

"Why aren't we moving back to New York?" Sylvia asked. She was the only one of the siblings that had been born in New York. Even though she didn't remember anything of the city, she always considered it where she belonged.

"It's not polite to question your father like that," Raymond's mother said. She passed a plate of baklava and honeyed cookies to the opposite end of the table, hoping that desserts would quiet everyone. For her, food was always a cure.

Raymond's father sat at the head of the table. His stern eyes and sharp nose stopped Raymond from asking any of his own questions. It was clear that his father had decided for the family, and there was nothing else to it. None of them knew that underneath the table, his father fidgeted with his handkerchief.

There had been too many hurricanes on the island, and one in particular, had destroyed the warehouse. The booming textile business was dwindling, and other Sephardic families in the area were moving on. The Mizharis were moving to New York. The Ades were moving to Colombia, and the Chaloms were moving to Panama.

"Are cousin Albert and Uncle Nissim moving too?" Raymond asked.

"Yes, Uncle Nissim's family is also moving," his father said.

"To Egypt? With us?" Raymond couldn't imagine a life without his cousin Albert.

"No, *chéri*," Raymond's mother was about to give him the worst news a seven-year-old boy could hear. "They are moving to Brooklyn, New York."

"I won't see Albert anymore?" Raymond asked. In his young mind, that wasn't a viable option.

"Not for now," Raymond's mother explained. "But you can write to each other as much as you want, even send each other little presents for birthdays."

"Why can't we go to New York with them?" Sylvia asked, desperation in her voice. "That's where we all lived before we moved here. Why can't we go back?"

"That's enough, *Rohey*," Raymond's mother said.

"Why can't we stay?" Rose asked.

It wasn't in the cards for the Blancos. Only a handful of families in their Sephardic community decided to stay. Nearly a century later, those who stayed had become the wealthiest families in all of Haiti.

After the initial shock wore off, the family settled back into their desserts. Raymond's mother did everything she could to keep the hysteria down, and his father did everything he could to encourage excitement for the move.

"Wait until you see the marketplaces," his father said, directing his attention to his eldest daughters. "They wind through Cairo and are full of dress shops. You can buy sweets and taste all the spices."

The idea of eating Egyptian sweets while browsing for dresses seemed to appeal to Raymond's sisters.

"And Raymond, we are going to get a motorcycle, and we are going to ride out into the desert together to see the pyramids," his father promised.

"A motorcycle? You know how to drive a motorcycle?" Raymond asked in disbelief. He had never seen his father on one before.

"Of course I do." Raymond's father's tone was absolute. "That's all I ever rode when I was growing up in Cairo."

"And you'll let me ride on the back?"

"Yes, just the two of us."

Raymond's smile was genuine enough to momentarily forget that he'd soon have to leave his childhood home.

"And when we're not going to the pyramids, we are going to play football. You're going to become one of the great football stars of Egypt."

Raymond's father was trying to keep it together for as long as he could. His stern voice hid his anxiety, but he was more scared of the move than all his children combined.

When the plates were empty, and their appetites were full, Raymond stood up from the dinner table and left his mother and sisters to clean up. He slowly found his way back to his bicycle in front of their house. His basket was still full of all the fruit he had picked. He breathed a sigh of relief that turned into a gasp of regret when he realized that he'd never have the chance to do it again.

Raymond wasn't sure if he was ready to move to Egypt. Haiti was the only home he'd ever known. It was the island that brought him into the world and watched over him throughout his early childhood. He learned to walk underneath the coconut trees and in the shaded afternoons was where he learned to talk.

He'd heard a lot about Egypt before, mostly from Albert. His cousin always spoke of how much he wanted to visit one day. Raymond found it unfair that the one person who would have loved moving to Cairo was moving to New York. Raymond wondered if they'd see each other again once they left Haiti behind.

As if he knew, Albert arrived to find Raymond sitting on the front steps. It was evident by the solemn look on Albert's face that his father had just told him the news of their upcoming move too.

"No one touched your basket," Albert said as he sat down beside Raymond.

"It would have been cruel if they did," Raymond said.

Albert bent down and picked a handful of grass. He twirled and twisted the blades in between his fingers and tried hard not to acknowledge their families' decisions.

"You're going to New York," Raymond said, his tone definitive. He didn't know any other way to start the conversation he didn't want to have.

"I don't understand why we can't go to Egypt with you," Albert said as he threw the fistful of grass into the air in front of him.

"And I don't understand why we can't go to New York with you," Raymond said.

"Our fathers must have their reasons." Albert surrendered to the idea that neither he nor Raymond had any control over it.

"One day, you will have to visit us in Egypt." Raymond's voice switched from despair to hope and promise. This pure optimism fueled his willpower and determination throughout his whole life.

Albert's smile was made brighter by the moon's shine. They both craned their necks towards the darkened sky. It was clear in a way that only came after hurricanes; the stars shined with all their might.

"If we are ever separated, I hope to find you again one day, underneath a sky full of stars. *Inshallah*," Albert said. God willing.

"*Inshallah*," Raymond said in agreement.

Raymond grabbed the biggest mango he could find in his basket and cut it open with his hands. Even though he was full from dinner, none of the New Year's sweets could compare to Haiti's fresh fruit. Fireflies lit up like loosely falling embers in the sky. Crickets hushed the day until it turned to full night. He sat on the steps of their front porch and already missed Haiti before he even left.

There was a different plan for Raymond. At the end of the day, he'd always considered himself American. If anyone were to ask, he was a New Yorker. It might have started in Port-de-Paix, Nord-Ouest, where his first cries broke through the clouds, and his father finally had a son, but it would ultimately be New York where he'd become a father himself. It was on the small Caribbean island of Haiti where Raymond learned how to crawl, but it would be in Brooklyn where he'd learn how to walk with his heart leading the way.

Haiti would always raise questions. It would forever be on his birth certificate and passports. When he traveled to places like London and Tokyo, and Hong Kong, it would always seem strange to others that a white Jewish man was somehow born in Haiti. His birthplace would sometimes raise more questions than answers, and it would always be the country that gave his words an accent.

When he found himself in a hospital bed in Brooklyn, New York, the Haitian nurses considered him their favorite nearly seventy years later.

"*Kijan ou ye?*" he asked them how they were as if he wasn't the one who needed to be taken care of. They spoke in their shared native language as if none of them had ever left the shores of Port-au-Prince. He became the talk of the third floor, the white man who spoke Creole.

But for Raymond, Haiti would always taste of fallen mangos after the storms came. It would always feel like bicycle rides at dusk and tropical heat that lined his spine's curve. It would mean being one of the only white boys in class and one of only a few hundred Jews on the island who learned how to read Hebrew from the Torah. It never struck him that his differences were about to make an identity no one else could claim.

The Haiti he knew was gone, and the Haiti he remembered followed down the same path. His childhood had to end sometime, and underneath a sky full of stars, with a ripe mango in the palm of his hand, that part of his life slowly hid behind the crescent moon.

Haiti was never meant to be forever.

That evening of Rosh Hashanah was a quiet one, the way it always was after a hurricane left. The heat dropped, and a steady trade wind breeze brushed up behind Raymond's ears. The juice of the mango dripped onto his knees, and the sugar never tasted as sweet. Haiti held her hand out for Raymond to hold. Her hand was resilient, and even when he needed to move on to somewhere new, something about the island would always keep him coming back.

They sat hand in hand, always one with the other, no matter how hard each other tried to escape. Resilience made up the backbone of the country and breathed life into everyone who called her home. Resilience made their houses stand underneath a year's worth of rain and made candy fall from the sky after every storm. It was resilience and love, above anything else, that would be a driving force in all Raymond did in his life.

He just didn't know it yet.

Two

Cairo, Egypt, 1939

"If Joseph is there today, ask him for some of the softer pitas. Make sure they are warm if they have them," Raymond's mother said. They stood opposite each other in what felt like the epicenter of Cairo. The bazaar almost didn't have a beginning or an end, but just a middle point where all of Egypt seemed to gather. "Tell him that your mother, Molly, wants some."

"Ok," Raymond said. "Do you want anything else?"

"Nothing else." She opened her purse and gave him money for the bread. She slipped him a little bit extra.

"What is this for?" Raymond asked.

"For you, *Rohey*." He loved when she used the nickname. "Pick up some chocolates for yourself, if you want."

The extra coins in Raymond's hand were about to unlock the sweet tastes of the market.

"When you're done, come meet us at the butcher," she continued. "We'll wait for you there."

Raymond nodded and went his separate way through the marketplace. It only took a single moment for his mother and Adele to disappear within the throngs of people at the bazaar. There was something reassuring about being surrounded by others; he was never truly alone.

Sunday mornings often meant winding walks through the Cairo markets. His mother sought out the freshest ingredients for her home-cooked meals and always brought one of Raymond's sisters with her to buy them. She wanted to teach her daughters how to cook traditional Egyptian food, which always started with finding the right ingredients. His mother wanted the girls to understand how preparing a meal for the family was an expression of love.

Raymond's mother made cooking seem effortless and only ever measured the ingredients in her recipes by memorization.

The only time Raymond ever went into the kitchen was when it was time to eat. It wasn't his role to help prepare a meal or to learn a family recipe. When life in Egypt was a thing of the past, he never picked it up either. As a bachelor, he had enough money to dine out often, and as a married man, he had a wife who loved to cook. He was very traditional in his ways and married a woman who was equally traditional in her own. Raymond never had to cook more than a fried egg most of his life, and like his mother's traditions, some things never changed.

He was needed in the markets never-the-less, even if he could never distinguish between cumin and cardamom. As the only boy in the family, Raymond's mother utilized his growing strength to help her carry their food from the market to their home in Heliopolis. While his mother and sister wandered the narrow passageways looking for all the ingredients they needed, Raymond's eyes wandered through all the stalls.

The bazaar was in some ways precisely what his father had described, but in other ways, almost muted compared to its reality. Stalls were packed to the roof with burlap bags of spices. Raymond couldn't tell the difference between the sacks of coriander, ground ginger, or aniseed, but these types of spices in the air made him feel at home. Baskets of dried apricots and sugary dates lined stalls throughout the bazaar, and each merchant swore theirs was the best. Raymond hadn't tried them all yet but had all intentions of doing so.

Rich coffee beans sat by the thousands in almost-overflowing coffee sacks. Raymond wanted to run his hand through the beans to feel every smooth surface. Loose tea leaves were sold by weight; the traditional flavors of mint and hibiscus were some of his sisters' favorites. If the stall's owner was in a good mood, Raymond was sometimes given a sample of the mint tea while running errands for his mother.

After five years, Raymond knew the marketplace by heart. He approached the Egyptian bakery, and the idea of fresh, chewy pita on his tongue made his mouth water. He hadn't realized how hungry he was until he stood before the bakery. A row of puffed pitas were brought out of the oven.

Joseph, the family's favored baker, was working at the bakery that day, and Raymond knew his mother would be pleased. He asked for some of the pieces of bread that just came out of the oven, and Joseph happily obliged. When Raymond had a bag full of warm pita in his hands, he ripped off a piece and ate the warm bread as he continued his way through the bazaar. There were very few things in life that tasted as good to him as fresh pita bread, even when he couldn't remember why.

He left the bakery for the chocolate shop. Raymond's father disapproved of him eating too many sweets, especially since he'd taken up football with some of his classmates. Raymond always insisted that he'd burn off the sweets when he ran for the ball, but his father wanted him to stay as healthy as possible for the sport. Sometimes it felt as if his father was living the game directly through his son, and Raymond was ok with that. The last thing Raymond wanted to do was disappoint him. Instead, he curtailed his dessert intake and limited it mostly to times when his father wasn't looking.

But when his mother slipped him a few extra coins to spend at the chocolate shop, Raymond had a hard time refusing. It was their little secret, and although it didn't happen often, it made the chocolates that much sweeter when it did.

Raymond liked to try new chocolates whenever he had a chance. At the stall, there were chocolate truffles made with cardamom and others with the refreshing flavor of mint. Raymond spotted a few pieces of chocolate-covered orange slices, something he never had before. He asked for a small portion of them, and the chocolate shop owner slipped a few in a small, translucent bag.

Raymond bit into one piece before even leaving the stall and was pleasantly surprised with the flavors of citrus mixed with the richness of the chocolate. It was a flavor combination that he'd love for the rest of his life, and his daughter would always buy him some on his birthday.

Raymond slipped into the middle of the crowds and walked towards the butcher to find his mother and sister. The narrow walkways were just enough to herd people from one stall to another. It was as if they were all swimming upstream to another destination. Raymond snacked on another piece of chocolate-covered orange as he walked until he only had one piece left. He tucked it back inside the translucent bag and saved it for Adele. It was always nice to get a little special reward for helping his mother out with the shopping, but it was slightly more rewarding when he could share it with his sister.

Raymond never minded going with his mother and sisters to the marketplaces. They were more than fascinating to him. He had heard of the bazaars in stories but always thought his parents were exaggerating. The buzz and excitement of a Cairo bazaar was something he'd never find anywhere else in the world, even after he traveled through most of it later in his life.

"Was Joseph there today?" Raymond's mother asked as he approached her near the butcher.

"He was," Raymond said. He held up the bag of pita. "He sends his regards."

"That's good," Raymond's mother said.

"What did you get from the chocolate shop?" Adele asked curiously. Raymond knew she was probably only asking because she wanted a piece of whatever he had.

Raymond lifted the small bag of his chocolate-covered oranges and offered her the last piece without words. Adele's smile lit up like the sunrise when she picked it out of the bag. He'd do anything to see any of his sisters' smiles.

Raymond's mother gave him some of the heavier bags to hold, which marked the end of their shopping. She began to usher her children towards the exit of the marketplace, which was sometimes hard to distinguish. While the inside of the bazaar was noticeably darker with all the stalls covered with makeshift ceilings, sunlight tended to pour in at the corners of the market where the exit stood.

They walked out onto the streets of the Heliopolis neighborhood and made their way back home. When they got home, Raymond placed the shopping bags on the kitchen table and left the cooking to his mother and sisters. Raymond wasn't exactly sure what his mother would make for dinner that evening, but he guessed it was kebab with rice, based on everything they bought at the market.

"Raymond! Raymond! Come quick! I need your help!" Sylvia screamed from the living room.

Raymond quickly dropped the last of the bags on the kitchen table and rushed towards his screaming sister.

"I think it went inside the closet!" she screamed. She stood behind her younger brother for protection as her eyes were glued on the closet.

"What did?" Raymond asked.

"Another scorpion!" she answered, still not toning down her pitch.

Without hesitation, Raymond opened the closet and did a quick canvas of the floor. Stuck in a corner was a small scorpion trying to climb into a shoe. Raymond quickly picked up the shoe by the opposite end and brought it outside the front door. He let the scorpion find its way out of the shoe and into the dirt, where it belonged.

When it came down to it, scorpion poison was nothing without a sting.

Raymond learned that the hard way. His father told him about the endless bazaars and the never-ending desert, but he never told him that there would sometimes be scorpions in the house. He found them occasionally in the bathroom, sometimes crawling up the bare-boned tiles in the shower or near the faucet. He learned that they liked the moisture in the bathroom, so he tried to keep it dry. One evening, he had found one trying to bury itself into a bag of rice. He had lost his appetite for dinner that evening but moved the bag from the floor so it would never find a home there again.

The scorpions preferred to hide in the dry dirt in front of the house, but a few always managed to make it inside. His sisters were terrified of them, especially at night, when they were most active. He made sure his sisters' shoes weren't out in the open, so the scorpions couldn't crawl in while everyone was asleep.

"Sylvia, make sure you put your shoes in the bedroom closet," Raymond reminded his sister. Out of his five sisters, scorpions found her shoes the most.

"Can you do it for me, just this one time?" she asked. After all the commotion simmered down, Sylvia found her way to the kitchen to help their mother cook. Egyptian sweets were being prepared in the kitchen, and their mother had almond-flavored dough all over her hands.

"Just this once," Raymond said. He would never say no to her or any of his other sisters for as long as they lived.

It wasn't the first time he'd put her shoes away or reminded the others to do the same, and it wasn't the last. When he realized that cats made for good pest control, he domesticated one so his sisters wouldn't be afraid of finding scorpions everywhere. Being his sisters' protector was one of his earliest purposes in life, and it was something he'd carry with him forever.

There hadn't been scorpions like that in Haiti. Like almost everything in his newly adopted home, it all took some getting used to. Even a few years after leaving Haiti, Raymond still thought about it from time to time. The lungs of Egypt breathed differently. Cairo's backyard was what seemed like an eternal desert, the dry heat of the Middle East rose through his nostrils, and the warmth never left. Olive trees replaced Haiti's banana leaves, and the Caribbean Sea was replaced by the Nile River. Sandstorms overshadowed hurricanes. It always took him a while to get all the sand out of his ears after one had departed.

There was undeniable grit to Cairo, but there was also something magical about it. The raw combination of it all covered the city in layers. Raymond felt like it was up to him to blow the dust off its surface to reveal an Egypt of the past, along with an Egypt of his future. It didn't take long for Raymond to feel grounded in a land he'd never stepped foot in before. Haiti would always be where Raymond was born, but Egypt was the place where he'd been for generations.

He picked up on the culture's ins and outs as he openly embraced it as his own. He also learned Arabic rather quickly, especially for it being such a different language than he was used to. The intonations of his voice and the harshness of its words came almost naturally. Arabic was coarse and heavy compared to Creole, but it glided off Raymond's tongue with ease. He only knew a few Arabic words before moving to Egypt, but it was Cairo's streets that taught him the language of his father and all the fathers before him.

Creole was quietly replaced almost entirely by Arabic in their household, but even though he and his family spoke it less often, it never truly left them. French always stayed by their side because it remained the dominant language taught in school. It was the only part of Haiti that followed Raymond to Egypt, and he was thankful to have it as a reminder of his treasured first home.

Dinner that evening was full of chicken kebabs, rice, and pita dipped in fresh hummus. Raymond left the table full. As he was about to go into his room, his father asked him to join him near the radio, as he did most evenings. Raymond felt grown-up whenever his father asked him to join. It was as if he was getting an invitation to an exclusive party only meant for adults.

Raymond's father made it a routine to catch up on the evening's news after dinner as if he needed the news to help his food settle. The radio was always the main source of information for the family, and it was their lifeline to the world outside of Egypt.

The radio was in Arabic, and Raymond's father insisted that listening would help his son perfect the language. His Arabic had become almost fluent at that point, but there were times that Raymond had to listen closely so he wouldn't miss some of the words. But for his father, Arabic came back to him naturally, because in reality, it never really left.

"Turn the radio on for me, Raymond," his father said as he poured himself a strong cup of Turkish coffee. "I will be there in a moment."

Raymond walked over to the lone radio in the house and turned it on to his father's news program. A radio broadcaster was in the middle of a heated sentence, and it took a moment for Raymond to understand that the topic of the evening was Germany.

"What's the news for tonight?" Raymond's father settled into his worn-out leather chair in the living room and took a sip of coffee.

"I didn't catch everything yet, but for some reason, they are talking about Germany."

Raymond's father's eyes turned to stone. Raymond noticed a shift in his posture almost immediately as if his father were preparing to bear the weight of a tragedy yet to come. Unease crept into Raymond's throat.

Raymond knew not to ask questions and kept silent as his father listened intently to the news. Hitler's Germany had gained massive traction in Europe. They had just invaded Poland, and it seemed like it was just the beginning. France and Great Britain formally declared war against Germany.

Raymond's father rested his cup of coffee on a side table. He took out his handkerchief from his pocket and wiped his mouth.

"They declared war?" Raymond asked.

"Yes, it seems so," his father answered.

"Why are the Germans doing this?" Raymond asked.

His father's protruding stomach rose and fell with a big heave of breath. "Because Hitler's brainwashing is working."

World War II was the first war Raymond would live through. Egypt somehow felt disconnected from the rest of the world as cities and countries were bombed and invaded. Listening to the radio that evening with his father was, in a sense, the first time he ever felt like an adult, and he wasn't sure if he was ready for it.

"Enough of this," Raymond's father said abruptly as he turned off the radio. Raymond wasn't sure if he was shielding his son from the news or if he was shielding himself. "Go to sleep early tonight, *Rohey*. We have something to do early in the morning tomorrow."

Raymond's ears perked up.

His father's stone-cold façade chipped away, for just a moment, to reveal the smallest of smiles.

"What do we have to do tomorrow?" Raymond asked.

"No details for now, just go to bed."

Needless to say, sleep was the last thing Raymond wanted to do. Cairo's streets turned dark with midnight, and Raymond lay in bed, anticipating what the next morning could possibly bring. His father hadn't given him any clues, leaving Raymond to think that maybe he'd need help fixing something around the house. Even though he could hardly contain his curiosity, thoughts of the war also stuck in the back of his mind. Raymond willed himself to fall asleep for a few hours as World War II raged on the other side of the world.

Night turned to day in an instant. A deep roar of an engine seemed to shake the house, startling Raymond awake. He jumped out of bed and looked out the window; a small part of him already knew what was waiting. When he couldn't see it from the window, he ran outside to see it for himself.

Raymond's father sat on a motorcycle, the corner of his mouth ticked upwards in a shy smile.

"*Yalla*, go get dressed," he urged.

Within minutes, Raymond sat behind his father on the motorcycle and held on to his waist as they sped through Cairo's streets. Raymond didn't ask where they were going, and his father didn't tell him either. Both knew what was in store for that Sunday morning, and it was located in Giza.

The silent sun rose above Cairo's densely packed buildings and cradled the Sahara Desert in its warmth. The concrete pavement of Cairo turned into sprawling stretches of untouched sand. It didn't take long for them to get to Giza, but Raymond felt a world away. And when they arrived, it all made sense.

Raymond finally understood why his father decided to move their family to Egypt instead of New York. Raymond bent down and scooped up a handful of sand. Its heat permeated through his skin and seemed to torch the veins in his body. His family came from this land, and moving to Egypt allowed him to see that. It wasn't just a country they happened upon, and it wasn't just a city they found a house in. Egypt was where life for them began, even before he was born.

Raymond and his father parked the motorcycle in a secure spot and started walking towards the pyramids. Thin streams of sunlight fell between his father's eyes as he led the way. He had finally come back to where he was supposed to be.

"We weren't really sure if we'd ever come back here, Raymond." His father placed his heavy hand on the top of Raymond's shoulders and gave it a firm squeeze.

"We?"

"Your mother and I."

Raymond waited for his father to continue.

"The last time we visited the pyramids was one week before we left Egypt. We thought we were leaving Egypt for good, for New York. No one could have ever predicted that we'd be back here."

"Is that a bad thing? That we're back here?" Raymond asked.

"Not at all, *Rohey*. Not for a minute."

They stood before the great wonder of the world, and Raymond wondered if the tips of the pyramids touched the clouds.

"We thought we'd make a home in New York, as there were other families in our neighborhood that were moving there. There was so much promise when we made a home there, but it didn't last. It's because our home has always been here."

Raymond stood quietly, waiting for his father to say more.

"Raymond, try to make homes in other places."

"What do you mean?"

"I mean, test things out. Go explore when you're old enough. Find out where you truly feel comfortable, what place really makes you happy."

Raymond nodded in agreement, even though it would still be years before he truly understood what his father meant.

"And if it happens to be here, in Cairo, so be it. But maybe it'll be somewhere else, and maybe that somewhere else will be all you ever hoped for. But promise me, you'll go find it."

Raymond promised his father, without saying another word.

He kept that promise his whole life. He searched for that place to call home, until he eventually found it. Being home was a feeling, more than a memory, especially when his memories faded with age.

"My father used to bring me here once a month," Raymond's father said. "We'd wake up as the sun was rising and make our way here before the heat got too unbearable."

"I'd love to do that."

Raymond's father squeezed his shoulders one more time, in agreement.

Raymond grew up on the back of that motorcycle en route to Giza. Every first Sunday of the month meant time away from modern Cairo's routine for the history of Egypt. It was where he felt closest with his father, in both proximity and spirit.

They talked about school and how Raymond wanted to be the first person in his family to attend college. His father was proud of his responsible nature. Their monthly visits to the pyramids were where his father always reminded him of the importance of caring for his family. It was where their motorcycle broke down in the middle of the desert, and they hitched a ride back to the city. The ins and outs of their relationship were learned and tested on their monthly trips. Raymond never wanted to forget it.

Those monthly trips to Giza were the more prominent memories Raymond held of his father until his memories started to disappear. Even though he wasn't always able to remember the details and the words that were spoken, the shared experiences and all the lessons his father taught him were woven into the person Raymond became.

They always made it home in time for lunch; a spread of homemade Egyptian food was guaranteed. Those monthly trips to

Giza filled Raymond's mind with ambition. Once a month after lunch, Raymond wrote a letter to Albert, a world away in New York City.

Raymond told Albert about the pyramids and how each of their points seemed to pierce the sun. He wrote about school and football. He was getting good at the sport, and his father was proud of him for it. Raymond tried to describe the winding bazaars of Cairo and the hookah cafés on the street. He hoped that when they were old enough, Albert could experience it for himself. He promised to find the best shisha in Cairo for his cousin's visit.

Albert wrote back almost immediately. He asked Raymond if he'd become fluent in Arabic, and Raymond sent a small vile of Saharan sand to New York, so Albert could touch the desert for himself. Their correspondence became frequent. They sometimes reminisced on Haiti's hurricane season, but that was a time and a place so far distant from where they each lived.

Albert promised to take Raymond to Coney Island if he ever had the chance to visit New York. He wanted him to see the boardwalk and taste a hot dog from Nathan's. Albert started sending him magazine clippings of places he went and places he wanted to go. He told Raymond about the magazines he read at home and how he decided that he wanted to write magazine articles one day.

He sent a clipping of Coney Island and a folded map of the subway. Albert explained how he'd ride the train with Uncle Nissim from the heart of Times Square to the edge of the Atlantic Ocean. The oceans of Brooklyn weren't the same as in the Caribbean, Albert said. But for Raymond, there were no oceans anymore. Only deserts.

Writing to Albert was the only thing that remained the same while the rest of their worlds changed. Raymond always looked forward to writing his next letter to his cousin, but more than anything, he anticipated what Albert would send in return. They swapped little trinkets and mementos of their childhood and adolescence from two very different countries, but each envelope always held the same sentiments of their unconditional bond.

In between all the letters back and forth between Albert, World War II stretched on for weeks and months. Almost every evening, Raymond listened to the news with his father on the radio. Raymond looked forward to every first Sunday of the month, not just for the time spent with his father but also to watch time stand still, away from the looming war.

One Sunday in 1940 was different.

It wasn't like his father to have guests over on a Sunday morning. This particular day, Raymond's father had a few of his colleagues, all Jewish men, huddled around the radio in the living room. Raymond knew not to disturb them but wanted to know if they'd still be taking their trip out to Giza.

One of his father's colleagues put his hand to his head and spoke words of dismay in Arabic. Another put down his Turkish coffee and ran his fingers through his hair in disbelief. Raymond's father fiddled with his handkerchief. None of them took their eyes off the radio as if they watched the words of their future come to life.

Italian Libya attacked Egypt in hopes of controlling the Suez Canal. It was the first time Egypt was brought into the war, and the uncertainty of the Jews' safety was felt throughout their tight-knit Sephardic community.

There was an unmistakable tension in the air, not between his father and his colleagues, but between them and what seemed like the rest of Egypt. They were all Jews, but most of Egypt wasn't. They were at risk and didn't know what to do next.

Raymond stayed out of their way. His father and his colleagues drank their morning coffee in the living room. The radio had been moved to the center of the room, the wire stretching as far as it could. They listened to the news as if the broadcaster were the only person in the world who could determine their fate. Raymond had never seen such looks of worry; the strongest man he knew seemed lost in his own home.

His father's colleagues left an hour later, but the air of uncertainty never did.

Raymond's father bid his goodbyes to his friends and closed the front door. He leaned his back against the wall, and the collective pain of their community pushed down on his shoulders. Raymond met his father's eyes and, for the first time in his life, saw what it meant to be unsure.

The front door opened again. A white mezuzah hung on its outer frame. Raymond's father took it down without any shared words and replaced it on the inside of the doorway. No one in Cairo was to know that a Jewish family lived there.

"Come with me, *Rohey*," Raymond's father said.

Raymond followed his father into his parents' bedroom and sat down at the foot of their bed. Raymond's father opened the top drawer of his dresser and took out a knife, protected in a chocolate-colored leather sheath.

"You will need this," Raymond's father said as he handed the knife to his son. "I want you to hide it somewhere in your bedroom, somewhere that is easily accessible if you ever need it quickly. Hide it somewhere your sisters will never see. They are never to know about this. Your mother is never to know about this either."

Raymond nodded his head in agreement and felt the weight of the knife in his hands. To him, it seemed as if all their lives depended on it.

That was the first night Raymond fell asleep with a knife hidden underneath his mattress. It was the last time he ever fell asleep as a child, underneath an Egyptian sky of dimmed stars. Every night after, he secured the knife in place before he dreamt of better days, until the day he was forced to leave Egypt for good.

Three

Cairo, Egypt, 1943

Raymond should have known that day would be different.

It was the first Sunday of the month, and he had just turned sixteen years old. The doors of Cairo opened up in a way they hadn't during childhood. The buildings didn't seem as imposing, and the streets held more promise. With his age came a bit more freedom, and with those freedoms came a bit more responsibility. Raymond embraced both almost equally because if there was anything he appreciated more than the chance to make his own decisions, it was the chance to prove himself a responsible young man.

Raymond's father revved up the motorcycle's engine, just like he did every month. The powerful strength of the early morning sun stood as their guiding light towards the pyramids. The pair of them zipped down Cairo streets and turned corners into wide boulevards. Cairo at dawn moved at a slower pace. Something was calming about the city as it stretched its arms for the day, as if a collective moment of renewal could somehow erase the day before.

Raymond and his father left Cairo for Giza, and as the pyramids came closer in proximity, his father stopped the motorcycle.

"What happened?" Raymond asked as they stepped off the motorcycle and onto a sandy stretch of road.

Raymond's father hardly cracked a smile, but when he did, it turned stone to dust. "Your turn, *Habibi*."

Raymond had been learning to drive the motorcycle here and there on less crowded streets and back alleyways when no one was looking. His initial surprise kept him frozen in place, but he knew not to ask any questions in fear that his father might change his mind. Raymond switched seats with his father and felt the earth shake with possibilities. The warmth of his father's hands remained on the handlebars, and as Raymond began to accelerate, he got his first taste of what it meant to have a purpose. It was that kind of intention that would eventually fly him around the world.

Raymond finally understood what it meant to hold someone else's life in his own hands. He was no longer the boy on the back seat. His father's calloused hands held on to Raymond's waist, and Raymond felt the rise and fall of his father's heavy stomach against his back. The roles of responsibility switched on a stretch of road that led to the pyramids, and the idea of it energized Raymond with the power of one thousand Egyptian suns. Even decades later, when Raymond's memory failed him of the times he spent with his father, it gave him a sense of renewed life to be responsible for a family of his own.

Within minutes, the ride was over, and they reached the pyramids. Raymond stepped off the motorcycle. Pride pooled at the tips of his fingers and toes.

"Well done," his father said as he straightened the corners of his shirt.

Raymond always sought his father's approval, not knowing that he could do no wrong in his father's eyes.

"Let there be many more smooth rides here, *Inshallah*." God willing, Raymond's father said in Arabic.

Raymond stored his elation deep within a portion of his heart that was kept only for his father. His father wasn't a man of many expressive emotions, and Raymond followed in his footsteps. They walked around the perimeter of the pyramids with only a handful of words shared between them, but an undeniable realization that what they felt, they felt it together.

Their footsteps moved in a deliberate fashion across the heated sand. It was as if they both felt the change in the atmosphere at just the same time, as if the balance of the world would soon rest on Raymond's shoulders and his alone. Raymond's father found a shaded area where the pyramids blocked the sun from striking them too hot and sat down at its base. There was something peaceful in the way the wrinkles on his forehead eased into his skin.

They never sat at the pyramids. Every first Sunday of the month, Raymond and his father parked their motorcycle and walked around the pyramids. Raymond usually had handfuls of stories to tell him about school, and his father had all the time in the world to listen. They never sat down, not even when the weather was more favorable, or the stories seemed longer.

But on that day, they sat down side by side and breathed in a shared air of tranquility.

Raymond didn't have many stories to share that morning, but they stayed a bit longer anyway. They lingered in the shade, and the grains of sand beneath them were surprisingly cool to the touch. Raymond grasped at handfuls of it and slowly released a thin line of sand as if his fist were an hourglass, the owner of time. Time in the desert was usually elusive. Even though the rest of the day waited for them, the high desert gave them an extra few undisturbed moments with each other. Had he known it would be the last time he'd ever visit the pyramids with his father, Raymond would have never left.

"Why today?" Raymond asked.

Raymond's father waited for his son to elaborate on his question.

"Did you think that I'd be more prepared to drive us today?"

Raymond's father dabbed his handkerchief at the corners of his forehead, where sweat began to form. "You have to trust the timing, *Rohey.*"

Raymond let his father's answer sink through his skin.

"Were you ready last month? Probably," his father explained. "But the timing wasn't right yet."

Raymond waited for his father to continue.

"This morning, the way you walked towards the motorcycle as if you knew the ins and outs of its mechanics and the way it is supposed to perform, you looked ready. You always have to trust the timing of things in life, or else what you're looking for will never find you."

Raymond didn't completely understand his father's outlook on time but sensed that one day he would. They sat together in silence as the morning sun continued to rise over the peaks of the pyramids. There was a comforting type of quietness that stretched over the Sahara Desert, one made of patience. He sat with his father and thought about their lives and how it all coincided to bring them to that moment. No amount of Caribbean hurricanes or Saharan sandstorms could have prepared Raymond for the calm before the storm.

"Should we get back for lunch soon?" Raymond asked. The mid-morning heat caused sweat to trickle down his back and made his neck tingle.

Raymond's father slid his hand behind his son's neck and gently guided him towards the motorcycle. "*Yalla.*" Let's go, he said.

Raymond drove them away from the pyramids towards the edge of Cairo. He switched places with his father one more time as they entered the city. Raymond sat on the back and held onto his father's waist one last time. If he knew it was to be their last trip to the pyramids, he would have held on a little tighter.

Raymond's father made a few turns, and Raymond realized they weren't going directly home. His father brought them to Groppi, an outdoor café that smelled of gardenias and jasmine. The line was long and stretched out the door as they parked and approached the storefront. Any other time, Raymond's father would have insisted they go home and come back another time, but that day, he did things differently. They found the back of the line. They waited together for one of the most memorable meals they would ever have.

"Eat some of your mother's food when we get home, *Rohey*," Raymond's father said as they walked back to the motorcycle. He took a bite out of his pastry. "She won't be upset that we stopped here for some food, but she will be upset if you don't eat her lunch also."

Raymond took a bite out of a buttery croissant and nodded his head in agreement. Cairo teemed with weekend happenings all around them, but at that moment, the only thing that mattered was each other.

Once they finished their midmorning snacks, they headed home. As they parked the motorcycle and walked towards the front door, Raymond felt he was one day closer to becoming an adult. His father sensed it too.

There was nothing routine about that Sunday, and it shifted the way Raymond thought for the rest of his life. Raymond would become a man of routine. Daily structure grounded him, and it kept him focused and organized. It gave him a sense of security and helped him forget that the day that his father wanted to do things differently was the same day that everything changed.

"How was your morning?" Raymond's mother asked as they returned home.

Raymond wasn't sure if his father wanted him to explain, but he got his father's silent approval.

"I was allowed to drive the motorcycle there today, for the first time."

Raymond's mother slipped a few words of disbelief in Arabic and French as she held her hand up to her mouth to keep any more from sliding out.

"He is a natural," Raymond's father reassured her. He squeezed the top of his shoulders and reassured both his wife and son at the same time.

"Is this true?" his mother asked for more confirmation.

"It's true," Raymond answered.

There was a quiet moment between all of them when Raymond wasn't sure how his mother would react. She was always one to wear her emotions openly, but that time, he couldn't read her at all. Not until she burst out laughing and hugged him tightly.

"I can't believe it," she said as she kissed both of his cheeks. "Ezra, when did our only boy turn into a man?"

"When we weren't looking," Raymond's father answered.

"*Yalla, Habibi*, come eat," Raymond's mother led him into the kitchen.

Raymond did as his father said and ate some of the food his mother made for lunch, even though the food from Groppi filled him enough. His father did the same and then retired to his worn-out leather chair in the living room.

His sisters trickled into the kitchen, and Raymond described to them the feeling of steering the motorcycle towards the pyramids. They followed his words and emotions as if they were on the back of the bike with him. He wanted to write it all down for Albert before the raw experience of it faded away.

There was a single letter sitting on his pillow when he walked into his room; it was where his mother always left any letters he received from Albert. Raymond ripped open the envelope and began reading.

Albert caught him up with everything that was happening in New York. He told Raymond about the trips he took to Manhattan and all the tall buildings that seemed to stretch upwards into the sky for miles. Albert sent another magazine clipping, this time of the New York City skyline glistening at night. Raymond always pictured New York that way, and he wondered if Albert lived in one of those tall buildings. He was still years away from understanding the difference between Manhattan and Brooklyn, where Albert actually lived, and how sometimes they could feel like night and day.

Raymond was taking out a pen and a piece of paper from the top drawer of his desk when the front door opened. Three deep voices greeted his father. Raymond left the stationery where it was and walked into the living room. His father's friends had arrived for an afternoon game of dominoes.

Within minutes, each man had a cup of coffee. Rachel helped their mother bring out plates of fruit and baklava as the men began their game. Cigarette smoke billowed in the space between them with enough force to power a train, and the overpowering smell of fresh tobacco could be traced back to Raymond's father's pipe.

Raymond knew how to play dominoes, but he only ever played it with a few classmates from his school. He wasn't invited to join the games with his father's friends, but he liked to casually watch as they slapped the bare tiles onto the wooden table. He could never see their tiles, as they knew how to keep them well hidden, but he followed their hands and kept track of who might have what.

Raymond sat in the living room and pretended to study his math lessons for school. He wanted to join their game but would never ask.

"Raymond, leave your studies for now," David said.

Raymond looked up from the book he wasn't reading and found his father's friend sipping on coffee.

"Come join us," David encouraged.

Raymond checked for approval in his father's eyes before joining the men at the dining room table. He pulled a chair from the living room and wedged himself next to David and his father. He was slightly uncomfortable despite their welcome.

"Do you know how to play?" David asked.

"Of course," Raymond answered.

Raymond's father sat in disbelief, both by the fact that his son could play and by his confidence.

Raymond gathered some tiles, face down, and pulled them towards himself. He looked at his tiles in secrecy, and the game began.

"How old are you now, Raymond?" Haim asked. The tips of his mustache were slightly wet from coffee.

"Sixteen, sir."

"Sixteen," Haim repeated. "This boy is almost a man, Ezra."

"I'd say so myself," Raymond's father responded, beaming with pride. "He drove us to the pyramids this morning."

"Did he?" Benjamin asked.

"He drove without a misstep," Raymond's father continued.

"It wasn't a problem at all," Raymond added.

Raymond's father's friends nodded in approval and continued the game.

"Sixteen-years-old. That must mean you're almost finished with school. What does the son of Ezra Blanco want to do after graduation?" David asked. He blew a thick cloud of cigarette smoke into the air. It nearly covered his entire face.

It was Raymond's turn to play, and he placed his tile down on the table. "Attend university here in Cairo, and then go into accounting. That's the plan."

The whole table nodded in approval once again.

"Soon enough, Ezra, he will be married with his own children, and your grandchildren will be playing in front of the house," Haim said.

Although Raymond couldn't fathom becoming a full adult, his father seemed to like the idea.

"I always tell him that life should be lived to make memories," Raymond's father said. "He needs to make more memories before he settles down."

"See the world, *Inshallah*," Benjamin said.

"Ezra, the man who always wants an adventure. What else is there to see?" David asked. "Do you want him to go to New York the same way you did?"

"It doesn't have to be New York, no," Raymond's father explained. "But there's more to see outside of Cairo, David."

"There are talks to make a Jewish state," Haim said. "Have you heard of it? Maybe Raymond can go there if you want him to see other places besides Cairo."

"A Jewish state?" Raymond asked.

"Yes, a part of Palestine," Haim answered. "A declared country for Jews, without any of the persecution, where we can have our own territory."

Raymond's father suddenly pushed his dominoes towards Raymond, and his cup of coffee flooded the table. The abrupt sound of the bare tiles clinking against Raymond's dominoes startled him. There was an involuntary heaviness in the way their tiles collided.

"Raymond, get your mother," his father said. He leaned towards Raymond's chair and clutched the back of it for support.

"Papa, what's wrong?" Raymond asked in a panic.

His father's face was losing color, and his eyes were losing focus. Raymond would never forget how quickly his father's cheeks turned ghastly pale and how he placed his hand to his chest as he tried to stop the heart attack from coming.

"Go do what I said, Raymond," his father said.

Those were the last words Raymond would ever hear his father speak. Even on days when things were forgettable, Raymond never lost sight of his father's last wish. He always did what his father said, long after he was gone.

The heart attack came on suddenly and left abruptly. It never gave Raymond the chance to look it directly in the eye. He never had a chance to wish it away or understand why it had struck until it was all said and done. In its wake stood a family broken in two. Raymond had a family before the heart attack and a different one after it.

His father was gone in moments. His handkerchief remained in his pocket, and his half-smoked pipe sat on the dining room table. His hair was neatly combed in place, and his pipe still burned, but he was still gone.

His father's body slumped over on the dining room table. His friends mumbled prayers and tried to shield him from the children. Raymond was the only one of his siblings who saw their father in his last minutes, something he'd never be able to share with any of them.

Raymond tried to catch the tears of his mother and sisters with his own bare hands. He always regretted that his hands were not large enough to pool the oceans they wept. They screamed and cried in agony and mourned in his arms of strength. He tried to hold them steady, and he tried to keep his family upright when everything else in the world was trying to push them down.

Raymond should have known that day would be different.

He went from learning to drive the motorcycle at sunrise to becoming the head of the household by the time the moon rose into the sky.

His father's friends helped arrange for the funeral, and their wives came by the house with platters of food that no one had the appetite to eat. When his mother and sisters had enough time to calm down from the initial shock, Raymond slipped out of the house with his deep blue velvet yarmulke in his pocket. It was the same one he wore on holidays in Haiti and the same one he used on the day of his Bar Mitzvah in Egypt. He walked for a few minutes and placed the yarmulke on his head at the doorsteps of a synagogue. He pulled open its heavy doors and sat down inside. He prayed for his late father.

The walls of the synagogue knew of his aches. Raymond prayed, but the weight of responsibility began to settle on his chest. There was no roadmap of where to go from there, and there was no signpost or direction of how to move forward. Raymond didn't know how he would help provide for his family and wasn't sure how he would become the head of the household. At the time, he didn't think his father had prepared him for this sudden shift, but when he looked back at it years later, Raymond realized that his father had been preparing him his whole life.

Word of his father's passing spread to family and friends throughout Cairo and to his family in New York. Every day for a week, relatives and colleagues came by to pay their respects. Raymond's house felt like a whirlwind of familiar faces, but none of them were the only face he wanted to see: his father's. Near and distant family from New York sent their condolences. Even though Raymond didn't necessarily know all of them personally, something about their words gave him a sense of reassurance. It gave him an extra push during a time when there was nothing else pushing him to do better.

It was quickly decided that Uncle Nissim and his family would move to Egypt to help with the household. In such a dark time, it was what Raymond didn't know he needed. Being Raymond's father's only brother, Uncle Nissim would take over the family business in Cairo and help provide for his mother and sisters. Raymond was to start working with Uncle Nissim when he wasn't in school, and there was nothing more Raymond wanted than to help contribute and protect his mother and sisters.

That also meant that Albert would be moving to Cairo too. If there was any sense of relief in the whole situation, it was knowing that he and Albert would be living in the same house together, sharing the same bedroom. There was nothing more that could comfort him than to be near his closest ally.

Raymond and Albert fell back into their place as best friends as if they were still young children riding their bicycles around Haiti. But they were almost adults by that point, in a land so foreign from where they were born. Whenever Raymond looked into his cousin's eyes, he saw scenes from yesterday but also saw what it might feel like tomorrow. A comfort settled over them in their shared bedroom, a feeling that Raymond knew was mutual.

With his father gone, Raymond had everything to prove. He was a few years away from being the first person in his family to attend university. When he wasn't working, he spent most of his time making sure that everything was in line for his higher education to happen. Raymond studied harder in school. He received exceptional grades and knew better than to associate with the wrong crowd. When he had some rare downtime, he continued to play football, but this time Albert joined him.

Where Raymond was headstrong and had a clear direction, Albert had other plans for himself. He was one year older than Raymond, and there was nothing about attending university that appealed to him. He was steadily counting down the days when school would be over, so he could work full time in the family textile business and spend his evenings writing in their bedroom. The idea of being trapped within the walls of a university while the world of Cairo sat idly waiting for him didn't seem appealing at all.

At first, Cairo was everything Albert wanted. It was a place so distant and unimaginable compared to Haiti's thick summer days or the cold winter months of New York. He spent his time exploring the cafés and outdoor movie theaters, he browsed the shops and took in live music at parks. Cairo was exotic, it was meaningful, and it had a long history. It didn't take Albert long to become conversational in Arabic. Raymond always assumed that Albert must have practiced for that moment back in New York.

Albert had a honeymoon phase with Egypt. It was only a matter of time before one of them fell out of love.

One early evening in 1948, Albert suggested that he and Raymond go to a shisha café he found not far from their house. Raymond had been too preoccupied with his studies that he hadn't properly been to a shisha café yet. Albert convinced him to take a break, as it was the weekend. Raymond reluctantly agreed, and the pair of them walked to the neighborhood café. Raymond felt like he was growing into adulthood and his cousin helped speed up the process.

Raymond and Albert sat down at a round, outdoor table and ordered glasses of mint tea. Tables around them were full of men playing either dominoes or backgammon. The smoke was thick and swayed in the air around them until it became too cloudy to see people's faces.

Raymond and Albert started a game of dominoes on their own as the smoke of their own shisha began to seep into the threads of their shirts. The evening had turned dark, and the stars of the night dotted the sky.

A man with wide shoulders accidentally stumbled into their table. It sent Albert's tea glass shattering onto the ground. The warm liquid splattered at Raymond's ankles, and the heat of the drink jolted him upright.

Albert mumbled what sounded like words of profanity but mostly ignored the man, assuming he'd return to his own table.

Raymond looked up at the man as he continued to stand above them.

"Where did you learn how to play so horribly?" the man asked Albert.

Albert peered at him through a cloud of shisha smoke. His bushy eyebrows almost met in the middle. Albert took another strong puff of shisha instead of answering the question.

"Probably from your Zionist father," another man, his friend, joined them.

Raymond's body tensed up. He looked them up and down for their height and weight and knew that it would be a tight match if anything were to happen.

"Gentlemen, have a good night," Albert said, trying to dismiss them.

"I think he wants us to leave," the first man said to his friend. "This man, in our country, with his American accent trying to speak Arabic. He wants us to leave."

The other man's laugh came from deep within his belly and echoed down the alleyways of Cairo. Albert stood up, and Raymond instinctively followed suit.

The man with the broad shoulders was probably only a few years older than Albert and Raymond but stood above them as if he governed them. He approached Albert, and the two men locked eyes in a standstill that made the earth pause.

"How about you take one more puff of your shisha and find your way out of this café, *Habibi*," the man said. "And when you leave, keep walking until you reach Israel."

"Both of them are Zionists, look at them," his friend said.

Albert took a deep puff of shisha and blew it slowly and directly into their faces.

Raymond wasn't sure what broke first, the other tea glass on their table or the hookah as it crashed onto the floor. The sharp sounds of crunching glass came from beneath their shoes. Deep shouts and muffled words erupted around the café. Raymond received a punch to the side of his face that made his ears ring. The adrenaline in his fists punched back as Albert shouted with rage. Raymond wasn't sure who threw the first punch but had a feeling it was his cousin.

The four men were trapped in a battle that no one would win, and in a way, it was an early representation of the fight they'd all face in Egypt in the coming years. The owner of the shisha café kicked all of them out and forbade them from ever returning. The other men continued to yell and instigate the fight's continuation, but Raymond faced Albert instead. There was vulnerability in his cousin's eyes, so he pushed him back by the shoulders and urged him to stop fighting. Albert's nose was bleeding, and droplets fell onto Raymond's shoes. Raymond wasn't sure if the blood on his shirt was his or someone else's.

Albert's body released and retreated. His shoulders relaxed, and he put his hands up to show he wasn't willing to engage.

Raymond and Albert backed away and walked home without saying a word. Neither of them knew what to say or how to feel.

Albert retreated in many ways after that fight. But instead of withdrawing into himself, inside their home, he escaped into the hidden worlds deep within Cairo. He spent evenings at other cafés, mingling with new friends, showing the world that he was not scared of anything it would ever throw at him. In a sense, he wanted to protest. He would never let anyone stop him from living his life in Egypt, even though tensions as a whole in the country were dictating otherwise. Albert stood as a young Jewish man at the cusp of his prime, and that was no longer accepted in Egypt.

Albert needed to find that kind of acceptance elsewhere.

Israel had become an official country by that point, and the levels of Jewish persecution on the streets of Cairo and Alexandria soared. They were increasingly unwelcome in a country that they called home for generations. The majority of Jews didn't have Egyptian citizenship, and it wouldn't take much to expel them from the Arab land. A tense community of around 80,000 Egyptian Jews walked carefully on a path made of delicate eggshells, careful not to crack too much before the entire road gave in. Raymond and Albert trod lightly as well, but they were planning their next moves with strategy and secrecy.

"Raymond, go put your shoes on," Albert urged as he walked into their shared bedroom. An air of excitement entered with him. It had been a couple of months since the fight at the shisha café, and Albert had rarely talked about it since.

Raymond was studying for an upcoming math exam, but Albert's enthusiasm was always contagious. He put down his pen and looked up at his cousin.

"Just close your books and get dressed," Albert repeated.

Raymond sat back in his chair, and although he was listening carefully, his books remained open. "You look like you have plans for us."

"I want you to meet some new friends," Albert started.

When Raymond agreed to meet them, he didn't realize that it would single-handedly be the reason why the rest of his life would change. When he closed his math books for the evening, he didn't quite know his studies would no longer going to be the ultimate driving force in the next few years of his life.

They met in an apartment not far from their own house in Heliopolis. The apartment was on the second floor, on top of a kebab shop below. The smell of grilled meat wafted through the open windows and reminded Raymond that he was hungry.

"Albert, come in, come in!" One of Albert's new friends greeted them both with firm handshakes. It was the kind that would always have a grip on Raymond's hand, well after that evening.

"Sami, *izayyak?*" How are you, Albert asked in Arabic as they walked into the apartment.

"*Ça va bien, Alhamdullah,*" Sami said he was doing well, thank God. He towered over them in both stature and personality. "Come have a seat."

"Raymond, this is Sami and Henry," Albert said as they sat down in the living room. It was surprisingly furnished for a pair of bachelors.

"Welcome, Raymond," Henry said. His hair was full of curls, and his Arabic had a thicker French accent that reminded Raymond of his mother's tone. "Would you like some tea? Or coffee?"

"That's fine, thank you," Raymond declined. His mind lingered on the kebabs downstairs, but he doubted he'd have any that evening.

Henry sat back against the couch and lit a cigarette. It was then that Raymond realized the whole apartment smelt of cigarette smoke. It was woven into the fabric of the couch and hung low on the drapes. It was thick and pungent, making the apartment feel much more confined than it was.

But even though the apartment seemed tight, Albert's new friends were welcoming. They were both Egyptian Jews, studying at the same university as Raymond. They were two years older than him and didn't share any of the same classes, but Henry was in an advanced level of accounting that Raymond was aiming for as well.

The four of them talked about school and introduced Raymond to cigarettes. They talked about their families and what they hoped for their futures. They talked about the oppressed state of Jews in Egypt and how they were going to be driven out of their own country if they didn't do anything about it. Raymond felt a quick connection with Sami and Henry. He understood how Albert found shelter in their friendship when he needed it the most.

Sami loved to hear stories about America, and Albert loved to tell them. Even though Albert had fully embraced his background as an Egyptian Jew in Cairo, a part of him still missed New York. He spoke of the city like it was above all the rest, like there could never be another New York even if the world started anew and tried to recreate it. Sami soaked it in like he was hearing of a long-lost sibling, as if he had lived in New York before, maybe in a previous lifetime.

"One day, mark my words, Albert, you and I are going to be in New York, eating hot dogs," Sami said with confidence. Raymond would never meet another person as confident as Sami.

"*Inshallah*," Albert said. "One day, I will buy you all the hot dogs you can eat."

Sami lit up another cigarette in the kitchen and brought a single folder to the coffee table before them. He opened the folder and spread out a variety of photographs on the table.

"This is what I was telling you about the other day, Albert," Sami said. He admired the photos as if they were some of his most prized possessions.

Albert raised a photo in front of his face to get a better look at it. It was an unassuming photo of a public library.

"I see," Albert said as he studied it.

"It's all so simple," Henry explained. "There really is nothing to it."

Albert nodded in agreement. Raymond didn't yet know what he agreed to.

Albert put the photo down and picked up another. It was a picture of a cinema theater not too far from their house.

"Someone will give us a list of places. All we do is take a photo of the building and send it back." Henry explained.

"Easy enough, isn't it, Albert?" Sami asked. He took a deep sip of his mint tea.

"It is," Albert agreed again. He placed the photos down on the table; he had seen enough.

"So, what will it be?" Sami asked.

Without saying a word, Albert nodded his head in agreement. It only took another few meetings for Raymond to do the same.

And what they both agreed to was espionage.

Four

Cairo, Egypt, 1949

His mother and sisters were the only ones who still called him Raymond. The rest of the world knew him as Ibrahim Youssef Nasim.

It was an artificial identity. Raymond went by his alias whenever he met new people, mostly at Sami's parties. His new name came with the strength of a thousand armies but also the weight of a thousand lies. Raymond knew not to take it lightly. Not just anybody got selected to be two different people in the same lifetime.

His new name was given to him under the watch of secret eyes and careful leaders. Raymond wasn't privy to his spy ring's complete hierarchy, which was probably for the best. He knew Sami and Henry were equally above him, and Tarek watched over them both. He only met Tarek on a handful of occasions and liked to keep it that way. Tarek's subdued temper made Raymond question what he was truly capable of. Raymond didn't know who was in charge past Tarek and how far the ladder stretched but knew it ultimately made its way to Israel.

Raymond had just finished university and graduated with the first college degree in his family, but finding a steady job as an accountant was difficult. Jobs were increasingly hard to come by for Egyptian Jews at that time. Nationalism and anti-Semitism grew like twins from the same womb. Raymond went to countless job interviews, but whenever a prospective employer met with him, they never asked him to return.

Despite all the roadblocks, he took care of his mothers and sisters in a way that would make his father proud. He continued to work as a bookkeeper for Uncle Nissim's textile business and provided for his family the way his father would have, with dignity and pride. Money came in, and food stayed on the table, but it wasn't enough to prosper. The golden era of Jews in Egypt didn't shine the way it once did. The sense of growth the community once shared dwindled before their eyes. It wasn't what Raymond sought for himself. It wasn't what his father ever wanted for the family.

When Raymond wasn't busy working with his uncle, he found other, more meaningful work to keep himself busy. He looked towards a growing network of young Egyptian Jews for support, as they all tried to find their place in a country that didn't want them anymore. It was only when his heritage was being stripped from him that Raymond got a true sense of its value. The country that raised him didn't have a use for him or his lineage any longer.

Even though he could trace his family back in Egypt to generations before him, it was that same Egypt that wanted him gone. His frustrations boiled internally until the blood in his streams almost burst into flames. There was a secret uprising underneath the surface of the political tensions, and Raymond wanted to be in its epicenter. His family would never know the truth, and he needed to keep it that way for the rest of his life.

When no one else was looking, Raymond transformed into Ibrahim. Ibrahim walked the streets of Cairo with a camera. He used it to take pictures for what he thought was the greater good of the Egyptian Jewish population. He scouted popular buildings in Cairo and took photos of their exteriors. He simply followed orders and never questioned the people above him.

Ibrahim had a political and religious agenda shielded in secrecy. It was easy to keep secrets when his life and his family's lives depended on it. Not one of his five sisters knew a single ounce of the truth, and he knew it was for the best. Once every two weeks, his mother was brought into the police station by Egyptian authorities. She spent hours there, almost full days, under the scrutinizing questions of police officers. They interrogated her about her son's involvement with Zionist organizations. But she knew nothing, and time and time again, the authorities let her go. The notion of secrecy was so ingrained in his heart that even in the latter part of his life, not even his own daughter knew the complete truth.

For two years, he became Ibrahim almost as much as he was Raymond. Each morning, he woke up as Raymond but quickly transformed into Ibrahim as he traveled through Cairo, always following his orders and always taking photos. He didn't immediately know what the photos were used for, but at the time, that was none of his concern. His body and mind took the shape of his new name. He learned to think in ways that only Ibrahim could. Every morning, he put on his pair of thin-wired glasses and saw the world behind a new lens, the kind that reminded him to watch his back at all times.

Albert had a new name too. He transformed into Max Labaton as if it were who he was supposed to be all along. An air of confidence sprouted in Albert's spine, and he soon walked into every room as if he commanded it.

"Max, tell us that story again, you know, that one with the bird?" Lily, a frequent guest at Sami's parties, encouraged him. A necklace of pearls lined her collarbone. Raymond had a feeling she came from a wealthy family and that her mother was French.

Albert took a sip of his drink and placed the sweating glass on the coffee table in front of them. "You love hearing that story," he said and gave her a wink.

Lily's cheeks flushed at the gesture, and she instinctively fiddled with the pearls on her necklace.

Albert lit a cigarette and leaned back into the couch.

"I was walking in Manhattan with my father, looking up at the tall skyscrapers, trying to figure out how they really make them," Albert began. "We just moved to New York, and it was my first time in Manhattan."

"Is New York everything they say it is?" Sami asked. He was always heavily invested in any story about New York.

"It's everything they say it is, and everything they say it isn't," Albert responded.

"Crowds of people everywhere?" Henry asked.

"And buildings that reach the clouds," Albert said. "But anyway, that's not the point of this." Albert took a long drag of his cigarette and continued. "My father and I were walking around Manhattan, and he wanted to show me the Empire State Building. On the way, he bought us two ice cream cones. His was chocolate, and mine was vanilla."

By then, Albert had the attention of most of the room, just how he liked it.

"I was too busy watching the buildings, and then all of a sudden, my father was yelling at someone. I looked at him, and I realized he's not yelling at a person, he's yelling at a pigeon. This pigeon was flying around, just above our heads, and its beady eyes were looking straight at our ice cream cones."

"It wanted to eat them?" a woman with waves in her hair asked. Raymond had never met her before; it must have been her first time at one of Sami's parties.

"It wanted both of them," Albert said with a grin. "My father started swatting at it to shoe it away, but by then, a few other pigeons joined in, and they managed to knock my father's ice cream cone to the ground."

The room started laughing. Albert's chest swelled as he relished in the spotlight.

"The pigeons swarmed around it on the ground and ate all the chocolate ice cream and the cone, nothing was left."

"But they didn't get yours?" Sami asked with a smirk on his face.

"One of them kept trying, but I managed to shoe it away. And as I did, it decided to go to the bathroom, on my head."

The room burst out in roaring laughter. Albert took another puff of his cigarette. Even behind a thick cloud of smoke, he was still the center of attention.

That's how many of Sami's parties went. They brought together a group of young Egyptian Jews, mostly in their twenties, who made a lifestyle out of mingling and searching for a good time in a country that wanted to limit their happiness. In between the constant cigarette smoke and laughter, Sami always made his way through the crowd of old friends and new acquaintances. Everyone felt welcome the moment they walked into his house, and he had a special way of bringing people together.

But underneath it all, Sami was recruiting. He scouted the crowds of friends, and friends of friends, for anyone he thought had the potential to join their covert operations. He looked for men who had the right physique to run from police if they had to, and he looked for women who could charm their way into and out of any situation possible. But mostly, he sought out people who were slightly vulnerable and highly passionate about their community. Sami especially loved meeting the "triple threats," anyone who spoke French, Arabic, and English. Those were the ones who could straddle a multitude of worlds without even trying.

Sami had an eye for it. Raymond wasn't the first person Sami recruited, and he surely wasn't the last. Even though Raymond worked closely with Sami, Sami still left out enough details and kept enough secrets for Raymond to never truly know him. Sami was in charge of finding other young Egyptian Jews, like Raymond, to play a role in a bigger purpose that none of them completely knew but trusted whole-heartedly. But other than his political beliefs, Raymond never got a chance to understand what made Sami tick.

Sami poured a drink for Raymond and placed a single napkin underneath the glass. When Raymond picked it up, he noticed that there was writing on the bottom of the napkin. He knew not to look at it and slipped it into his pocket when no one was looking. It took all the courage in the world for Raymond to keep the napkin hidden, and it brought him all the purpose in the world, knowing that he was needed to play a part for the greater good.

When he returned home, he returned to being Raymond. He was the man who told his family lies and bounced between two worlds when no one was looking. He'd always be Raymond, to his sisters who needed his guidance, to his future wife who never knew him otherwise. He'd always be Raymond to his daughter, who wouldn't arrive for decades and would never know him in any other light, until she began to dig deeper into his past. He went to sleep as Raymond every night, knowing that Ibrahim would be needed the next morning.

A few evenings after Sami's party, Raymond turned on the lamp in his bedroom. He studied the writing on the napkin as if he hadn't already memorized the location and address of the public library. It was one that he had gone to often when he was still in school. It was a central library, one that he knew well. It was almost always crowded, both inside and around the perimeter of the building. He knew he'd have to be careful if he wanted the mission to go well.

"You've been staring at that napkin for the past 10 minutes," Albert said. He sat on his bed, propped up by a pillow behind his head, as he thumbed through a National Geographic Magazine. He brought an older copy with him from America, and it still stood in mint condition.

Raymond looked up from the napkin and finally placed it neatly on his nightstand.

"If I had to guess, I'd say you're a bit nervous about this one," Albert assumed.

Raymond took off his glasses and placed them on top of the napkin. "Nervous isn't the word for it."

"Concerned?" Albert guessed.

"Hesitant," Raymond finally admitted.

Albert stopped turning the pages of his magazine and gave his full attention to Raymond.

"Hesitant," Albert repeated.

Raymond nodded in agreement.

"Why the sudden hesitation, Raymond?" Albert asked. "Either you go there tomorrow, or you don't. There's no in-between."

"It's just that I know this library well. I've been there dozens of times."

"So that should make it even easier for you. You know exactly where to stand to get a good photo of the building from the outside."

"It's not that, though."

"What is it then? You're getting cold feet?"

"You know what will happen to this library," Raymond said. "We both know."

"That's the way this works." Albert didn't seem the least bit concerned. "Honestly, it's none of our business what eventually happens to the library, or anywhere else we go. You trust Sami, don't you?"

Raymond paused. He wasn't even sure there was a correct answer.

"If you don't trust him, then don't go tomorrow," Albert said.

"I do trust him," Raymond finally admitted, even though there was still a piece of him that didn't.

"Look, we are part of something greater than just taking photos of buildings. This is something you'll look back on in fifty years and tell your children and grandchildren about, don't you understand that? We are taking control over what is right."

Raymond breathed out a long exhale. "There's no other way."

Albert smiled from his side of the room and flipped onto the next page of his magazine. "There's no other way," he agreed.

There was a maturity in the way they approached life then as if all of it rested in their hands and their hands alone. They moved and breathed as if they walked on the edge of the earth and the air around them was the only guiding force towards clarity.

It was an uprising that the world didn't know of yet. Their Sephardic bloodline's earthy roots were buried under layers of Egyptian history, and only now were they breaking from beneath the surface. The country that once welcomed them home was trying to cut their roots, and if someone was going to do something about it, it had to be them.

And if there was no one way to be accepted into the country they had always loved, they had to find a way out. At the end of the day, it was one thing to be buried, but another thing entirely to be buried alive.

The following day came and went, and Raymond found himself outside of the central library he knew all too well. A continuous stream of people walked in and out of the building, many of them university students like he had recently been. It was only a camera, but it seemed to nearly burn the skin off Raymond's palms with the undeniable meaning and consequences if he were to be caught. After a few quiet clicks of the camera's shutter, it was done. Raymond left the camera in a prearranged drop-off zone and knew Sami wouldn't be too far behind to pick it up. As the sun swapped places with the moon, Raymond sank into his bed with his shoulders lifted. He'd wait for his next orders. There was simply nothing else to it.

Raymond read books and magazines from America in his free time, but Ibrahim learned how to read and write in invisible ink when no one else was looking. He learned about the intricacies of photography and knew his way around a camera without second-guessing himself. Drop-offs were spread throughout Cairo and never in the same place twice. The trickle-down world of espionage meant that the photos he took eventually ignited delayed-action devices and letter bombs. Libraries were bombed. Post offices shook with the force of homemade explosives. Parts of Cairo came under attack, and every fiery ember that fell from the sky had parts of Raymond and Ibrahim in them.

Somewhere along the way, he received false identity papers that solidified himself as Ibrahim, if anyone were to ask. And people did ask, eventually. He tucked the papers away alongside the knife underneath his mattress and prayed that his family would never find out about his secret life. In some moments, he questioned whether he could ever go back to just being Raymond again because Raymond would feel all the guilt that Ibrahim couldn't.

Guilt wasn't something that Albert ever understood. Raymond was spared the details but knew well enough that Albert was steadily climbing the ladder of espionage with ease. He invested himself in the cause and didn't bat an eye at the repercussions. Every day, he went out with new missions and came home every evening to escape into a world in a National Geographic Magazine. Albert always pointed out his favorite magazine clippings to Raymond and never gave up on the idea that one day, he'd write magazine articles about exotic travel destinations too.

In between the missions of secrecy and Egypt's ever-changing political and social world, Sami's parties continued. They weren't just filled with middle-class Jews anymore. Upper-middle-class Egyptian Jews with well-known family businesses gathered and mingled, and they all somehow knew Sami. On a handful of occasions, Egyptian movie stars even made their way into some of Sami's parties, and it was then that Raymond understood that his world of espionage had infiltrated much deeper into their community than he could begin to imagine.

"Gentlemen, I'd like you to meet Bridgette," Sami said to Raymond and Albert in the middle of one of his lavish parties. Sami's hand was placed on the small of Bridgette's back, and his abiding love for her covered him with a shield of grace.

"It's a pleasure to meet you," Bridgette said as she delicately shook both of their hands.

"This must be the young lady you haven't stopped talking about," Albert said as he playfully pushed Sami's shoulder.

Bridgette blushed at Sami as he kissed her on the forehead.

"This is the beautiful young lady," Sami confirmed. "She is studying at university now, she wants to become a chemist."

"Wow, that's impressive," Raymond said. He immediately wondered if her knowledge in chemistry had anything to do with homemade explosives.

"Thank you," Bridgette answered. "I still have one more year to go."

"I don't know how you find time to study when you have to put up with this man's nonsense all the time," Albert teased Sami.

Sami took a puff of his cigarette. A chuckle and a cloud of smoke came out of his mouth in unison.

"He's been very supportive," Bridgette said. "When he's not too busy with his own work."

Raymond questioned if Bridgette knew what kind of work Sami did. From the casual way she mentioned it, she probably had no idea.

"Bridgette, can I get you a refill?" Sami asked as he eyed her almost empty glass.

"Please," she answered.

Within a moment, Sami came back unexpectedly with two glasses of champagne. Sami gave her one as the look of surprise washed over her face. He clinked a fork against his glass and raised it in the air.

Sami placed two fingers in his mouth and made a loud whistle. "Can I have everyone's attention?" Sami asked. The room was full of some of his closest friends, and his smile bounced from one person to another.

A hush fell upon the room as all his guests settled down. All eyes were on Sami, and he didn't waste a moment of it.

"Thank you all for coming to the party this evening," Sami said. "I told many of you that we'd be celebrating something special," he said. He turned his focus onto Bridgette. "And I hope we do."

Bridgette smiled, not knowing what was about to happen.

Sami placed his glass of champagne down on a table, and in the same motion, knelt down on bended knee in front of Bridgette. He took out a velvet box from his pocket and opened it for her to see.

"Bridgette, I love you dearly, now and until forever. Will you marry me?"

Bridgette's shock jolted the crowd of party onlookers. For a moment, she didn't speak.

"Yes! Yes, of course, I will marry you!" she exclaimed.

The whole party erupted in applause as Sami picked her up in his arms and spun her around in a jubilant circle. Friends began congratulating the newly engaged couple. Raymond was sincerely excited for them both. It was exactly how Sami's parties always went. They lived in an inner world where discrimination and persecution didn't exist. It was always filled with love and happiness.

The people at Sami's parties somehow always worked for tomorrow, but lived so much in the moment that the future didn't pose a threat. They never questioned where they would live, if it weren't in Egypt, or if their future children would know their traditions and culture if they didn't experience it firsthand in Cairo. None of those things were ever discussed, at least not at Sami's parties, because that was the only place where they were untouchable.

Within six months of the engagement party, Sami and Bridgette were married.

To this day, their wedding was one of the grandest celebrations Raymond ever attended. It seemed like the entirety of their Egyptian Jewish community was invited, and not one detail was overlooked. A feast of the finest foods was offered to the guests, and they danced to the loudest, most vibrant music on that side of the Sahara Desert. It was the last official party Sami ever threw.

The weeks turned into months, and before either Raymond or Albert realized, a year had gone by. Discrimination against their community continued to escalate, and there seemed to be no concrete end in sight. Some of their closest friends talked about leaving Egypt altogether, and others already did. Raymond focused on the work that needed to be done for Sami but felt that time was running out. Albert continued to complete one mission after another, but it was clear that his love and patience for Egypt had already vanished.

"This nonsense wouldn't be happening in New York, I can guarantee you that," Albert said out of frustration. Albert and Raymond sat on their own beds in their shared bedroom. Albert had been searching for a new job outside of the family business but always came up empty-handed. Raymond flipped through one of Albert's National Geographic Magazines while Albert smoked a cigarette out of the window.

"What makes it that much better than somewhere else in the world?" Raymond asked.

"Spoken like a person who has never seen New York before," Albert said. "Raymond, no one was joking around when they say that America is the land of opportunity. I would find a job if I still lived there. There's no question about it."

"Sure, but what makes it better to live in New York than somewhere else, say Paris?" Raymond asked.

Albert took a puff of his cigarette and blew the heavy smoke into the evening Cairo sky. "You walk down the street there, in America, and you can be anonymous, or you can be the most celebrated person in the world. You walk down the street there, and you will find someone who comes from where you're from, or you will meet someone who comes from the other side of the world. But no one cares. They don't care about differences there. They take those differences together and make something new out of it. That's how they made New York. I just don't know if anywhere else in the world does it the same."

"Are you planning on moving back one day, when all of this is over?"

"Who knows? Your guess is as good as mine," Albert said. "Eventually, yes, I'd like to find myself in New York again. I don't miss the winter when it snows, and it's hard to walk on the streets, but other than that, it's one hell of a place to live."

Raymond wondered if that was what his cousin truly wanted or just thought he wanted.

"How about you, Raymond?" Albert asked. "You and me, move to New York together one day?"

Even though leaving Egypt was becoming an inevitable reality, Raymond hadn't seriously thought of what came next.

"What about Israel?" Raymond asked.

"What about it?"

"Would you ever want to move there?"

Albert took another drag. "I'm not sure," he said. "I'm curious, yes. But they are just starting out. They don't even have a solid foundation yet, and it seems like the whole world is against them. Maybe it would be a good place to move to. We could be there right when the country is getting its footing. Or maybe that's a horrible idea."

Raymond agreed with him when he heard the words out loud. At that moment, he made a mental decision that if he ever had a chance to move to New York, he'd take it in a heartbeat. New York City showed no signs of slowing down, and if Albert were right and its citizens were as welcoming as he said they were, Raymond could make a life for himself without anyone ever knowing about his life in Egypt.

"All I know is that I don't want to be here anymore," Albert finally said. "I thought Egypt was going to be one thing, but it's turning out to be something entirely different. New York though, New York never hides what it always has been and what it always will be."

In his formative years, Raymond was brought up in a land of ancient Egyptian history and generations of tradition. At the same time, across the world, Albert became a New Yorker through and through. It was the years spent apart, in those late childhood and early adolescent years, which created a real divide between how they saw the world. If Raymond had to leave Egypt, all he wanted to do was see a little more of the world. And if Albert had to leave Egypt, all he wanted to do was return to New York.

Raymond's wishes eventually came true, but Albert's never did.

In between their late-night talks in their shared bedroom and countless missions and drop-offs, time moved on. The seasons of Cairo came and went, and as they neared another year gone by, Hanukkah turned bittersweet. It was unknowingly the last one they'd ever spend together as a whole family in Egypt.

"Raymond, you say the prayers this time," Uncle Nissim said as the family stood in front of the menorah.

Raymond stood shoulder-to-shoulder with Albert as he led the family in the nightly prayers. The candles' subtle light bounced off the familiar silver stitching on both Raymond and Albert's yarmulkes.

1949 turned into 1950, and talks of leaving Egypt started to escalate within their spy ring and amongst friends and family in the community. Families that Raymond knew from his late childhood began to pack up and go. Some of his neighbors moved to Italy and America. Childhood friends he used to play football with left for

France and Argentina. Egyptian Jews weren't welcome in their own country anymore, so they sought out refuge elsewhere.

Raymond wondered when the time would come for his own family to leave Egypt. It felt like Haiti all over again; neither home was meant to be forever. Raymond didn't know when his family would be forced to leave but had a feeling it would come in a rush. His father always believed that the timing had to be right for Raymond to find what he was looking for. Life in Cairo turned into a waiting game.

The timing of everything started to unravel when winter turned to spring. Raymond received his next mission, and for the first and last time in his life, it wasn't related to photography. An increasing number of Jews needed to leave Egypt, and he was to be in charge of ensuring their safety out of the country.

But what that really meant was that he had to leave for good too.

Raymond and Albert each packed one bag. It was all they were allowed to bring, but at the end of the day, it was all they needed to start their lives over.

"Make sure your bag is light," Albert reminded him. "You don't need an unnecessary bag weighing you down."

"It's light, don't worry."

"Oh, believe me, Raymond, I'm not worried." Albert smirked as he continued to fold a couple of shirts into his bag.

"The man who is never worried about anything," Raymond said.

Albert's smile grew along with his ego. "Why should I be worried? I'd be more worried if we were staying here in Egypt. But now we're onto new places. There's nothing to be worried about."

Albert had a realistic way of looking at things.

"Here, take this," Albert said as he gently threw a copy of his latest National Geographic Magazine onto the foot of Raymond's bed.

Raymond picked it up and flipped through the pages. "Why are you giving me this magazine?"

"You'll need something to read on the long journey," Albert said. "Trust me."

And Raymond always did.

When they were both finished packing their bags, Albert was quick to get into bed. He insisted on sleeping early, something he rarely did, but their new circumstances were something that rarely happened.

"Don't forget your lighter." Albert teased. He knew Raymond couldn't go long without a cigarette, not since he started smoking at Sami's parties.

"I'd never leave home without it." Raymond laughed.

"And don't forget your comb," Albert continued. "We wouldn't want that thick head of hair of yours to fall out of place." Albert always found a way to joke about Raymond's slicked-back hair, especially during tense situations.

"One more thing. Don't forget what I said in Haiti," Albert said before he turned off his light. "If we are ever separated, I hope to find you underneath a sky full of stars. *Inshallah*."

"*Inshallah*," Raymond agreed. God willing.

Raymond sat down at his desk and traced the solid woodwork on the front drawer. He took out a single piece of paper and a pen and began writing a note. It didn't take much effort, as he had it all planned out the moment he knew he'd be leaving Egypt. His whole family was intended to read it, and he hoped it would help them sleep better at night.

Raymond's most expensive brown suit hung in the closet. Raymond asked his mother to press it earlier that morning, and she made the creases extra sharp as if she knew he was about to go places. He picked out a tie to match; it was a solid caramel color he only wore on special occasions. It had a certain sheen to it that made him appear distinguished.

Raymond picked up a pair of shoes and a shoe-shining kit from the bottom of the closet. He sat on the edge of his bed and waxed each shoe until tomorrow's reflection looked back at him. They were a sturdy pair of shoes, and they had to be because they were about to bring him around the world. He placed the shoes at the foot of the bed for the morning. His single bag held a few changes of clothes and a handful of mementos, including a keychain that once held the keys to his father's motorcycle and all the magazine clippings Albert had ever sent him. He slipped in the copy of a National Geographic Magazine Albert had tossed him and zipped up his bag.

Finally, he neatly folded a handkerchief and settled it onto his nightstand. Embroidered at the bottom corner of it were his true initials, V.B., and the richness of the deep red thread rose from the cloth with purpose. He placed a pocket-sized comb on top of it because he knew it would probably be windy. He never left home without a full pack of cigarettes, so he made sure those were in place.

He checked for his paperwork and knife under his mattress one last time, then reread the handwritten list he already memorized. He tightly rolled the thin piece of paper in his hands. He slid it into an empty toothpaste tube and turned off the light.

Five

International Waters, 1950

There would always be something magnetic about Egypt at sunrise. It would forever remind Raymond of motorcycle rides with his father to the pyramids, when the ancient sun met them for a new day. Mornings in Cairo were when the city's landscape stood unfiltered and unapologetic in its stillness, before the rest of the earth began to shake. It would always be the time of the day where Raymond sorted through his thoughts with clarity and uninterrupted purity.

It was as if Egypt knew he had to leave. The clouds from the day before disappeared overnight. The usual grit and smoke of the country retreated that morning as if parting the way forward. The routine street noises and traffic seemed to level off. The sun switched places with the moon as an early morning quietness settled overhead. It was the last time he ever saw Egypt underneath a honey-colored light. Egypt kissed him once on each cheek and bid him farewell. He'd always be grateful for that.

Raymond tightened the cap of the toothpaste tube. He double and triple-checked that it was secure before he slid it into the breast pocket of his jacket. He smoothed down the lapels of his suit and put his hands in his pockets. A single handkerchief sat in his pocket, and Raymond squeezed it for reassurance, just like his father used to.

He posed as a businessman on the way to France. He had the paperwork to prove his travel purposes if anyone asked. Raymond's slicked-back hair forced sunlight to bounce off it. It made him look aristocratic, like he had important business to attend to across the Mediterranean Sea. He found a previously uncovered confidence in his bones and muscles as he boarded the ship. He needed as much poise as he could muster if it were all going to work.

"Have you heard about the French women?" Albert asked as he leaned against the railing of the ship. "The carefree type, so much different from Egyptians."

Raymond didn't answer. He had heard of the French women, yes, but the toothpaste tube in his pocket was his only main concern at that moment.

"We will take a trip to Paris when the time comes," Sami said. "Visit the Notre Dame, see the Eiffel Tower. We'll find our way through all the arrondissements."

Albert smiled and chucked the butt of a cigarette into the water below. "You can't forget about the Moulin Rouge, Sami."

Sami cocked his head towards Albert. "That will be our first stop, of course."

Albert took out a fresh cigarette from his pack and lit it. He only chain-smoked when he was nervous.

"How are you feeling?" Sami asked Raymond. "You've been strangely quiet this whole morning."

"I'm fine, *Alhamdullah*," Raymond's answer came out more as a reflex than anything else.

"That's what I want to hear," Sami said. "We made it, look at us."

"On the way to France," Albert said in a dreamy tone.

Standing on the top deck of the ship made Egypt look significantly smaller than Raymond expected. From within its streets, Cairo was an almost never-ending maze of livelihood. Raymond had spent the better part of his youth constantly moving around those streets, but Egypt sat still for once from the port. The country welcomed him home when he was just a young boy, but now it was the country that expelled him as a young man.

Raymond regretted that life in Egypt didn't work out. Even though the region's politics were completely out of his control, he couldn't help but wonder how things would have been if he weren't being forced out of his home. Life in Egypt could have been glorious, but the alignment of his life with Cairo's just wasn't in the cards.

Egypt found clever ways of expelling the Jewish community. Finding work in the country as a Jew became almost impossible. In both the private and public sector, upwards of 90 percent of employees had to be legal Egyptian citizens to gain work. The majority of Egyptian Jews, like Raymond, never gained proper citizenship in Egypt. With no work came no hopes for a thriving future. The country made it an inevitable reality that all the Jews would be expelled one way or another.

The community that once prospered in Cairo and Alexandria was reduced to people who had to leave with only what they could carry. The majority of their personal property had been taken away by the government. They sewed their gold jewelry into the seams of their clothes and packed them neatly in the few suitcases they could carry. They had to find ways to hide just a little bit of their wealth as if it were something to be ashamed of.

The Egyptian Jews on the ship carried a *laisser-passer*, a one-way travel document. With it, there was no returning. Egypt wiped its hands clean of its Jews, and for most, it meant leaving a home that didn't want them anymore.

They looked across the sea for a new life and never looked back.

Egypt would forever be the mold that shaped Raymond into the man he was for the rest of his life, no matter the circumstances of his departure. The tastes of freshly made hummus would be a thing of the past, and the touch of the Sahara's sun on the back of his neck would only burn in memories. Days of football with his classmates and motorcycle rides with his father existed in a country that wasn't meant for him anymore. But more than anything he left back on the shore, Raymond would miss his mother and five sisters the most.

He woke up that morning when the moon was still high, and the city was still quiet. Albert's bed was already made, and his single bag was packed and sat at the foot of it. Raymond folded his hands in his lap and sat silently, one last time, in his bedroom. He stretched one hand out to touch the wall. The thick walls and the foundation of the house cooled in the evening and early morning hours. He touched it like it was a lasting hug from a home he'd never see again.

Raymond donned his prepared suit and shoes. He slid on his glasses and neatly combed his thick head of hair. Before he walked out of his bedroom, he kissed the note he had written and left it on his pillow. He wondered which one of his sisters would find it first but hoped his mother would beat them to it.

He wasn't sure when he'd see them again but knew that he was partially doing this for them. He needed to be the first in his family to leave so that he could be the first to bring them over to a new home one day. He hoped he'd see them again under better circumstances, in a land where they were accepted. Raymond secretly wished that place would be America, but it was so far out of reach he never thought it to be possible.

If there was ever one person who regretted his leaving the most, it was his mother. She always suspected that Albert had influenced Raymond. Although she wasn't entirely pleased by what she saw as a negative impact, she had to let Raymond be the man of the household and didn't say a word about it. She found his letter and read it for what seemed like one hundred times. Her hands never stopped shaking as she read his words. He explained how he was forced to leave in a hurry but had faith that they would be together again one day.

Raymond's sisters had never questioned his activities before he left. They were too busy with their own lives as young women to be concerned with what he did and were unaware of his other persona. Decades later, when they asked him if he was involved in espionage in Cairo, he'd only smile and change the subject.

The toothpaste tube in his pocket felt like a thousand bricks. Rolled into it was a single piece of paper with the names of all the people he was responsible for. There were families on board with children who had to leave Egypt. There were single men fleeing the country and newly married couples who wanted to make a home elsewhere. Raymond was responsible for all of them. Once they got to France, they'd be on their own. But until then, he needed to take care of them.

Over one hundred names were written on the rolled-up paper within the toothpaste tube, and their identities were one of the biggest secrets he ever had to keep. The people on his list were all immediate family members of his fellow spies. Raymond was in charge of ensuring their safety to France before Egyptian authorities found them. Each name represented a life in his hands, lives that made the painful decision to leave their home in Egypt for a better home, somewhere else. He carried their names in a toothpaste tube, in a pocket close to his heart. He didn't know where else to put them.

He thought he'd never forget those names. He read the rolled-up piece of paper so many times that he'd memorized each one. Not because he had to, but because he felt like he needed to. The letters and the words became a permanent fixation in his mind. He thought he'd never forget those names, but one by one, he eventually did. By the time he reached ninety years old, none of those names meant anything to him, but the toothpaste tube always did.

"Just a few more minutes, gentlemen," Sami said. He was always so sure of himself. "Drink it up one more time because who knows if we will ever come back."

Sami leaned his forearms against the railing before him and seemed to be at peace with leaving Egypt. He'd send for Bridgette once he was settled in France. If there was ever a moment when Sami seemed still, it was then. There were no more missions and no more orders from higher-ups. That was the final time they worked together, and it was ultimately to help their own community thrive and survive somewhere else. At the end of the day, it was all Sami ever wanted.

Albert ran his fingers through his hair and looked up at the sky, then down onto Egypt, as if he were better than it all. France would be the first stop, but Raymond knew that Albert still had his heart and mind set on returning to New York. Albert's life had taken one detour after another, but he never lost sight of home.

As the ship swayed ever so lightly against the dock, Raymond was washed with waves of regret and guilt. It overshadowed his last few moments in Egypt. It took away from the country's beauty and the significance of what they were involved in. For one last moment, he felt Egypt's pulse within his own and hoped he'd be able to come back one day. But in reality, that day would never come.

"Sami," Albert said softly as he nudged him with his elbow.

Sami and Raymond followed Albert's gaze to the shore. A handful of police cars with flashing lights and whining sirens raced towards their docked ship.

"*Yalla*," Sami said. His voice remained calm, but his deep tone said otherwise.

And just like, the three of them left the top deck of the ship and went their separate ways. For the rest of his life, Raymond always had a hard time saying goodbye because of that one moment never gave him the chance to.

Raymond retreated to the interior of a lower cabin while the beating of his heart swelled in his ears. He and Albert went over this situation multiple times together, and Raymond had rehearsed this scenario on his own countless more. There were a handful of sleepless nights, especially most recently, when Raymond planned what he'd do if anyone were on to them. Never in his wildest dreams did he think it would happen, but then again, he didn't dream much anymore.

Their plan was simple. If the police came looking for them, all they had to do was blend in with one of the families they were escorting to France. Raymond had their names memorized into his heart and already knew some of the families personally from years of living near them in Cairo. All he had to do was find a family to attach to, just for the time being, while his own family had no idea what kind of circumstances he was caught up in.

But when it came down to it, rehearsal and reality were two separate entities.

A horn with the force of a thousand shofars blared from above. Its voice was loud enough to wake up all of Egypt. A handful of birds fluttered into the air from the initial surprise of the noise. The ship stepped back from the dock within a moment, and Egypt slowly seemed out of reach. Raymond walked through the middle-class cabin and searched for a few familiar faces, but everyone seemed to be strangers. He needed to find a hidden refuge, and it needed to happen quickly.

The ship continued to move away from the shore. The floor underneath his feet rocked back and forth, and an uneasiness rose in his throat. From the confines of the interior cabin, it was almost impossible to know how far they were from the dock or if the police had made it onto the ship. Raymond hoped for the best but knew to prepare for the worst.

He listened closely for the Egyptian police. In between the engine's roars and the chatter among the passengers, Raymond's ears became finely acute to any outside threats. He searched for their deep and aggressive voices in the crowds, but they hadn't found him yet.

Raymond maintained his composure, no matter how jumbled his insides felt. He scanned the middle-class cabin for familiar faces, as if in a sea of strangers, he would somehow find his own family. He searched for neighbors and faces he knew throughout Heliopolis, faces that matched the names inside the toothpaste tube. He looked for a family when his own was somewhere still onshore. He never knew the unwavering need to belong until those few moments, when he didn't belong anywhere.

Raymond eyed a woman with an infant and a toddler. Her name was Jacqueline, and Raymond was an acquaintance with her late husband. His stomach rose to his throat. Being a recent widow, Jacqueline gave him a chance to hide within her family to pose as her husband. His backbone disappeared, and he regretted the decision even before he approached her, but he had no other choice.

"Jacqueline, hello," Raymond said as he walked towards her and her children.

Jacqueline's eyes widened into two full moons. She wasn't supposed to have much contact with Raymond during the whole journey to France. Regardless, she smiled with pleasantries, as if this were a routine trip and not a journey out of the country and into another world.

"Good morning, Raymond. Are you well?" Jacqueline asked as she held her infant in her arms.

Raymond whispered a few quick details to Jacqueline, and her back stiffened. She nodded in agreement and allowed Raymond to play with her toddler as if the child were his. Her son was luckily a friendly young boy who was eager to play with him. In between joyful games and small bits of laughter, Raymond caught one last glimpse of Egypt through a round porthole window. The Egypt he knew shrank in size, in unison with his heart.

Jacqueline held her infant daughter tightly to her chest as the baby began to cry. "Sssh, *mon chéri*," Jacqueline whispered to her baby. It was clear that aside from comforting her daughter, she didn't want to cause any sort of commotion that could potentially lead the police to them.

Raymond had no sense of time anymore. He wasn't sure how many minutes had passed as he played the role of husband and father. He had never wanted so desperately to have a family of his own until that moment, when he understood how quickly it could be taken away.

Heavy footsteps clamored up the ship's steel stairwell. The commotion was undeniably forceful, and the approaching sounds made some passengers nervous. The bodies attached to those footsteps moved with intention. Raymond fidgeted with the handkerchief in his pocket. His fate was finding its way to him; he just didn't know it yet.

Their voices became increasingly louder. Arabic flew off their tongues with aggression and a deep, hoarse undertone. There was no doubt in Raymond's mind that the armed police officers were coming closer, no matter how hard he tried to believe otherwise. They were looking for him, along with Albert and Sami and a small handful of other men from their group if they hadn't found them yet.

Raymond took a coin out of his pocket and put it in the palm of his hand. He flashed it in front of Jacqueline's toddler son and played a handful of disappearing tricks with him. He wished with all his might that he could disappear, the way the coin did to the young boy. But he had to remind himself that even with the most well-trained hand, the coin never truly vanished.

The young boy giggled when Raymond revealed the location of the hidden coin. "Again! Again!"

Raymond smiled and tousled the boy's thick head of hair. He prayed that the young boy would have a beautiful life in France.

Raymond always did what he was told. He performed the classic coin trick one more time, and for that last moment, he was suspended in a world of innocence. The police approached, but Raymond's breath was surprisingly calm. Underneath his most expensive suit, beads of sweat dotted his back and trickled down the back of his neck. In his pocket, Raymond's fingers fumbled with his handkerchief again. On the outside, he remained calm. If this were how fate would have it, so be it.

The police officers opened the door from the stairwell of the ship and barged into the cabin. All the passengers shook with surprise. They held their family members and belongings closer, which was all too common for Egyptian Jews to do those days.

Two police officers, dressed in identical utility uniforms, walked into the cabin as if they were ready to flip it upside down. They were fueled by anger and determination, and for a moment,

Raymond realized they shared some common ground. Raymond knew anger and determination all too well, as they were the driving forces that made him flee Egypt to begin with.

The two police officers started to walk past some of the passengers. They were clearly looking for certain faces in particular. Raymond knew his face was one of them.

"Don't hide him anymore!" one police officer shouted. His tall stature gave him an advantage when searching through the crowds. "There is no point in going down with him, just to protect him!"

Jacqueline tightened her hug on her baby. Raymond regretted ever getting her involved.

"Where is he?" the other police officer yelled. He held a baton in his dominant hand with his wrist cocked to the side as if getting ready to swing it at anyone who got in his way.

"Show yourself now!" the tall police officer shouted. "We know you are here. We already captured your co-conspirators."

A gust of air got caught in Raymond's throat and burned all the way down. Sami and Albert were smarter than that to get caught. It had to be a bluff.

"It is time to give up. Surrender yourself."

Raymond almost laughed at the idea. As if anyone would give up that easily. Surrendering himself to the Egyptian authorities would never be an option, not under any circumstances. He continued to play with Jacqueline's young son as he methodically tried to figure out his next move. He knew the blueprints of the ship with such detail; it was as if he had constructed the ship himself. He knew the exits and the corridors, which doors led inwards, and which doors led outside.

But there was ultimately nowhere to go. The ship had already left the dock and was sailing in the open waters. All his escape plans were based on still being onshore. He found himself in an entirely different situation, one that he had no plan for.

The police officers started going to every passenger one by one and looked into their fear-stricken faces. Raymond regretted that any of them had to get involved because of him.

"*Yalla, Habibi!*" Albert screamed from the opposite side of the cabin. He only had eyes for the pair of police officers, and in an instant, they only had eyes for him too.

Raymond's attention snapped to his cousin, the last time it would ever do so. Albert stood in the doorway of a stairwell, his arm draped upwards against the frame, a cigarette hanging from his lips.

The police officers left their frantic search and ran towards him. In between all the unsettling commotion, Raymond and Albert caught each other's eyes. Their lives aligned, one more time before it was all gone. No matter how many backup plans or escape routes they rehearsed together, neither of them ever planned on saying goodbye. Not like that.

And even though that moment seemed to string along in the world between them for a second too long, Albert had to leave. He retreated into the stairwell and darted away from the police officers as fast as he could. The heavy footsteps of their boots traveled across the middle-class cabin and followed Albert wherever he led, until it was out of earshot.

Raymond sat quietly still near Jacqueline and her children. His chest heaved in and out as if there was not enough air in the room to fill his lungs. The palms of his hands were cold to the touch with sweat, and every ounce of him knew that he should stay put. But regardless, he gathered enough energy to get up and leave. He needed to find a better hiding place, somewhere away from all the people he was trying to save. Being around them wasn't going to do anyone any good.

Raymond should have gone downstairs. He should have found a hidden utility closet or cargo area to hide until the ship docked in France. But his quickening footsteps led him upstairs, and all he could do was hope they led him towards Albert.

A handful of voices shouted at each other in Arabic. The shouts undeniably guided Raymond closer to the police officers, but he also held on to the belief that it took him closer to his cousin too. For one of the first times in his life, Raymond's plan was not to have one. Raymond never believed in violence, but in that instance, the pocket knife his father gave him seemed to have a purpose.

The door leading to the upper deck opened up to a sun-bursting sky. The sea surrounded the boat in all directions, and the horizon line swayed ever so slightly with the ship's motion. It took a moment for Raymond to gather his bearings and adjust to the mid-morning brightness. The inner cabins were dark and full of a communal worry, while outside spoke of light and hope.

Raymond stood by himself on the top deck and spun around in a quick circle as he searched for anyone familiar. But there was no one. And there was nothing around him except the stretch of the Mediterranean that connected his old home to his new one. Egypt was long gone, and it seemed like Albert was too.

The ship swayed over the sea's waves, and Raymond tried to steady his footing. The voyage to France continued on its way, regardless if there were police officers and spies on board or not.

The short minute of silence disappeared as a frantic rush of Arabic shouts came back. The police officers yelled and cursed at anyone who would listen. Raymond fine-tuned his ears to pick up Albert's voice, but he didn't hear his cousin anywhere. He found a short wall near the stairwell to hide behind. He pressed his back against it and held his breath as if the sound of his breathing limited him from hearing Albert's voice amongst the shouts. There was still nothing.

The two police officers scrambled around on the opposite side of the deck. Raymond peered around the edge of the wall just as the officers ran towards the deck's railing. They hunched over the bars, just enough to look down without falling. It was as if they were looking for someone who jumped overboard, and in Raymond's heart of hearts, he knew that person was Albert.

In between his deep breaths and the continuous thrashing of the sea, Raymond picked up another voice he knew all too well. It was Sami. His voice echoed up from one deck below. Raymond couldn't make out what he was saying or who he was talking to, but even on the brink of captivity, he kept his charisma. Knowing Sami was still there gave Raymond a sudden surge of hope that maybe they were all ok for the time being.

"Officers, please!" a man shouted. His accent was French, and Raymond never realized until that moment how comforting that language had become. Raymond turned around as the boat captain and a handful of crew members walked onto the top deck.

The two police officers turned around to face them, but in the midst of it, one of them caught Raymond's eyesight.

"*Yalla*, there is one of them!"

Raymond shuffled around the corner of the wall as the two officers started running towards him, both holding their batons.

"Gentlemen, as the captain of this ship, I must order this to stop immediately!" The captain shouted. No amount of batons seemed to hinder his intentions.

Neither officer paid him any attention. They kept their sights on Raymond like predators, ready to strike.

"Arrest him!" the taller officer shouted.

Raymond peeled himself off the low wall and ran in the opposite direction of the officers and captain. He found the nearest stairwell, and he ran so fast down the stairs he skipped many along the way. Just as he was nearing the doorway to an inner cabin, the heavy breaths of the police officers lined the curve of his neck. One officer grabbed him by the collar of his suit and knocked him down the remaining three steps. Raymond's back hit the cabin's door like a bulldozer and a sharp sting shot through the entirety of his right side.

"One more Zionist caught," the taller police officer said and went on to beat Raymond with his baton. He took blows to his side and back as he tried to scramble up from the bottom steps.

"I order you to stop this immediately!" The captain ran down the steps and met the police officers at the landing.

At that point, there was nothing anyone could say to get in between the police officers' batons and Raymond.

"Release him! Release him this instant!" The captain pushed the officers out of the way and stood as a physical shield in front of Raymond.

"As the captain of this ship, I order you to release this man," the captain continued. "This ship is in international waters, and you no longer have any jurisdiction."

The Egyptian police officers both gave Raymond one more fierce kick as he started to stand.

"This man is under my protection," the captain said. "And I assure you he will arrive safely into France."

Raymond pulled himself off the floor. He wasn't sure if the blood dripped from his mouth or his nose. The pair of police officers released a string of curses in Arabic, none of which the captain understood. They continued to stand in a fighting stance, breathing hard with adrenaline.

In what was one of the longest moments of his life, Raymond stood behind the captain, bleeding from the wound inflicted by the hands of people he once considered his countrymen. Raymond's body shook with pain, but he stood with his shoulders squared and his glasses on straight. The country he had once called home wanted nothing to do with him, while a man from another country welcomed him with no questions asked.

No one wanted to back down. The Egyptian police puffed their chests. The taller officer's nostrils flared with the intensity of his anger. The captain continued to stand his ground. After a few more terse moments, the police officers retreated in unison. They took a step back but kept their hands on the sides of their belts, close to their weapons.

"Gentlemen, please," the captain said. He motioned them towards his onlooking crew members as if they were old friends. "Please allow my crew to escort you from here."

Two crew members led the police officers out of the stairwell and into the middle-class cabin. They looked back at Raymond one last time, and he recognized in them the eyes of people ready to get rid of him as if they represented the home that didn't want him anymore. They ultimately disappeared, but the sense of being unwanted stayed with Raymond for years, well past France and well into adulthood. Even when his memory started to fade, he recalled how their eyes looked at him with disgust.

And just like that, a man named Captain Pierre Montague from Marseille, France saved Raymond's life.

Raymond stayed to himself for the rest of the long journey to France. Captain Montague heard about Raymond's mission and found a sense of virtue in it. He set him up in an unused crew member's room for the remainder of the trip. As Raymond walked through the cabins to get to the empty room, he searched through the passengers for Albert and Sami. He tried to find Sami's charismatic voice in between conversations with passengers, but he was nowhere to be found. He tried to find Albert's slender stature and immaculate mustache, but it was as if it had all vanished from the Earth. Rumors were going around the ship that other spies had been arrested before the captain had the chance to intervene.

Within the small but safe confines of the crew member's room, Raymond lost track of time. There was no way to know how long it had been since the police officers tried to arrest him, and there was no way to know if they had gotten to Albert and Sami. It made Raymond sick to his stomach to think that he was the only one who managed to escape.

Raymond took off his suit jacket and placed it on the back of a single chair in the room. His most expensive suit lost its luster with the new bloodstains. He tried to spot-clean it. He needed France to know that he was a decent man. He meticulously dabbed at the bloodstains on his suit until his fingers rubbed sore. He eventually fell asleep but didn't have the capacity to dream.

And after all of that, the ship found its way to France.

The shores of Marseille, France, were beautiful. It was the most peaceful coastline he had ever seen, and even into his later years, the South of France would always be one of his favorite places in the world. It wasn't just because the South of France was built around the marvelous coasts along the Mediterranean Sea or because of the laid-back sunshine days throughout the year. But because Marseille would always remind him of freedom.

As the ship approached the shore, Raymond's mission was almost complete.

Raymond disembarked with the group of Egyptian Jews he was in charge of. All the names on the rolled-up paper in the toothpaste tube, all the families and individuals he memorized, had finally made it safely to France. He never gave himself enough credit for what he did; he never truly acknowledged how many lives he took out of harm's way. He never found out that Jacqueline's son eventually had a beautiful life in France.

As his group followed him onto a bus, there was soft chatter about the captured men. It was all hearsay, but Raymond clung to every word as if it were the last he'd ever hear of Albert and Sami. As the bus lead them away from the docked ship, he finally felt that he was on his own. There was no Albert or Sami to lean on for guidance anymore. Raymond pictured his mother and five sisters weeping over his farewell letter in Cairo as he made his way to a vineyard in the South of France. There would be no more walks through the enchanting bazaars of Cairo, no more weekend drives to the pyramids with his father.

Raymond never saw Egypt again.

The bus had one more stop before Raymond's. It approached a smaller farm, and a family of four prepared their belongings to get off. Raymond knew the Cohens well; their school-aged children would never need to worry for their futures in a place like France. As they walked off the bus, Raymond knew that it was all worth it, no matter how hard the journey had been.

A slim, familiar man walked from the back of the bus to sit down in the seat next to Raymond. Raymond, distracted by the rolling hills outside of his window, didn't turn to him immediately. But when he did, a needle in his spine forced him to sit straight up.

"Next stop is yours," the man said, his full head of curls still carried the same bounce it always had at Sami's parties. It was Henry.

"Yes, one more stop," Raymond said in all seriousness. He didn't even know Henry had left Egypt with them, let alone got on the same bus as him.

"I must keep going," Henry said. "For a few more hours."

Raymond looked at him for more clues and dug into his words for a deeper meaning.

Henry reached out his hand for a handshake, and Raymond took it. The crisp edges of a small piece of paper crinkled softly between their warming palms.

"Marseille is beautiful in the evenings," Henry said as he slipped his hand away. He spoke as if he knew the city like an old friend. "Find some time to visit the port and try an *éclair au chocolat*."

"Will do," Raymond said.

"Send my regards to Albert tomorrow, under a sky full of stars. *Inshallah*," Henry said.

"*Inshallah*," Raymond repeated. God willing.

Raymond looked down at the small piece of paper. On one side, there was an address in Marseille, 712 Quai du Port, and on the other side, an address in Paris, 818 Rue du Juliette. He slid the paper into his pocket and gathered his bag to leave.

The bus driver dropped Raymond off at his stop. His mission was done. He tried to wipe his hands clean of everything he ever did on the streets of Cairo and wash himself of the man he had grown to become. He found himself on a meticulously maintained tree-lined road that led straight to a French vineyard. It was where he had the chance to start anew, but even decades later, he never stopped cleaning the bloodstains off his suit.

Six

Marseille, France, 1950

The air of Marseille sat differently in his lungs. It breathed of the Mediterranean Sea. It tasted of raw oysters and salt. It was delicious, it was peaceful, and with no other choice, it became home.

Raymond was early like he usually was for important occasions. He leaned his back against a bistro chair at an outdoor café and adjusted the gold watch on his wrist. It was only 3:15 PM, and nightfall in Marseille was still hours away, but he waited anyway. He didn't want to miss anything, even though he wasn't sure what he was looking for. According to Henry, Marseille was beautiful in the evening. That had to mean something.

Raymond took the small piece of paper out of his pocket and laid it flat on the table before him. He drank his black coffee while he memorized the addresses on either side in case he ever lost the paper. He didn't want to ever lose its memory.

712 Quai du Port.

And that was where he waited. The address led him to an unmarked building, one that didn't have any meaning to him. Its limestone façade blended in with an identical row of buildings that lined the portside street, its familiar design stretched out in all directions of Marseille. Nothing was disconcerting about the building, no special significance in the address, absolutely nothing that stood out to Raymond. But he knew better than to question the obvious. There had to be something more.

Raymond trusted the process. It was all he'd done in the past few years in Cairo, and even though he expected his mission to be over the moment he stepped on the vineyard in France, he knew it wasn't. It wouldn't be over until he knew Albert was safe.

So he waited. He waited for hours at the Old Port of Marseille for Albert to appear. He sat out in the open and didn't try to be discreet. If there were ever a time that he needed to be seen, it was then, because he wasn't willing to accidentally go unnoticed by his cousin. Raymond had all the time in the world to wait, so he remained vigilant and trusted that Albert would show up.

In those hours of limbo, Raymond stole moments in time where France took over his imagination. There was no more Haiti and no more Egypt. He found his way to France, and as he sat at the outdoor table facing the mysterious address, he imagined what life would be like there. He wanted to casually dine at an opened-air table over plates of coq au vin and watch the locals move around him as the salty breeze ran through his hair.

In those stolen moments from reality, Raymond's attention was drawn to a nearby bakery. Adjacent to the address where he waited was a corner bakery whose large storefront windows allowed him a glimpse into a sweet world within. A woman stood behind the counter, and every time she smiled at a customer, his world began to shift. He wanted nothing more than to go inside and learn her name. He wanted nothing more than to share in her smile. But that was not his purpose that day, and as time spun clockwise on his gold watch, Marseille's afternoon dimmed to night.

Henry was right; Marseille was beautiful in the evening. The city had an undeniable grit, but it also had a soft side that could only be a product of its Mediterranean shores. Storefronts switched on warm lighting, and neighborhood cafés lit candles on their outdoor tables. People strolled along the streets and boulevards with a sense of ease rather than a rush of purpose; the sea breeze rocked babies to sleep in their strollers.

But regardless of the beauty, no one came. Raymond spent hours looking for a familiar face in the crowds of strangers. He searched everywhere for a glimpse of Albert's prominent mustache. He heightened his sense of hearing for Sami's contagious voice. He looked for any possible signs that would point him in the right direction, but as evening turned into the thick of the night, there was nothing to hold on to except for the slow and steady rocking of the boats in the marina. There was no trace of Albert, no signs from Sami, nothing to make him believe they were near.

Raymond waited until each restaurant closed for the night, and every last table and chair was empty. He waited until the moon climbed to the top of the sky and settled in behind a blanket of scattered clouds. No one came for him, and there was nothing left for him to find. He would have waited an eternity if it meant seeing Albert just one more time. But when he couldn't wait any longer, he got up from his chair and prayed that his cousin made it to France safely because praying was all he had left. Raymond left the Old Port of Marseille as a sky full of stars lit the path forward, and for the first time in his adult life, that path didn't include Albert.

When there was no one left to wait for and nowhere else to go, he went home to the vineyard. When days turned into weeks and a month went by without a sign from Albert, he pushed away his worst fears and quietly hoped that their best days together were yet to be seen. Raymond walked each day with a special kind of optimism that fueled him for the rest of his life. It was what kept him resilient, it was what pushed him forward, and later in his life, it was the medicine that always made him feel better.

As Raymond tried to track down Albert, he visited every corner of Marseille and searched for him on a neighboring farm where Albert had previously planned to stay. But there was no trace of him ever being there, and Raymond's life had to go on. He worked at the vineyard until early afternoon on most days. His hands traded the sand of Egypt for France's rich soil, and his fingers were stained with the deep undertones of the grapes he picked. The work was manual labor, and his university education didn't matter at that point, but the job kept him sheltered and fed. If there was one thing that France taught him, it was that safety always waited for him if he searched in the right places.

Raymond's job was stable enough in a time when stability was all he needed. He learned how to harvest grapes and watched as they transformed into wine. He was never a man with a deep taste for alcohol, but after months of understanding the soil and the grapes of the region, he learned to admire the process of winemaking. The vineyard on the outskirts of Marseille took him in when no one else would. He owed his existence to the soil and earth of the South of France. Raymond would eventually travel to over thirty-five countries and lived in many of them, but the South of France would forever be his favorite.

The ship ride from Egypt to Marseille stood only months in the past, but it might as well have lived in another lifetime. On most days, Raymond's newly adopted home stood as a distraction to the past. But there were times when a police car's whining siren made him freeze in place. His near-capture by the Egyptian authorities haunted him; it brought an acidic taste to his mouth that he couldn't swallow. At those moments, Raymond had to actively remind himself that he made it to safety, that no more officials were searching for him, that he had left it all behind in Egypt.

He was far away from Egypt in miles and memories. It was a place of the past and would forever be just that. Raymond would never return, not when the region's politics died down, not when tourism made it a desirable destination, not then and not ever again.

Life in Cairo was quickly replaced with quieter days in France. Cairo's everlasting noise and layers of dust cleared the way for portside sunsets and boats bobbing at the docks. Arabic disappeared, but French always stayed by his side. Into the later part of Raymond's life, French was the language that would roll off his tongue with ease even when he had difficulty finding the right words to speak.

Cairo would always remind him of coming of age, but Marseille would remind him of freedom.

Marseille was the kind of place that asked you to stay just a little bit longer. It wasn't like Port-au-Prince with its unforgiving hurricane seasons or like Cairo with its relentless sandstorms. Marseille sat at the edge of the Mediterranean Sea with its toes in the water and its head in the clouds. The colors of Marseille were more vibrant, the sun more relaxed. It coated Raymond's skin until it turned olive but never left a burn.

On most days when the weather in the South of France was favorable, and his daily work on the vineyard was done, Raymond rode a Vespa into town. It had a handful of rusted spots he meant to fix, but it got him from place to place with ease. Raymond steered it through the outskirts of Marseille, and every time he held onto its handlebars, he could almost feel the weight of his father's hands holding onto him on the last day they visited the pyramids together. The Vespa was a far cry from his beloved bicycle in Haiti or his father's motorcycle in Egypt, but those days belonged to another era.

Haiti looked nothing like the rolling hills of the European countryside. Egypt seemed like a mythical land of exotic spices and sands that could never exist elsewhere. France was another world entirely, one that had wider skies and open doors.

Raymond rode into the Old Port of Marseille. Rows of limestone buildings lined the perimeter, and outdoor cafés spilled onto the sidewalks. Tables and chairs invited pedestrians to come and sit for a while. A flock of small birds fluttered their wings in a fountain. The Europe of Raymond's daydreams could have never predicted how perfect the air would feel on the back of his neck.

Raymond parked in a narrow alleyway and walked along the edges of the port. His innate sense of exploration ignited on the streets of Marseille. He spent as much of his free time as he could wandering its historic streets and tasting its rich French flavors. The French way of life felt like a home he never knew existed, and its undeniable welcome came on quicker than any of his other homes ever had. He pretended he was a local and hoped they couldn't see right through him.

Raymond often wrote letters at the Old Port. His once-monthly letters to Albert during their adolescence were replaced with a monthly letter to Uncle Nissim. He needed contact with his family as much as he needed their forgiveness. He wanted them to understand, but he couldn't tell them the truth. He needed to know they were safe and felt an unwavering regret that he'd ever put them in harm's reach.

The first letter he wrote was the hardest. Raymond was fluent in three languages but didn't know enough words to properly say sorry. So instead, he wrote about beautiful Marseille. Each line of his letter shared meaning and insight but held an edge of sorrow and regret. He spoke of life on the vineyard and how everything was fine. Later on in his life, Raymond willed himself time and time again into believing everything was fine, even when it wasn't. And even when it wasn't, Raymond only ever saw the beauty during tough times.

Raymond explained to Uncle Nissim how he and Albert had worked for the greater good of their community over the past few years. Raymond was good at keeping secrets and steered clear of all the espionage details. He explained how they had to leave Egypt on a minute's notice, and even though he spared him the specifics of the journey to France, he made sure Uncle Nissim knew that Albert helped save his life.

The truth tried to escape Raymond, but he was strong enough to hold it in. Uncle Nissim and the rest of his family never needed to know the details; all they needed to know was that he was safe, and everything was ok. They never knew the extent of his involvement in the spy ring, but it was for the best. It was the first of many letters to Uncle Nissim, which comforted and pained him to write. And on the last line of his letter, he explained how he lost contact with Albert, and for that, he would always be sorry.

Albert was everywhere he looked, but nowhere at all. So many things about France reminded Raymond of his cousin, even if neither of them had ever been there before. Raymond walked the streets of Marseille and stared through the crowds in hopes of a miracle. Dozens of men smoked cigarettes the same casual way Albert did, the butt hanging loosely on their lips. There were others whose slender physique mimicked Albert's, but at the end of the day, none of them were him. Raymond traveled much of Marseille on foot, and even though his eyes constantly explored the city, they were searching for Albert at the same time.

Raymond began to learn the ins and outs of Marseille. Whenever he ventured into town, he tried not to spend too much of his money, but when he did spare some cash, he made sure to try a new café. The flavors of France were rich, and he wanted to sample them from all parts of the city. An extra amount of money sat in his pockets that day, as he had just gotten paid for the week. It came right in time for his birthday, even if he didn't have anyone to celebrate it with.

As Raymond spent the afternoon walking around Marseille, his attention was taken by a familiar, quaint bakery. At second glance, he realized it was the one next to 712 Quai du Port. It seemed etched into the corner of the limestone façade as if it were an afterthought. The few extra coins in his pocket rattled against each other as he walked towards the bakery for the first time, not knowing it would be the first of many.

The front door stood wide open, and the Mediterranean's air mixed with the warm fragrances of flour and fresh yeast. There was a welcoming warmth in the bakery. Even though France's scents and herbs were unlike what he grew up with in Egypt, an identical quality of nurture and love helped remind him a bit of home. The bakery's immediate comfort was the place he didn't realize he yearned for.

A handful of patrons stood inside the bakery. Parents ordered pastries as their small children stared with excitement into the glass showcases of the shop. A young couple held hands as they waited their turn to order. Their silhouettes covered the bakery showcases, and even though it took a moment for Raymond to see clearly through the rows of pastries, he noticed her immediately.

She stood behind the counter. Her crisp white apron was tight enough to shape her torso into a slim hourglass. Wisps of chestnut-colored hair hung loosely around the lines of her face. She smiled at every customer as if they were a part of her family. Raymond would soon learn she treated everyone with that kind of affection, something that would ultimately be both her greatest asset and downfall.

Raymond approached the counter and ordered a cup of coffee and a chocolate éclair on a whim. He was too unfocused to think clearly. Everything about her distracted him. A chocolate éclair was the only thing he could come up with at the spur of the moment.

He wanted to talk to her. He wanted to know what her favorite pastry was and if the sunrise made her smile. He wondered if she was the store's principal baker or if it was a family-run business, the way many bakeries were. He had so many questions for her and hoped she had all the answers. Raymond had never felt so strongly intrigued by anyone in his life, and the momentum of his natural feelings almost threw him off his feet. But instead, he left with his coffee and éclair, without even learning her name.

Raymond took his food outside and left her behind. The bakery set up a handful of quintessentially French, round marble tables and bistro chairs out front, where customers enjoyed some sweets and the heartbeat of Marseille at the same time. Raymond found an empty table and sat on a chair facing outward towards the crowds of people walking by. He took bites of the rich éclair as he read a book without absorbing any of the story. He had nothing on his mind except the beautiful woman in the bakery. His shyness ultimately overshadowed his courage, and as the afternoon slowly turned to evening, he felt like his chance to say hello was gone. He snuck in one last look of her through the bakery's windows. Her smile made the world erupt.

Time on the vineyard moved slowly. He harvested grapes like a well-oiled machine but paid it little attention. His mind only had room for her. She wasn't the kind of woman who faded away when the sun rose the following day; her smile wasn't the kind anyone ever forgot. Raymond wanted to tell the world that he found the woman he was going to marry, but there was no one there to listen to him. Albert would have been happy for him, but he was nowhere to be found.

A handful of days passed until Raymond found enough courage to go back to the bakery. He toyed with the idea ever since their paths first crossed, but he often retreated into himself, unsure what he would even say to her. On the fifth day, as late afternoon approached, Raymond got back on his Vespa and rode it until it brought him to the corner bakery. The doors stood open as they previously had. He flattened the sides of his pants as he walked into the bakery.

A man with a perfectly round belly stood behind the counter and greeted Raymond with a hearty *bonjour*. Raymond searched in between the pastries and baguettes for her beautiful face, but her smile wasn't there to ignite the room. He ordered a coffee and a chocolate éclair, unable to think clearly once again, but this time it was caused by her absence.

As the late afternoon shifted towards early evening, the Old Port of Marseille began to dance with fluidity. Young couples filtered through the sidewalks, held hands across tables and spent the evening hours wondering about what their tomorrows together would bring. Families brought their children out to the marina after dinner and before bedtime to let them run off any extra energy before the moon's gentle glow lulled them to sleep.

Raymond sat alone at a table and sipped his coffee. It was something he had gotten used to in France. Up until life in Marseille, Raymond never knew what it meant to be alone. There was always someone nearby, whether it was his father with an unlimited amount of generational knowledge to pass down or his mother with a spoon to taste. At least one of his five sisters always came to him for that kind of protective brotherly love they couldn't get elsewhere. And there was Albert, the person who always held the match up to the wick within Raymond without hesitation. But in France, there was no one.

A kaleidoscope of human relationships moved before him. The people of Marseille gave Raymond a sense of anonymity. No one questioned who he was or where he came from. And even though Raymond was thankful to finally fall under the radar, he missed the connection.

A few weeks went by without Raymond trying to meet the woman at the bakery. He spent lots of time thinking about her but didn't want to face a recurring sense of disappointment if she wasn't at the bakery when he searched for her. So instead, he spent his downtime exploring other parts of Marseille. He searched for similar bakeries and other beautiful smiles. He watched the boats dock at the port and thought of how his mother and five sisters would love it there.

It took a while, but Raymond finally received a letter back from Uncle Nissim. Even before he opened it, the handwritten envelope flooded him with a strong sense of homesickness. He took a deep breath before he read it.

According to Uncle Nissim, things were taking a turn for the worst in Egypt. Nationalism was on the rise, and all prospects for a future were seemingly obliterated for the Jews. Uncle Nissim was going to give up on the country that he loved too. He was going to move back to New York, this time for good. He had a job lined up as a salesman in an electronics business with a few colleagues who were already in New York. A Brooklyn address was listed for Raymond to find him. Uncle Nissim promised that Raymond's mother and sisters would eventually join him once he got settled. At the very end of Uncle Nissim's letter, he asked if Raymond had heard anything about Albert. At that point, it had been nearly four months since Raymond last saw him, and he hadn't.

The first letter to Uncle Nissim was hard to write, and the follow-up wasn't any easier. There was an unmistakable pain in his words as he explained how he had no new information on Albert's whereabouts. Raymond hadn't heard from his cousin since the moment Albert taunted the Egyptian authorities. He hadn't seen his cousin since the moment he stood in the doorway, one cigarette loosely dangled from his lips as if he had no cares in the world. Raymond wanted to believe that Albert hadn't been captured on the boat, he couldn't stomach the idea that his cousin had jumped over the railings. He needed to believe that Albert found safety in another part of France, but it became increasingly hard to hold onto that hope. Raymond thought about Albert whenever he lit a cigarette, whenever the sun came up for the day, and whenever the moon rose with the night. He was sure that Uncle Nissim thought about him even more.

Raymond focused his letter on positivity instead. He let his uncle know that he had been in Marseille for a few months and saved most of his money to move to Paris. There was something about the city of lights that captured Raymond's imagination, and he knew he had to experience it for himself. He toyed with the idea of moving to New York to be with his uncle, but Paris had his heart for the time being.

A couple of weeks flew by on the vineyard as it became peak harvesting season for the grapes. Raymond's manual work made his muscles ache, and his skin turn gold, but it also filled his pockets with more money than he had ever made. He worked longer days and picked up extra work on the weekends, just to save every penny towards his move to Paris.

The woman from the bakery had almost disappeared from his mind until he got a day off from work. Without even realizing it, he steered his Vespa in the direction of the bakery and looked for her one more time. All the luck in the world aligned because as he walked through the open doors, there she was.

It seemed as if she remembered him by the way her eyes widened when he approached. Even though they hadn't had a proper introduction, he sensed they had already met. He ordered a coffee and a chocolate éclair and finally asked if she would join him when she was done with work.

She agreed.

Raymond waited at an outdoor table for one hour until her shift at the bakery was over. It was the quickest and longest hour of his life.

She walked out of the bakery with her apron still on and held a plain white box tied with a delicate string. Raymond stood up from the table and pulled her chair out as she approached him. It was at that outdoor table for two where he learned all about her.

Her name was Odette. She had the most perfectly round eyes the color of caramel, and when he looked closely, they seemed speckled with gold. Her skin was much fairer than his and didn't absorb the Mediterranean sun the way his did, but she blushed at jokes, and the corners of her mouth pursed tightly when she tried to hold in her laughter.

Odette opened the bakery box and revealed an assortment of handmade French petit fours. She made them herself and insisted he try them all. Raymond's sweet tooth flourished because of that afternoon with Odette. Even when he was long gone from Marseille, he would never shake off his craving for sweets. Odette explained that the bakery wasn't just a place where she worked, but it was a part of her family. The man with the perfectly round belly was her father, and their family had owned the bakery for the past four generations. Flour, sugar, and butter were in her blood.

Raymond took Odette for walks around the Old Port of Marseille and watched the boats bob in the marina until the sun went down. He didn't have much money but tried to treat her to dinner at restaurants as much as he could. He opened doors for her and pulled out chairs, he walked her home on late evenings, and he fell in love with everything about her.

"What made you want to move to France?" Odette asked. Their shoulders touched side by side as they sat on a bench overlooking the marina.

The strings in Raymond's heart tightened as he concocted the only lie he'd ever tell her.

"My cousin and one of our friends. They always talked about how wonderful it would be to go to Paris." Although it wasn't entirely false, it wasn't entirely true either.

"Paris," Odette responded as if she were on an evening's journey of her own through the city of lights.

"Have you been to Paris before?" Raymond asked.

"Never," Odette answered. "I have only ever been here, in Marseille. But one day, I will make it to Paris."

"I will too," Raymond agreed.

"Paris has the best culinary schools in the world," Odette continued. "I want to study there."

"Do you?" Raymond asked. He didn't think she needed to learn anymore. Her baking was already perfection.

"I do," Odette said. "Everything I've learned came from my family's recipes and techniques. None of us are professionally trained in baking, but we somehow know what tastes right and the perfect way to knead dough. But I want to learn from the real masters in Paris."

"Does your father know about this?"

"He's known since I was ten years old," Odette said, completely sure of herself.

Raymond was sure of her too.

Their romance came on with the force of a summertime downpour. She covered him in bliss and washed away much of Raymond's secretive past. With her, he didn't need to look back at Egypt, and he didn't need to regret some of his earlier decisions. Raymond made sure Odette never learned of his involvement in the spy ring and why he truly left Egypt.

The only important thing was that they both had their sights on Paris. With no trace of Albert in Marseille, all he had left was a Parisian address scribbled onto the back of that small piece of paper. He wondered if Albert had somehow made his way there. The only way he'd find out was if he went there himself.

Raymond and Odette spent late afternoons and early evenings by the marina, planning where she would attend proper culinary school and how he would try to find an accounting job in Paris. They took walks around the majestically grand Abbey Saint-Victor and drifted around the old streets of Le Panier. The Basilique Notre Dame de la Garde always guided them like the northern star atop the hills of Marseille, and underneath its guidance, Raymond found a sense of peace. In a city where he had known no one, he found the person who knew him the best.

When the time was right, Raymond bought the most expensive diamond ring he could afford and asked Odette to marry him. And when she said yes, the remainder of his tomorrows became all hers.

Seven

Paris, France, 1951

Odette sprinkled a measurement of flour into a mixing bowl as she stood at the kitchen counter. She cracked a couple of eggs and folded the yolks into the ingredients. There was a delicate pressure in the way her hands worked, the kind that could only come from a lifetime's worth of apprenticeship and a heart full of dedication. Raymond sipped his afternoon cup of coffee at the kitchen table, and although he wasn't sure what she was going to bake, he knew it would be delicious.

"Save some of your coffee for this," Odette said as she wiped her flour-covered hands onto her apron.

"What are you making?" Raymond asked.

"Some madeleines. Chef Charlie gave me a new recipe to try," Odette said. She often spoke about her new culinary teacher with high regard, as if he could do no wrong.

Raymond put his mug down on the kitchen table, and even though it would take a while to bake, the wait would be worth it.

"Camille will bring the wine tonight," Odette explained. "And Charlie is making a beef bourguignon. They should be here by seven o'clock."

Raymond stretched out his left arm and turned his wrist sideways until his gold watch stared back at him. It was only late afternoon, and his appetite already grumbled for dinner.

"Is there anything I can do to help?" Raymond asked. He already knew that everything was probably taken care of, but it was still hard for him not to offer the help.

"There's nothing, *chéri*," Odette said with a smile that made the early spring evening feel like the height of summer. She turned around and got back to the batter.

It didn't take long to settle into Paris; it was as if the city had been waiting for them all along. Their one-room flat was modest, but it was all they needed at the time. The flat came sparsely furnished, and Odette added a few decorative touches, but none of that mattered when they set their eyes on the nearly floor-to-ceiling windows. A sweeping view of the French city gave their flat an elegant sense of vibrancy. A small balcony off the living room brought in a breath of fresh air, and on the other side, the distant Notre Dame peeked through the wrought-iron railings. When Paris went to sleep for the night, the sky opened up to another world of possibilities.

Life started off easy in Paris. Raymond secured his first accounting position and finally felt like he was on the right path towards providing for himself and his soon-to-be wife. There was nothing more that he liked more than knowing that he was able to keep her safe in a warm apartment and give her anything she wanted. Odette quickly found work at an upscale bakery. It was far different from the family bakery she was used to, but it taught her more techniques in a month than she had learned in a year. She began her studies at the culinary school and often came home smelling of flour and sugar. For Raymond, her happiness became his.

Even though they weren't married yet, Raymond and Odette's new life was like a continuous honeymoon. Paris served as the perfect backdrop for their love, with its everlasting romantic gardens and classically European boulevards. Odette took them to local markets where they smelled bunches of lavender and sampled French cheeses. Raymond found neighborhood cafés, and when he sat across small candlelit tables from Odette, his whole world felt right in front of him. They walked along the River Seine and listened to outdoor music performances. He felt richer just by walking down the streets of Paris, even if his wallet hardly held money. With her, anywhere felt like home.

Odette spoke passionately about her studies. She lit up with enough energy to light the moon whenever her new colleagues came to their flat for an aperitif. Camille and Charlie were both bakers themselves, and even though Raymond never had to cook a day in his life, watching Odette share recipes and techniques with her newly acquired friends made his life with her taste even sweeter.

The madeleines came out of the oven, and seven o'clock came around before Raymond even noticed. With a knock on the door, Camille and Charlie arrived at their flat with dinner and wine in their hands. Raymond sat around the small dining table, and even though there was hardly enough room for all of them, the kitchen was full of fresh aromas and warm laughter.

"The shower wasn't working this morning," Camille said.

"That's not entirely true," Charlie said with a slight smirk on his face. "The hot water wasn't working properly, but the shower was working."

"Yes," Camille agreed and took a deep sip of her glass of pinot noir. "The hot water wasn't working, so in my opinion, that means that shower wasn't working."

Odette laughed as she lit up a cigarette. A thin ring of smoke rose above her head like a halo.

"I asked Charlie to run downstairs to Marc, he lives on the first floor, and he fixes those types of things in our building."

"I go downstairs and find Marc, but when we come upstairs, there is Camille, barefoot and wrapped in her towel."

Raymond and Odette found Camille's eyes in unison, with the same look of questioning and astonishment on their faces.

"He was taking a long time," Camille tried to explain but couldn't hold back her laughter. "I just peeked out of our door and looked down the stairs to see if they were on their way."

"And then the door locked behind her."

The group of them erupted in shared laughter. It wasn't a surprise that Camille managed to lock herself out of their flat, and it wasn't a surprise that Charlie found it amusing. Odette glowed in the presence of her new friends. Raymond didn't notice as her smile drifted into Charlie's line of sight or when Odette and Charlie stole a moment away from the others.

Once the beef bourguignon was eaten, and their wine glasses were topped off, they brought the dinner party out onto the balcony. Odette served a plate of freshly made madeleines, and Paris served a horizon full of dancing lights. Cigarette smoke traveled from their mouths into the open evening air, and wine traveled the course through their bloodstreams. In that moment, there was nowhere else Raymond wanted to be, and Paris suddenly felt like it could be forever.

Paris allowed them to feel secure. Gone were the days and the homes of the past, and even though Raymond was physically far from his family in Egypt, Odette helped fill that void. Albert's disappearance managed to get pushed temporarily into an unutilized corner of Raymond's mind, if only for a short period of time because Odette had the power to help him forget. Paris stood as a beautiful distraction from what would always matter the most to him. In between the wide boulevards and seemingly endless romanticism of his new life with Odette, Raymond started to lose a sense of what he truly needed to do.

It was a bright spring Saturday morning when a string in Raymond's heart started to pull the curtains closed on their honeymoon, not knowing that Odette's heart was already doing the same. They had spent the early morning hours at an outdoor market, and through every cheese stand and bushel of fresh herbs, Raymond's mind started to fill with Albert, while Odette's started to burn for Charlie. It was a silent wall they started to build one brick at a time.

It wasn't until their walk back to their flat when Raymond spotted a copy of the latest National Geographic Magazine in a bookstore window. Until that point, his time in Paris had unknowingly been a much-needed distraction, but like all other distractions in the world, it came with an expiration. Raymond stood in front of the bookstore's window and stared at the National Geographic Magazines as if he were eye to eye with Albert.

"Raymond?" Odette asked. She had taken a few steps in front of him, quietly thinking about Charlie's latest batch of strawberry macarons, before she realized Raymond had stopped to look in the window.

"Yes, sorry," Raymond said. He tried to snap himself out of it, unsuccessfully.

"What are you looking at?" Odette asked. She joined his side and looked into the bookstore.

Raymond pointed to the signature yellow magazine. "My cousin, Albert, he used to read those magazines."

Odette stood beside him but didn't respond. All she knew about Albert was that somewhere along the way, Raymond lost contact with him and that he was forever regretful for it.

"Those were his favorite," Raymond said. "He always told me how he wanted to write travel articles like the ones in National Geographic."

"Do you want to go inside?" Odette asked. "Do you want to buy a copy to read at home?"

Raymond took his gaze away from the bookstore's window and looked into her soft, caramel eyes. "No, we can go."

Odette nodded in agreement, and they walked silently back to their flat. Even though Odette returned to casually enjoying the weekend walk through Paris, everything in the city suddenly reminded Raymond of Albert. Men with neatly pressed suits reminded him of Albert's style. People who smoked cigarettes on park benches and young boys running around, up to mischief, made Raymond miss his cousin tremendously. The remainder of the walk home made Raymond realize that even though home needed to be with Odette, it also needed to be near his family. He wasn't sure if Paris could ever be that place to him.

When they returned to their flat, Raymond opened the French doors and walked out on their balcony. Springtime tulips were beginning to bloom in the flowerpots scattered across its perimeter. A single wrought-iron table and two chairs took up most of the space. Raymond sat down at the table with a pen and a sheet of paper. It had been a while since he wrote to Uncle Nissim, and now more than ever, he felt like he needed him.

He told his uncle about the accounting job he secured in Paris and how he and Odette were planning on getting married next year. He hoped his family could somehow make the trip to Paris for the wedding, but more than anything, he wished Albert would stand by his side during it as his best man. It had been more than a year without a single trace of Albert. Neither of them had any new information on Albert's whereabouts, and even behind the shielded screen of a letter, Raymond could tell that it took a toll on Uncle Nissim. Without openly saying it, Raymond always feared the worst, but Uncle Nissim's correspondence helped him find the energy to hope for the best. He had a feeling his uncle felt the same.

The weekend morning in Paris shifted things for Raymond. An overwhelming need to find Albert, one way or another, pressed against his chest with the heaviness of rain-filled clouds. Where Odette had her priorities in Paris, Raymond had his elsewhere.

Uncle Nissim was always prompt with his responses. A letter came back sooner than Raymond expected. His uncle's letter wrote of New York and how well things were going there, compared to

Egypt's decline. Uncle Nissim always tried to convince Raymond to move to New York with him and promised that he could arrange for all of it. The idea of moving to New York was always a possibility, but for the time being, Paris was where he needed to be. Uncle Nissim always ended each letter asking about Albert, as if Raymond has extra information that he wasn't telling him.

Odette fit into Paris. She bloomed under the Parisian skies and grew into a confident baker at culinary school. She surrounded herself with like-minded people and found a sense of permanence in Paris. She wanted to spend her days learning and perfecting her baking, and she wanted to spend her evenings surrounded by those she enjoyed the most.

Odette liked to invite a handful of her culinary school classmates to their flat, where they shared bottles of wine and compared ideas on life. Raymond joined them but mostly kept to himself; he enjoyed being a spectator rather than actively participate in their world. His appreciation for wine grew from being around them, but it often allowed him to retreat and give the spotlight to Odette.

"Charlie, do you mind opening the bottle of Malbec?" Odette asked as she lit another cigarette. The smoke flew away from their balcony and disappeared into the Paris night.

"Had enough of the Sauvignon Blanc?" Charlie asked as he obliged and opened another bottle of wine.

"It's not that I've had enough," Odette answered. "But it's always good to try new ones."

Raymond took a sip of his wine and silently agreed.

"Did I ever tell you that Raymond used to work on a vineyard in Marseille?" Odette asked her friends from culinary school.

"Is that so?" Camille asked. She leaned into the conversation as if Raymond all of a sudden had something more to offer.

"Just for a short time, before we moved here," Raymond said, trying to downplay it.

"That is a dream," Charlie said. "One day, to open up my own vineyard in the South of France."

"But what about baking?" Odette asked.

"I can do both; I don't see why not," Charlie answered.

"I'm sure we will love to visit your vineyard one day," Raymond said.

Charlie took a sip of his wine and placed the glass down on the wrought-iron table. "Has anyone ever asked you about your accent?" he asked.

Raymond's spine sprung up into a straight line. "My accent?"

"Yes, your French is impeccable, but I can tell there is an accent there. I can't pinpoint where it's from."

Raymond never considered that he had an accent.

"It's a mixture of things, really," Raymond answered vaguely. It was always hard to explain why his French sounded a bit Haitian and why his Arabic sounded a bit French.

The night continued with talks of their French childhood, something that Raymond was excited to hear about but couldn't relate to, no matter how hard he tried. He shared stories of trips to the pyramids and shopping at the bazaars, but while they were all interested, they eventually settled back into the comforts of their own French lives. Underneath the fullness of the French moon, Odette was where she was supposed to be, but Raymond wasn't sure if he could say the same about himself.

It went on like that for months. Ever since the moment he saw the National Geographic Magazine in the window, he hadn't been able to shake himself of the idea that he belonged elsewhere. He knew Odette was mostly clueless about it; he had only mentioned it to her one other time. Paris would always be beautiful, and for some people, Paris would always be perfect, but for him at that time, Paris wasn't meant to last forever.

He got so wrapped up in his new life in Paris that he felt guilty for not looking for Albert sooner. He finally decided to find the address on the piece of paper: 818 Rue de Juliette. It was a bookstore, but it was closed. Raymond didn't understand why the address led there at the time and never would.

As Raymond went to the bookstore to look for Albert, Odette put on lipstick and a splash of rouge on her cheeks right before opening the apartment's door to Charlie. As Raymond searched behind the bookstore's closed gates and in between all the shelves of novels, Odette kissed Charlie as if her lips were meant for his, forever.

As Raymond returned to their flat, Odette walked in with a couple of shopping bags. She had just been to the markets and was always excited to share her local finds with Raymond.

"Raymond, you have some mail," Odette said as she put the shopping bags on the kitchen table. She handed him a single, white envelope.

Raymond took the envelope in his hands, not knowing the weight of its message would always rest on his shoulders. He scanned the envelope for a return address, but there was none. He opened the back of the envelope delicately and was initially disappointed when there was no letter inside. Instead, Raymond pulled out a single magazine clipping, one that showed Nathan's in Coney Island, Brooklyn.

And in the very bottom right-hand corner, scribbled in black marker, was a language he hadn't read in years. It was Creole, and all it said was, "I'm ok."

Raymond sat down at the kitchen table and traced his thumb over the Creole words. He tried to feel for Albert's handwriting; he wanted to know definitively that it was Albert who sent it to him. There was no way of tracing the letter back to him, but there was no way it could have come from someone else. Raymond read and reread that magazine clipping a dozen times, searching for something tangible to hold on to. The magazine clipping brought a quick sense of calm but also created more questions than answers. It was as if Albert was right there in the palm of his hands but still nowhere to be found.

"Raymond, can you reach those wine glasses up there, please?" Odette asked as she pointed to the top shelf of the kitchen cabinet. She had been busy unpacking the groceries that she didn't even notice Raymond's sudden realization. Raymond slipped the magazine clipping into his pocket and snapped back into their shared reality.

Raymond took them down as she pulled out a bottle of wine from one of her shopping bags. Raymond picked up the bottle and read the label. It was a bottle of wine from the Marseille vineyard where he used to work. He wondered if his hands touched the grapes inside that very bottle.

"Let's go outside," Odette said as she started walking towards the balcony. She held a fresh baguette and a plate of cheese in her hands.

Raymond followed her and stepped out onto the balcony. The late summer evening sky had just begun to fade from pastel pink, and the air had begun to cool. Their flat's interior had become suffocating, and the magazine clipping burned a hole into his pocket. There was so much he wanted to tell Odette, but an unspeakable hush kept his lips sealed. There was still one thing he had toyed with, and time had come to make the move.

"Try some of this Roquefort. Charlie suggested it; it is aged in a medieval town in the south of France. He said it is simply the best piece of cheese he's ever tasted," Odette said. Her enthusiasm for the flavors of France was unparalleled.

The harsh cheese melted in Raymond's mouth, and he sipped his glass of wine for an aftertaste.

"A few of my classmates and I are going to browse some of the markets again tomorrow morning. Some specialty farmers are coming to Paris for the weekend, and we heard it shouldn't be missed. Do you want to join?"

"You go ahead and enjoy it," Raymond said. "I don't want to get in your way."

Odette nodded and took a sip of wine. The sun sank, and the moon rose at the same time, behind her caramel eyes.

"I received another letter from Uncle Nissim recently," Raymond said.

Odette broke off a piece of the fresh baguette and topped it with a bit of cheese.

"I am worried about him," Raymond continued. "It's been too long now, without any word from Albert. It seems like Uncle Nissim is getting very lonely in New York without any of the family there."

"That's really such a mystery," Odette said. "Why would he plan to move to France with you and then disappear?"

Raymond's chest transformed into stone whenever he thought about how little Odette knew of the truth. "It's so hard to say."

"But where else could he have gone if he didn't stay in Marseille? Don't you think he would have resurfaced by now? That he would have somehow found you or his father?"

Odette spelled out the truth the way he never wanted to hear it but knew it was the most likely scenario.

"I have to keep hope, Odette. If anything, I have to keep hope for Uncle Nissim. Albert is the only child he has."

Odette took another sip of her wine and leaned back into the wrought-iron chair.

"What do you think about moving to New York?" Raymond asked. "Once you are finished with culinary school? I am sure you can find a very respectable baking job in Manhattan."

Odette's smile was coy as she finished her glass of wine. "Move to New York?"

"Yes, I want to move to New York. I've only ever heard good things about it, especially from Uncle Nissim and Albert. I would like to be near my family, especially once my mother and sisters arrive there."

Odette's smile faded as quickly as the setting sun. "You're serious?"

"Of course I am serious. I wouldn't ask you if I weren't serious."

Odette shook her head in disagreement. "No, Raymond. We cannot move to New York like that; it is not that simple."

"What is not so simple about it?"

Odette's face had turned stone cold, and it was the first and last time he ever witnessed it. "Raymond, no, just stop."

"Stop what? I am serious, Odette. I need to be near my family. Uncle Nissim was there for me when my father passed away, and now I need to be there for him as we try to find out where Albert is."

Odette sat quietly for a moment.

"I will not go," she responded with finality.

Her answer took his breath away. He had never imagined that she would say no.

"Odette," Raymond began.

"Is this what you want?" Odette asked. "Are you absolutely sure that you want to move to New York? And there is no convincing you otherwise?"

Raymond sat across from her without speaking. Once his mind was made up, there was no changing it.

"I'm sorry, Raymond. I won't move to New York."

Raymond placed his glass down on the table, and the tides turned before him.

"My life is here, in France. My family is here, my school and friends are here. There is nothing for me in America. I want to become a pastry chef here, in France, where it is genuinely appreciated as an art form. I cannot live in New York." Odette took a long sip of her wine. "And Charlie is here."

Raymond's otherwise soft eyes turned sharp and pierced through her truths. He frantically searched the corners of her mouth for words unspoken and into the rounds of her eyes for a lost sense of familiarity. He had never caught on to their affair, but with no other words needed, she shattered his heart as if it were made of glass.

They finished the bottle of wine and watched the clouds pass over the moon. Odette slipped the diamond ring off her finger and placed it back into the warmth of Raymond's palm.

It was decided that Odette would stay in Paris and continue living in their flat, without him. Within a few weeks, Charlie moved in with her.

And within a few weeks, Raymond left for New York.

Eight

Brooklyn, New York, 1952

The traffic light swayed precariously overhead with the seaside breeze.

"*Yalla*, hurry up. The light is about to change," Uncle Nissim said as he picked up the pace. Raymond followed Uncle Nissim's lead and their footsteps found synchronicity as they hurried across Surf Avenue.

They stepped up onto the corner, and the immediate fragrances of the unfamiliar swayed in the air. Raymond stood at the intersection of Surf Avenue and Stillwell Avenue in Coney Island. Even though he was miles away from Ellis Island, it was at the edge of Brooklyn where he had an overwhelming feeling that he finally made it to America.

What stood before him was the original Nathan's location. It boasted its history with a sign that read 'World Famous Frankfurters Since 1916'. Its yellow awnings and green writing were equally bright in the day and lit up with neon at night. Even though it was only Nathan's and it was only famous for hot dogs, everything about it was what he always envisioned America to be.

It was exactly how Albert had described it.

Raymond followed Uncle Nissim to the back of one of many long lines. Brooklynites packed into the establishment. Some were dressed in their best weekend casual attire like Raymond was, and others were coming from the beach to grab a mid-afternoon lunch. Raymond didn't know much about Brooklyn yet but already had the impression that it stood as the world's crossroads. It seemed like no two people were alike in the city. Each of their different backgrounds came together to make a collective culture; it built the spine of New York City from the tips of her toes to the top of her crown.

"What would you like?" Uncle Nissim asked.

Raymond eyed the menu on the wall. It was simple and easy to read, but he still didn't know where to start. "I've never had a hot dog before."

Uncle Nissim's hearty laugh sent vibrations down the line. He nudged the top of Raymond's shoulder as if he were silly for not knowing better.

"Let me order for you then," Uncle Nissim said.

Raymond nodded in agreement. They neared the counter, and Raymond eyed an open-concept kitchen behind a row of cashiers. The counter facing them was lined with hot dogs and fries. Cashiers served up trays of hot dogs to customers ahead of them in line, and Raymond quickly realized how important Nathan's was to the people of Brooklyn. Later on in his life, he'd bring his daughter to Nathan's on the Fourth of July for its annual hot dog eating contest. The boardwalk would always be packed, and the heat made them sweat the day away, but everything about it made him feel American.

Uncle Nissim ordered two hot dogs for each of them, two sodas, and an order of fries to share. Each hot dog had a line of ketchup and mustard on it, and the order of fries was pierced with a miniature red pitchfork. He'd never had a meal like it before, and even though he ate his way through many countries before the United States, that one would sit differently.

It was standing room only in Nathan's, but Uncle Nissim knew the right spot to take them. He led them out of the restaurant and down the block to the boardwalk. Raymond realized he had never seen a boardwalk before either. Its wooden planks stretched in both directions for what seemed like miles. Coney Island's Wonder Wheel and Cyclone amusement rides seemed to grow from the edge of the sand, and the famed bright red parachute jump stretched into the sky. The beach was dotted with umbrellas, and the Atlantic Ocean was full of people going for a swim.

A single bench opened up for them. Its surface was hot from the midday sun, but it gave them an optimal view of the shore and its crashing waves. Raymond and Uncle Nissim sat down together with their lunch in between them. It took years for them to get to that point, but as they stood at the edge of New York City, Raymond understood how much it was worth the wait.

"*Bon appetite*," Uncle Nissim said as he raised his hot dog in the air.

Raymond did the same and took a bite of the hot dog. Uncle Nissim looked on curiously and anticipated his reaction.

"How do you like it?" Uncle Nissim asked.

Raymond chewed his bite down and took another one. "This is delicious."

Uncle Nissim's laugh bellowed across the wooden floorboards of the boardwalk. It had been a long time since Raymond heard his hearty laugh; it had once been the soundtrack to family gatherings in Haiti and Egypt, but Raymond had slowly tuned it out as he grew up and spent more time out of the house. He now realized how much he had missed it.

"I had a feeling you'd like these hot dogs. Best in New York City, that's for sure."

Uncle Nissim finished his hot dog and took a deep sip of his soda. He looked comfortable lounging against the bench, with his sights set on the ocean. Raymond couldn't help but feel as if Uncle Nissim were a natural local, as if he had been born and raised by the streets of Brooklyn. Even though Raymond grew up near his uncle in Haiti and Egypt, Uncle Nissim never truly seemed settled. It was as if he knew those homes would never be permanent. But somewhere along the shores of Brooklyn, New York, his uncle found his home.

Raymond found solace in having his uncle with him in such a new and foreign place like New York City. It was the city he'd heard of his whole life when his parents reminisced on their old apartment in Bensonhurst and when Albert told him fantastical stories of Manhattan. His curiosity for New York had always been beneath the surface, but life got in the way and seemed to push those dreams aside. He was never entirely sure if he'd ever find his way to America, and it wasn't until the heat of the bench radiated onto his back when he realized that he finally made it.

"Monday morning, you'll come with me to the city," Uncle Nissim said. He wiped his mouth with a clean napkin. "You'll meet David, and he'll set you up with a schedule."

Raymond took a bite of his hot dog and nodded. He hadn't been into Manhattan yet and wondered if the buildings were closer to the clouds.

"Thank you again for getting me the job." Raymond had already thanked his uncle probably a dozen times, but there wasn't enough appreciation for how grateful he felt to be in New York City with him.

"Enough with the thank you," Uncle Nissim teased. "Thank me by showing up to work on time and doing an exceptional job. Don't make me regret it."

"Of course," Raymond's tone was serious and assuring.

"We'll take the train together. It's just walking distance from our house. You'll take it a couple of times, and before you know it, you'll be able to take a nap and wake up at the right stop."

Raymond nodded in agreement. He'd have to become a natural at it. He gave himself no other option.

"I always thought Albert would be working with me one day," Uncle Nissim said. He scanned the beachgoers as if somewhere in between the towels and umbrellas and swimsuits, he would find his son.

Raymond sat quietly and looked over the ocean. He wondered how far Albert stood on the other side of the Atlantic.

Uncle Nissim took a long breath. "Raymond, are you sure he didn't say anything when he left? He never mentioned where he wanted to go?"

He had replayed their last few conversations in his mind like a broken record, searching for something that he might have missed. He shook his head in disagreement. "He'll come back to us one day, *Inshallah*," Raymond said.

"I just need him to be safe. It's ok if he doesn't come back to us or doesn't want to be in New York. I just need to know that he is safe, wherever he is."

More than anything, Raymond needed that too. He wanted to reassure his uncle that Albert was safe, that he had found some sort of success after he left Egypt, that he was happy. But at that point, they didn't have any tangible evidence that Albert was ok, and the unconfirmed speculation lingered between them like a truth they couldn't escape.

"I haven't stopped looking for him," Uncle Nissim said as if confessing something Raymond didn't already know. "The day both of you left, I reread that note you left on your desk probably one hundred times. I read it and reread it, and then took a break and read it again. My son and my nephew, working for the greater good of the Jews in Egypt." He never referred to them as spies. It was almost as if they had a shared agreement not to.

Raymond breathed in the salty air of the ocean, and he swallowed his regrets. Uncle Nissim, the man who was always the light-hearted comedian of the family, had lost his jovial attitude since Raymond last saw him in Egypt. The gray hairs that were once only in his sideburns stretched up the sides above his ears, and even though his laugh could still make the earth shake, it held a weightiness from grief.

"I understand," Uncle Nissim said and locked eyes with Raymond. "I understand why both of you did it."

Uncle Nissim's sincerity caught Raymond by surprise. It was the first time in over a year that Raymond let go of his reservations.

"You understand?"

"Of course I do," he assured him. "What are young people supposed to do when the only home they know doesn't want them to live there anymore?"

What his uncle said was true: that was why Raymond had helped in the espionage acts to begin with. A home that had once been so full of opportunity had become a barren shell of a promising era gone by.

"I always knew it would be you who you reach out to me first," Uncle Nissim confessed. "I waited and waited, but I knew there would be a letter from you, telling all of us that you were ok."

Raymond never realized how well his uncle knew him. He spent his childhood in Haiti looking up to his father while his uncle watched and loved him from the sidelines. He spent his adolescence in Egypt wanting to become as strong of a man as his father, while his uncle had been a silent role model. Uncle Nissim was the extra boulder that propped the family up and never stopped providing the stepping stones for Raymond to climb mountains.

"Albert wouldn't be the one, it would always be you," Uncle Nissim added. Uncle Nissim was right about that. Albert wouldn't be the one to reach out. "I'll be honest, when I found out that both of you left Egypt, I had a feeling we'd find ourselves here. You and I, without Albert. But it doesn't hurt any less."

Raymond shifted his weight on the bench and took out his wallet from his back pocket. He opened it up to the little money he had and took out the piece of paper he received from Henry on the bus in Marseille. He unfolded the paper delicately, as if it were his most prized possession, and handed it to his uncle.

"What is this?" Uncle Nissim asked as he read the address in Marseille.

"Do you remember our friend Henry?" Raymond asked.

"Yes, of course, the son of Jacob Lagnado. The boy with that head of curls."

"He left Egypt with us."

Uncle Nissim's eyes widened with surprise.

"Henry Lagnado?"

"Yes," Raymond answered.

"Henry worked with you and Albert?" Uncle Nissim asked in disbelief.

Raymond nodded in agreement and realized how little his uncle truly knew. "He gave me this piece of paper when we got to Marseille. One side has an address in Marseille, and all he said was to give my regards to Albert there. So I went there, and I waited, but no one ever came. The other side has an address in Paris, and, eventually, I went there too. It was a bookstore, and it was closed."

"Can I see the paper?" Uncle Nissim asked.

Uncle Nissim studied the address as if it were the most important piece of information he would ever read. He read it out loud to himself a handful of times as if repeating it into his memory would make it real. But the address meant nothing to him, and a bookstore in the middle of Paris didn't hold any importance.

"I will ask around," Uncle Nissim finally said as he handed the paper back to Raymond. "Maybe someone in our area is familiar with these addresses. If Henry was working with you both, this must link back to him somehow."

Raymond agreed but wished he knew how the link could bring Albert home.

"And I received this in the mail too, right before I left for New York." Raymond took out a folded magazine clipping and showed it to his uncle.

"What is this?" Uncle Nissim asked as he looked at the photo of New York City.

"I think it's from Albert."

Uncle Nissim's eyes lit up like fireworks over the Hudson River. He scanned the clipping as if he were searching over the features of his son's face. He held the paper as if he cupped his son's cheeks in his own hands.

"But this is an article about Nathan's, right where we are now," Uncle Nissim said, not able to understand how this could connect back to Albert.

"Albert and I used to write letters to each other all the time when we left Haiti. And he always sent me these kinds of magazine clippings. It was always of places he wanted to visit or places he'd seen. He loved to send me clippings of New York. He used to tell me that one day he wanted to write travel magazine articles like these."

Uncle Nissim looked down at the clipping in a new light.

"And look at the bottom corner there," Raymond said as he pointed to it.

"*Mwen byen*," Uncle Nissim read out loud in Creole. *I'm ok.*

"I think it's from him," Raymond concluded. "I think he's trying to tell us that everything is ok, wherever he is."

Uncle Nissim held onto his breath for a moment longer than usual. "Can I keep this, for now?"

Raymond agreed as it was the least he could do.

Uncle Nissim's worn-down hands traced the two Creole words. He folded up the magazine clipping and slipped it into his pocket.

"He will come back to us, one day." Raymond made empty promises that felt almost useless in the grand scheme of things, but there was nothing else he knew how to do.

"*Inshallah*," Uncle Nissim said. God willing.

Low tide dragged the shoreline deeper into the ocean. Slow waves lapped at the edge of the coast, and children splashed in the sea-salted waters. Raymond wanted to run into the sea and have the water swim in between his toes. He wanted to search every face on the beach for the familiar look of Albert's; he wanted to track down his cousin so his uncle wouldn't feel lost without him anymore. But there was nothing he could do. He couldn't bring him back if he didn't want to be found.

"There is a playground, a little further down that way." Uncle Nissim pointed east towards the expansive beach. "I used to take him there when we moved to Brooklyn, right after we left Haiti. He wanted to come here even when the weather got colder in the winters. Both of you never felt winters in Haiti, it was a real surprise for Albert."

"I still don't know what a real winter feels like," Raymond reminded his uncle.

"Don't hold your breath," Uncle Nissim responded with a chuckle. "I'd trade it for the heat of the Caribbean any day. It's the only part of New York that I can do without. But Albert loved it here in the winters. He loved the snow, the way it fell from the sky in thick puffs of cotton."

"He wrote to me about a snowstorm once. It must have been the first winter we were apart after we moved to Egypt, and you and Albert came here."

"He was absolutely thrilled to tell you all about it," Uncle Nissim said. "It was all he talked about on the way home."

The idea of Albert as a young, naive child made Raymond see his cousin in a new light. It was hard for Raymond to remember a time when Albert was vulnerable, when he wasn't wildly pursuing his next adrenaline rush or bouncing to his next adventure. It was clear that for Uncle Nissim, Albert would always be that boy who found pure joy in watching snow fall from the sky.

"I would have done the same," Raymond said.

Uncle Nissim took a sip of his soda and placed it down on the bench. "You two, always in search of the same things. Your father and I didn't know what it was, but we noticed it immediately. It's funny how you both are so different in your ways but still so similar in the paths you chose."

Raymond's supportive smile masked how much he missed his cousin.

"Promise me this," Uncle Nissim said, "if you hear anything from him if he somehow tries to reach out to you, you'll tell me immediately?"

"Of course, Uncle Nissim," Raymond assured him wholeheartedly.

"Even if he wants to keep it a secret. We all know he's good at keeping secrets."

Raymond nodded in agreement.

"Even if he doesn't want to be found."

Although Raymond held onto hope more than anything else, his painful assumption was that something horrible happened to Albert on that ship ride towards France. He mentally ran through all the possibilities of Albert getting captured and tortured, even killed for his role in the spy ring. But never once did Raymond think that Albert just didn't want to be found after all they had been through. Not until that moment on the bench in Coney Island.

Without saying another word, they rose from the bench together and threw out their trash at a nearby garbage can. They walked in silence along the boardwalk and followed the shoreline's crashing waves. Raymond's outlook tilted under the realization that maybe his cousin didn't want them to find him. He couldn't understand why.

Raymond and Uncle Nissim walked the Coney Island boardwalk together from end to end. Uncle Nissim pointed out the best shop to buy saltwater taffy. He explained the history of the Cyclone and how the wooden rollercoaster always left him sore after the ride was over. He reminisced on Albert's favorite carnival games and almost bought them a spool of cotton candy as if Raymond were his own son and a kid again.

When they both had soaked in enough summer sun and memories of days long gone, they left Coney Island for their newly adopted neighborhood.

Bensonhurst was a shared space between a large Italian population and the growing community of Sephardic Jews exiled from Egypt. When Raymond stepped onto the sidewalks of Bensonhurst, he felt an odd sense of belonging, despite only having been there for a couple of weeks. He had neighbors who spoke French and Arabic and shop owners who sold the spices his mother always used in her home-cooked meals. It was nothing like Egypt but everything like home.

Uncle Nissim's house felt like stepping back fifteen years in time. Raymond wasn't sure where he got the furniture, but he had a sense that the couch and dining room chairs were not new. Everything looked sepia and antiquated. It made him feel like the world wouldn't progress into the future. They were stuck in a place and existence where things were the same, even though everything had changed.

The one part of the house that was meticulously decorated was a wall in the living room, which housed framed pictures of their family. There was a portrait of Uncle Nissim's late wife, Suzette, before she was pregnant with Albert. There was also a portrait of Raymond's father, smoking a pipe and standing in the middle of a field in Haiti. There was a group photo of all the cousins, Raymond, and his sisters, along with Albert, in the high desert of Egypt.

There was a single picture of Raymond and Albert riding their bikes in Haiti as kids. Raymond didn't necessarily remember that particular day of the photo, but he remembered it felt like they lived atop the clouds when he rode alongside Albert, underneath the shade of the coconut trees. They were inseparable, they were invincible, and Albert was all he ever needed.

Raymond sometimes found Uncle Nissim sitting on his leather chair in the living room, admiring the photos on the wall as Egyptian music played on a record player. It was as if he were admiring a way of life that didn't exist anymore, but Raymond couldn't figure out whether his uncle loved it or missed it. Uncle Nissim sat there, waiting for the moment Albert would walk through the door like nothing had ever happened.

"One day, Raymond, you will have a wife and children of your own, and I will add their photos to this wall," Uncle Nissim said one evening. He had just put on the record player and lit a fresh cigarette.

"*Inshallah*," Raymond said. "I would like that very much." If there was anything Raymond genuinely wanted, it was to have a family. It would take some time for him to get to that point in his life, but when he did, he wouldn't need anything else in the world.

"Maybe you will have five girls, the way your parents did."

Raymond laughed and sat down on the couch with a drink. "I will be happy if I have just one. I am not sure I can handle five."

Uncle Nissim took a long drag of his cigarette. "You will be able to handle anything that you are given, Raymond. Don't think otherwise."

It was a truth Raymond already knew too well, even without realizing it.

"I would love to see you with children someday."

Raymond took a sip of his drink and silently agreed.

"Albert is all I have," Uncle Nissim continued. "One day, he will come back to us. He has to come back to us."

They spent the rest of the evening listening to a mixture of older Egyptian songs on the record player as Uncle Nissim chain-smoked his way towards midnight. The heaviness in the air was partly due to the cigarettes but mostly due to the unease that never left their shoulders. Without knowing where Albert was, it was as if Uncle Nissim couldn't move forward. But without knowing that Albert was truly gone, it also gave him an exponential amount of hope that tomorrow would be the day he'd come home.

When the start of the week rolled around, Raymond commuted with his uncle to Manhattan for the first time in his life. He stood on the train, shoulder to shoulder with strangers, and never felt so accepted. He climbed up the stairs from the underground train station and walked onto Midtown's sidewalks as promises of a better life rained down from the tips of the skyscrapers. From that day on, there was nowhere else in the world that he'd ever call home the way he did New York.

There was nothing about New York that Odette would have liked. Even though he had spent a considerable amount of time with Uncle Nissim since he arrived in the United States, his mind still floated towards Odette with small thoughts of regret. He regretted how their paths had diverged, but with every step he took in Manhattan, he knew with all of his heart that it was best he did it on his own, without her.

Raymond eased into his new job at the electronics store seamlessly. He had spent enough time with cameras in his latter days in Egypt that selling them was almost effortless. The store's customers were a mixture of avid photographers and well-to-do tourists. None of the customers knew that Raymond's knowledge of cameras came from spying, and although he wanted to keep that part of his life in the past, it wasn't as easy to shake off.

Raymond found contentment in a daily routine. It was nothing like he knew of in Egypt or France. New York felt much more permanent; small roots started to grow from the soles of his feet into the concrete sidewalks of Brooklyn. He walked a handful of blocks to the train station every weekday morning and made sure to stop at the neighborhood corner store for a copy of the daily newspaper. He read every single article he could in the time it took to get into Midtown and continued to teach himself English until he knew it as well as French.

He never threw away the newspaper after the subway ride. He kept it for the evening commute back, where he meticulously read through all the job opportunities. He was grateful for his job at the electronics store but knew that America had something bigger in mind for him. He circled every accounting job that he could find and sent his resume to them all.

One by one, he went to interviews, and one by one, he was looked over. The interviews were often held on high-level floors of skyscrapers, and the views from the offices made Raymond never want to look away. The interviews usually went well, but not well enough. They were intimidating and sometimes a bit overwhelming. Even with a perfectly pressed suit and a borrowed briefcase from Uncle Nissim, Raymond was still turned away from one opportunity after another.

Each elevator ride up was always promising, but on each elevator ride back down, he contemplated that maybe he just wasn't American enough yet. Interviewers sometimes asked him to repeat himself because his English was mixed with a French and Arabic accent. His degree wasn't from the States, and neither were his aspirations.

Raymond left the office of an accounting firm on 53rd Street in Manhattan. The interviewer asked decent questions, and Raymond answered with as much confidence and poise he could muster. He knew he had done well but wasn't sure if well was simply good enough.

A gray ceiling of clouds hung low above the city's skyline on that late winter afternoon. Raymond looked at his gold watch and realized that he had time before he had to get on the subway for Brooklyn. He found a small diner tucked in between Midtown's corporate offices; it was the first time he ordered a slice of apple pie and a cup of coffee in New York. It would forever be his favorite dessert, even well into his life in New York, because it was what made him begin to truly feel like an American.

Raymond didn't know it yet, but the clouds that lingered above him were full of snow. They were the deep gray that only appeared in the winter. They stretched across the sky from one end of New York City to the other. There was a heaviness in their weight and solemnity in their darkness, but when they burst open, it turned the world into a wonderland.

The first time Raymond ever felt snow, the flakes landed on his eyelashes and the tip of his nose. The snowflakes melted onto his skin, and when they hit his lips, they tasted of purity. Raymond walked along the busy streets of Manhattan as the snow covered his shoes and layered onto his shoulders. It didn't matter that he shivered or that his ears turned red from the cold; he stood underneath snow clouds, and he couldn't wait to tell everyone back in Egypt.

Even though he was still unsure of how his interview went, he virtually erased it from his mind by the time he got home. He wrote a jubilant letter to his mother and sisters; they had never seen snow either.

One week later, Raymond received a phone call at home from the accounting firm. He got the job.

Three months went by at the accounting firm, and Raymond finally found a purpose he could fully stand behind. He was at the starting point of building a career, he knew the soles of his feet were settling into place on the streets of Brooklyn, and he could only patiently wait for the day when his mother and sisters would join him. New York was the place he called home; it was the city that welcomed him when some of his other homes had kicked him out. There was nothing better than living in New York City, and even though he wasn't one yet, there was nothing more he wanted than to be an American citizen.

But the United States had other plans for him.

"There's some mail for you," Uncle Nissim said as he walked into the house's entryway with a small pile of envelopes. Uncle Nissim handed Raymond a single letter and then began to skim through his own bills and letters.

Raymond hadn't received any mail since he moved to Brooklyn and hoped it was a letter from his mother and sisters. He wasn't sure if anyone else even had his new address, aside from them.

The envelope struck him as formal and serious, not something that would come from Egypt. He neatly tore open the envelope and read through the letter.

"What is it about?" Uncle Nissim asked as he looked up from his own mail.

Raymond's English fluency had grown exponentially since he moved to New York, but he still had to reread the letter to fully understand what it said.

"It's from the United States military," Raymond said. He looked at his uncle. Both of their faces turned from permeable to stone.

"The United States military?" Uncle Nissim asked as if he truly hadn't heard Raymond clearly in the first place.

"I've been drafted into the Army."

Nine

Stuttgart, Germany, 1953

Home never felt so far away.

Raymond sat across the table from his fellow soldiers Allen and Michael. No one talked as they shoveled heaps of mashed potatoes and gravy into their mouths. The turkey was a bit dry, but there wasn't anything they could do about it. The chow hall was crowded, as it always was at dinner time. A humming buzz of conversation filled the air as many of Raymond's brothers-in-arms ate what was supposed to be a traditional Thanksgiving dinner. But nothing was traditional about celebrating the American holiday in Germany. It was unconventional for all of them to share that meal in a land so far from their own during the end of the Korean War.

It was Raymond's first-ever Thanksgiving dinner, and he wasn't quite yet sure what to make of it.

"Are you about done?" Allen asked Raymond. Allen always seemed to be in a rush.

Raymond took one last bite of the green bean casserole. He had never had green bean casserole before; it wasn't something he ate in Haiti or Egypt. He secretly wanted to have another bite but didn't want to hold them up.

"I'm done," Raymond conceded as he pushed his plate away from him.

"What did you think?" Michael asked. Where Allen always seemed to be in a hurry, Michael's Southern Californian attitude spoke of ease. Ever since meeting Raymond in the barracks, Michael had been interested in Raymond's diverse background and the fact that there was still so much Raymond didn't know about being an American.

"Everything tasted good," Raymond answered truthfully.

"Don't lie." Allen nudged him as if an extra boost would spill the truth.

"Honestly," Raymond answered. "I thought it was all delicious."

Allen and Michael shared a laugh together, and Raymond couldn't help but question if he just wasn't American enough yet to understand fully.

"It was alright," Michael said, "but I'm sorry this had to be your introduction to Thanksgiving."

"I agree," Allen said as he stood up from the table. Raymond and Michael followed his lead and brought their empty plates to the tray stand. "Once this is all over, you'll come to my family's home in Pennsylvania. My mother will cook you a real Thanksgiving dinner, not like some of this garbage."

"And then when you're done with that," Michael said, "you'll come out to Southern California and have Thanksgiving with me by the beach."

The three of them walked out of the chow hall and into a colder than expected evening. Raymond zipped up his coat as high as it could go and jammed his bare hands into its wool-lined pockets. He'd only been in Germany for a couple of weeks, and as winter was starting to ramp up, he was reminded of his desert blood and how he wasn't born for winters. Stuttgart Army Base at the edge of winter was home, whether Raymond was prepared for it or not.

Allen took out a pack of cigarettes and tapped the edge of the box a handful of times. "I think I forgot my light."

As if on cue, Raymond took out his lighter. Raymond lit his cigarette as well, and even though Michael wasn't much of a smoker, he bummed one off of Allen for the hell of it.

"Man, I'm glad we get a break," Michael said. They were on leave for the next four days for the holiday. The unified cloud of their smoke traveled around them and up into the German skies.

"You're telling me," Allen said. "A few days off is exactly what I need right now."

"You all want to head into town tomorrow?" Michael asked. "Grab a couple of beers? My Staff Sergeant told me about a beer hall that brews their beer on the premises."

"I don't see why you want to wait until tomorrow," Allen said with a coy smile on his face. If Allen could do everything immediately, he would.

The three of them finished their smoke and stomped out their cigarettes on the cold pavement. Instead of going back to the barracks for the evening, they left base for the nightlife in Stuttgart. The German streets flowed differently than in France, and even though Raymond found himself in Europe once again, it was a Europe with which he was unfamiliar.

Allen led the way to the German beer hall. As they walked into the expansive bar, Raymond's eyes were drawn to the exceptionally high-arched ceilings and a row of oversized wheel chandeliers that lit the space. They found a section of empty seats at one of the dozen long, communal tables and ordered the first round. Within minutes, their steins of beer were full, and a couple of soft, oversized pretzels sat in front of them.

"Now, this is why I joined the Army," Allen said as he took a big swig of his lager. "There's no way I could see something like this in Pennsylvania."

Raymond wasn't sure what he meant. Joining the military, at least in Egypt, wasn't something you volunteered to do. And definitely not to see the world.

"You always planned on enlisting?" Michael asked.

"Since I was in elementary school," Allen said. "I had a poster for the United States Army hanging up on my bedroom wall." Allen was made for a life in the military. He would always be the most motivated soldier Raymond had ever known. The Lance Corporal that he was at the time would eventually rise to the highest enlisted rank of Sergeant Major.

"Your pops was in the Army too, wasn't he?" Michael asked.

"Pops was in the Army, and so was my grandfather," Allen answered with pride. "World War I and World War II veterans."

"A family full of combat heroes," Michael said as he raised his stein in the air. "Cheers."

The three soldiers raised their steins and clinked them together before taking a sip of their German beers. In between the cold beers and the warm conversation, Raymond had to do a double take. Just weeks prior, his life hadn't yet intersected with Allen and

Michael, yet there they were, in the middle of a German beer hall, spending an evening together as old friends do.

"You were drafted, weren't you, Raymond?" Allen asked.

Raymond nodded in agreement as he drank his beer. "I was."

"That must be one hell of a feeling to get drafted the way you were," Michael said. He tore off a piece of the warm pretzel and dunked it into a small bowl of mustard.

"It was the last thing I expected," Raymond answered.

"Can you believe it? You just move to the United States from France, of all places, and then end right back in Europe again," Allen said.

Raymond laughed at how ironic it was. In a way, that's all he could do.

"I didn't know you came from France," Michael said. "I've always wanted to go to Paris, and we are so close to it now. It's like I can almost see the beautiful French women in front of me." Michael stretched out his arm in front of him in a wide sweeping motion as if the beautiful French women he spoke about were right there before him.

Allen shoved Michael's shoulder in a tease. "Are you going to take leave and go to France?"

Michael's face lit up like a Christmas tree in a darkened room. "I never thought of that."

"I'll go with you if you want company," Allen said. "Raymond, why don't you show us around your old home?"

Raymond didn't intend to return to Paris anytime soon; he had always thought he'd stay put by the time he got to New York. His life had other plans for him, and even before he could picture the idea of walking down the familiar Parisian boulevards, he agreed to accompany his new friends to France.

They spent the rest of their evening ordering a couple more beers and planning when they'd take their trip to Paris. Allen had never once left the East Coast, and Michael had never even been out of California before joining the Army. Both had the type of eagerness that came from suddenly being unleashed from a cage. They asked Raymond a thousand questions about Paris's restaurants and nightlife; they both had an urge and excitement to see as much of the city as possible. Raymond happily answered all their questions but was slightly apprehensive of going back to the place that only recently broke his heart.

Raymond's sense of home had been wiped away during basic training in Aberdeen, Maryland. Home wasn't in the plantation-style house in Haiti or the desert of Egypt. He thought home was in Brooklyn, but that home was put on hold. Home was in the United States Army; it was in boot camp's early morning hours and his drill instructor's shouts. Home was wherever the military sent him, which happened to be the last place Raymond ever thought to look.

Raymond's drill instructors in basic training tore him down to build him up again. A heightened sense of discipline was instilled in him during his time in boot camp, and it was that type of discipline that he carried with him for the rest of his life. It taught him what it meant to care for strangers as if they were his brothers. It taught him that home didn't necessarily come with four walls and a roof above his head but traveled with him wherever he went.

Raymond's boots touched down on the ground in Germany soon after he finished basic training. The United States was nearing the end of the Korean War. Even though Raymond hadn't been an active duty service member for too long during it, he'd still always be considered a combat veteran for his service during America's forgotten war.

He had no choice but to pack his military gear and ship out to Germany, in the same way that Germany had no choice but to accept him in. Europe was different for him that time around. The Europe of Raymond's past meant falling in love on the coast of the Mediterranean Sea and having his love extinguished underneath Paris's eternal lights. Europe the second time around meant working in the ammunition supply shop and taking orders from his Staff Sergeant. Raymond wasn't an infantryman fighting in Korea but supported the war by sending supplies out to the men who did.

Raymond couldn't have imagined that his time in the Army would become a stepping stool to the rest of his life in the United States. The military had never been a prospect he wanted to conquer, but he rose to the occasion when required. He wasn't even a citizen of the country yet, but there was nothing he wouldn't do to protect the place that welcomed him home. He eventually lost contact with Allen and Michael and forgot the beautiful details of the beer halls in

Stuttgart, but always kept an intricately carved beer stein on display in his Brooklyn living room.

Raymond lit a cigarette and finished his beer. The rush of nicotine reminded him of Uncle Nissim's nostalgic living room, where they smoked and listened to classical Egyptian music on the record player. As Allen and Michael continued their talk of Paris, Raymond's thoughts drifted back to his family, now scattered across the world. If he tried hard enough, he could almost picture Albert sitting across from him at the long wooden table of the beer hall, his mustache perfectly trimmed, adventure in his eyes. Raymond later wrote to his uncle from the barracks and told him about the beer of Stuttgart. He wrote to him often and never missed a chance to ask about Albert.

His letter correspondence with Uncle Nissim continued throughout his time in Germany. Uncle Nissim updated him about life in New York and how his mother and sisters wanted to join him in Brooklyn. Raymond could hardly contain his hope that by the time he got out of the military, his family might be on the way to him in the United States. Raymond updated his uncle about life on base, and even though there were some talks about Albert, neither of them had any new information on his whereabouts.

Winter melted into spring. Raymond, Allen, and Michael had their leave approved and were geared up for their upcoming trip to Paris when Raymond received a rare phone call from Uncle Nissim.

"Lance Corporal Blanco of the United States Army." Uncle Nissim's voice was loud and boisterous, but, more than anything, it was proud.

"Uncle Nissim," Raymond said in return. "*Comment ça va?*" Raymond asked how he was doing in French.

"*Ça va bien, Alhamdullah.*" Uncle Nissim responded in a mixture of French and Arabic. He was doing well, thank God.

"Raymond, listen," Uncle Nissim said. "I asked around the neighborhood about those addresses that you had, the one in Marseille and the one in Paris."

Raymond's eyebrows arched with interest.

"I spoke with Jacqueline and David Cohen. They live on 21st Avenue. David recognized that address in Paris."

"He did?"

"Yes, he did. He had to look it up in his address book, but there it was, written down. I even saw it myself. 818 Rue de Juliette. Jacqueline and David's niece is Lily."

Raymond's mind spun backward in time to Sami's parties, where Albert was initially introduced to Lily and fell in love with her instantly.

"And Lily's brother," Uncle Nissim continued.

"Is Henry," Raymond answered for both of them.

"Yes."

"Lily and Henry, but what do they have to do with that address in Paris?" Raymond asked.

"David said they live there."

"Live there?" Raymond asked. "But when I went to that address, it was a bookstore."

"That is all they said."

"Did they mention anything about Albert?"

"They didn't mention anything about Albert, no." Uncle Nissim said. Even though it seemed like he came up empty-handed, the ring in his voice sounded of hope.

"Uncle Nissim, I am traveling to Paris soon with a few friends."

Uncle Nissim was speechless on the other end of the phone line. "You're going to Paris," he repeated.

"Just for a few days."

"Can you go back to that bookstore one more time?" Uncle Nissim asked.

"Of course, yes."

"Write down the address."

But Raymond didn't have to. He had the address memorized since the moment he first read it on the bus ride in Marseille. Raymond promised his uncle he would visit the bookstore again in hopes that it would uncover answers rather than more questions.

Paris was different the second time around.

Raymond sat on the train. Michael sat beside him, reading the newspaper, while Allen sat in the row in front of them. The train ride took more than six hours, and Raymond watched Germany turn into France from the window. It was an unexpected way to return to France, with the companionship of his Army buddies. They relied on him for his fluency in French, and he leaned on them as mild distractions from the memories of what Paris might bring up.

Paris held a little too much heartbreak. He hadn't realized how much of Paris belonged to him and Odette and how much of it was still hers. Her essence was in the way the trees and flowers lined the boulevards with the sole purpose of bringing beauty, and how the Eiffel Tower glimmered in the evening with the purpose of being breathtaking. She was the glass of Sauvignon Blanc over dinner and the weekend market that set up shop next to their hotel. The bakeries would always remind him of her. Odette had been all of it, and Raymond thought he had moved far away enough to forget about her, but it would still take years for that to happen.

But Paris that time around held a different meaning altogether. Aside from being the designated travel guide for his friends, Raymond had to keep his promise to Uncle Nissim. Raymond wanted to drop everything he was doing and run to the address that Uncle Nissim gave him. But Raymond had to be patient. It wasn't time yet.

Raymond took Allen and Michael around Paris as if it were his hometown. He remembered the ins and outs of each arrondissement as if they were the neighborhoods that had raised him. He never realized how much of a home Paris had been to him and how much of it he left behind until he showed up at its doorsteps one more time.

It wasn't until the second to last day of their trip when Raymond was able to steal some time away for himself. He had a feeling that this endeavor would lead him right back to where his journey started. But Raymond knew he had to go find out for himself if this new lead could bring him slightly closer to his cousin.

The address was still the bookstore that had absolutely no meaning to him. The last time he stood at its doors, they were locked. A steel grate had covered the storefront, and a sign in the window had let him know that it was closed for business. This time around, there were people inside. A woman and her young son opened the door and walked out of the bookstore just as Raymond approached its glass façade. A single bell jangled against the door's glass as the woman and boy left the bookstore, and the bell jingled one more time as Raymond walked in.

The bookstore wasn't anything extraordinary. If anything, it was a bit old and smelled the way years of untold stories do. The front of the shop was narrow, with stocked bookshelves that seemed to touch the ceiling and a carpet with a faded center from years of customers treading upon it. Raymond wondered how many books stood under that one roof.

Raymond walked down an aisle of the bookstore as if he were looking for something in particular. He walked towards the back of the shop, where the rows of books suddenly opened up to a communal reading area. A handful of mismatched couches and wingback chairs filled the space. Three larger wooden tables and chairs anchored the area. Patrons of the bookstore sat in the quiet reading room with books wide open, and as each of them took in a different story, they sat together, creating their own.

Raymond wasn't sure what to do from there. He found a magazine section towards the back of the shop and unconsciously picked up National Geographic Magazine's latest issue. He didn't realize what he held in his hands until its signature bright yellow cover stared directly back at him. He wondered if somewhere in the world, Albert had read this latest issue too.

He took the magazine and sat down at one of the wooden tables. Raymond rubbed the palms of this hands against his pants as they were starting to sweat. He flipped through the pages of the magazine without absorbing even one word. He hid behind its contents but peered around the bookstore for any sign of familiarity, something that would make him understand why that address had become the only tangible lifeline he had to his cousin.

Thirty minutes went by before Raymond cohesively gathered his thoughts. A young man, maybe only a few years younger than him, stood post at the front of the store and rang up the customers. A somewhat steady stream of people bought books that afternoon, enough for Raymond to never have an entry into a conversation without getting in someone's way. Once it seemed like the crowds had dissipated, Raymond approached the front register and introduced himself.

"*Bonjour*," Raymond said. His fluency in French hadn't left him, even after being away from France for a while. It never would.

"*Bonjour,*" the young man had a courteous smile reserved for the customers of the shop. "May I help you find something? A certain book?"

"Not exactly," Raymond answered. "But yes, I do need help finding someone."

"Someone?" the man asked. The nametag pinned to his shirt read that his name was Louis.

"Maybe I can speak to the owner of this bookstore?" Raymond asked.

Louis' face twisted in apprehension. "He is not here today."

Raymond's shoulders heaved downwards. He hadn't realized how tense they were. "I see. Well, like I mentioned, I am looking for someone, and I believe he may have some affiliation with this bookstore."

"What is his name?" Louis asked.

Raymond was hesitant to give up that information, but he didn't have any other choice. "Albert Blanco."

At the name, Louis' eyes scanned Raymond's with a sense of urgency, as if he knew a million little secrets that Raymond hadn't been privy to.

"Please, don't move," Louis said.

"I'm sorry?" Raymond asked. He hadn't intended on leaving.

"I apologize. I know that Henry has been waiting for you," Louis said as he began to scurry behind the register.

Raymond's throat swelled with a taste from the past. Henry.

"Please, will you come with me?"

Raymond nodded in agreement. Louis left the front of the store unattended and led Raymond towards the back of the bookstore once again. He motioned for Raymond to have a seat at one of the tables, where Raymond had spent the past half an hour waiting for this moment to come. Without saying another word, Raymond obliged, and Louis disappeared into a back office.

It only took a couple of moments before Henry appeared before him. He pulled out a chair and sat across from Raymond the way an old friend would do. Henry knew a lot more about Albert's whereabouts than even his closest family.

"Raymond, *bonjour,*" Henry said. His eyes were as green as Raymond remembered, and the curls in his hair bounced just like they once had before.

"*Bonjour*," Raymond was unable to hide the surprise in his voice.

"My family and I have been waiting for you," Henry said. "I regret that you didn't come sooner."

Raymond couldn't form proper words.

Henry went straight to the point as if he had waited a few years to do so. "It might be too late."

"Where is Albert?" Raymond asked.

"I don't know," Henry said, and with just those few words, Raymond believed him.

"Why did you give me this address back in Marseille?" Raymond asked.

"Is this the first time you made it here since Marseille?" Henry asked.

"No," Raymond said as if defeat had already started to take ahold of him. "I came once while I lived in Paris. But the store was closed."

Henry's eyes penetrated his.

"My uncle—" Raymond began.

"Yes, your uncle is Nissim Blanco," Henry stated.

"He's been searching for Albert since the day we left Egypt. He spoke to some neighbors in New York, and the only information they had about this address came back to you and Lily."

"Yes, our grandfather, on our mother's side, owned this bookstore," Henry said.

"I don't understand. I thought this address was your home. That maybe Albert was staying here?"

"He was. And it is our home. Our family lives upstairs." Henry pointed to the ceiling. "And my family, since we left Egypt, went through Marseille and came here to my grandfather."

Raymond looked up at the blue-painted ceiling and tried to picture the few apartments above the bookstore.

"And Albert was here?" Raymond asked.

"Yes, Albert was here once," Henry answered. "After leaving Marseille, he and Lily came here."

Raymond didn't even know Lily was onboard the ship and wondered what else Albert kept from him.

"But they aren't here anymore?"

Henry looked Raymond directly in the eyes as if he regretted that Raymond didn't know the whole truth. "I'm sorry, Raymond. He thought you'd come sooner."

But he had. Raymond had been there before; he had stood at the front doorsteps of the closed bookstore, not knowing what it was or its significance. He had been closer to Albert than he realized, but there would always be some sort of invisible gate that kept them apart.

"Are you saying that's all the information you have on their whereabouts?"

"Raymond, give me a moment," Henry said as he stood up from the table. He retreated back into the office and closed the door.

Raymond sat motionless in the reading area. He was scared to breathe as if doing so would blow away the opportunity. He still didn't know why Albert was so closely linked to Lily. The only person who seemed to know anything was Henry, but he was withholding the information for some reason.

Just like he promised, Henry appeared just a moment later. He sat down opposite Raymond once again and handed him a large manila envelope. Raymond took it without hesitation.

"Albert gave me strict instructions."

"That means he is alive?" Raymond asked quickly, with an overflow of enthusiasm.

"He was," Henry said. "I don't know where he is now."

"But he made it off the ship? He wasn't captured?"

Henry's hesitation allowed Raymond to believe that he was about to divulge a secret he wasn't supposed to share. "He was never captured. And he made it here alive, yes."

The ground beneath Raymond seemed to shift.

"But that was then, Raymond. He gave me this envelope before he left Paris. He knew you'd try to find him, and he knew your search would bring you here. And if you came too late, he wanted me to give this to you."

Raymond held the envelope gently in his hands, he feared that his sweat would bleed through the papers.

Henry began to get up from the table. "I'm sorry, Raymond, that is all the information I have for you. Please, stay in our bookstore as long as you want, if you want to open the envelope here."

Raymond tried to find the words to ask him to stay but couldn't.

"I hope we meet again, under better circumstances," Henry said. *"Inshallah."*

Raymond's grasp on the envelope tightened. *"Inshallah."*

As Henry disappeared into the back office, the bookstore's walls seemed to close in on him. Raymond never considered himself claustrophobic, but the blue ceiling seemed to hang low, and the millions of stories that circled him seemed to tell everything but the truth. Raymond got up from the table and left the store without making eye contact with Louis at the register. He didn't know where he was heading until his footsteps brought him to a quintessential French garden, just one avenue away from where Albert once stood.

Raymond sat down on a bench that overlooked a peak spring bloom of tulips. He had no time to appreciate its vibrancy or take in the aromas of the May afternoon. He didn't have the space to enjoy the sounds of children playing or focus on the French air traveling through his lungs. The envelope seemed to burn his skin, but a piece of him was scared to let go.

He opened the manila envelope and pulled out a pile of unevenly cut magazine clippings. There must have been at least ten different clippings inside the envelope. There were some of New York, a couple of clippings about Israel, and one of London. Raymond quickly skimmed through a magazine clipping about the South of France, but he came up empty-handed of the clues he wanted. He continued to browse through the clippings, through some about Asia and one that focused on Brooklyn. Albert only ever sent him magazine clippings from places he'd been or places he wanted to go. Raymond couldn't help but think that in the palms of his hands was where he could find his cousin.

After what seemed like an hour of searching through each clipping, Raymond slid them back into the envelope. As he did, a single sheet of paper slid out, one that Raymond had initially missed. Raymond unfolded the paper and realized it was a letter from Albert.

Dear Raymond,

It's too late. I hoped you'd find me sooner. I hoped that when Henry gave you the address in Marseille, that I would find you there. And I am sure that you waited for me, but I had to leave sooner than expected. We left for Paris, and if you didn't see me in Marseille, I hoped you'd leave for Paris too. Please know that I waited for you as long as I could, but we had to leave.

I'm not sure where you live, and you won't know where I am either. At this point, it's best that you stop looking for me, Raymond, because I will not be able to be found. It is better this way. You can move forward without me holding you back. This will be my last letter to you. If you are near my father, please give him one more hug, and tell him I'm sorry.

I hope we will meet again one day, underneath a sky full of stars.

Inshallah,
Albert

As he sat in the center of the city of lights, Raymond's everlasting hope of seeing Albert again dimmed. He only needed to read the letter once; he didn't search for any other clues or hidden messages in his cousin's words. Raymond folded up the letter and slipped it back in the manila envelope. He stood up from the bench and pushed his left sleeve up over his gold watch. He was already ten minutes late to meet back up with Allen and Michael, and if the Army taught him anything, it was to be punctual. Raymond tucked the manila envelope underneath his arm and walked out of the Parisian garden.

At that moment, Raymond stopped searching for Albert. It was clear that he didn't want to be found.

Ten

Brooklyn, New York, 1958

Raymond accomplished a lot during his four years in the United States Army. He learned to drive Humvees and obtained an official American driver's license. Raymond's time in the military taught him to be regimented and organized, where everything had its place and purpose. He learned to hurry up and wait, which made him perpetually early for everything the rest of his life. It was something that only began to slip when he was well into his 90's, when his relatively short time in the Army stood as nothing more than a blur.

He became a combat veteran in the Korean War. The conflict was coined "America's forgotten war," but he held onto his time in the Army with a humbled pride. He was honorably discharged as a Corporal. He had a chance to reenlist as an officer, but even though he found fulfillment in service to his country, he decided to move on.

The most defining thing the Army gave him was citizenship. Raymond entered the military a citizen of nowhere. Even though he was born in Haiti, he was never given citizenship because his descendants came from elsewhere. It was the land where he took his first breath, but it never recognized him as its own. When it came to descent, his roots were grounded in Egypt, but Egypt turned the other way, and Jews struggled to get formal citizenship in the country their ancestors had called home for lifetimes. France ended up being a steppingstone, and Raymond never had his heart set on staying long enough to be a citizen. But when it came to the United States, he never wanted to leave.

As an active duty service member of the United States Army, his newly adopted country sped up his immigration process exponentially. What normally took years was cut much shorter, and Raymond developed a sense of permanence in America. It was the first citizenship he truly held, and he thanked every star and stripe on the American flag for its empathy and acceptance. The chevrons on Raymond's uniform hung quietly in the back of his closet as he eased back into New York, the city that had been waiting for him all along.

Regardless of all he accomplished, a part of Raymond still came back defeated.

Defeat didn't come because of the Korean War; it came because of Albert. His cousin had put a sudden stop to their familial bond. Albert took it into his own hands to cut ties with Raymond, and it saddened and disappointed Raymond that he had no say in it. Raymond came back from Europe empty-handed; his calloused palms cradled the burden of unanswered questions. His love for his cousin still sat in the corners of his heart. He tucked it away gently to give it enough space to breathe. He tried not to have it weigh down his mind but kept it safe in case Albert ever came home.

Home had a new meaning that time around.

There was grit to New York, an air of superiority, and a sense of independence that was strikingly refreshing. After years of living in Europe and traveling through many of its countries, each new breath on American soil brought clarity. Raymond touched down in Brooklyn for the second time in his life and knew that time around held permanence.

Uncle Nissim kept Raymond's bedroom perfectly intact during the four years he had been gone in Germany. His old position at the electronics store waited for Raymond if he wanted it. Life was paused, and all Raymond had to do was press play again. It was as if Uncle Nissim was waiting for both his son and nephew to come back and knew which one would.

Raymond didn't have much of a chance to wear civilian clothing while he was in the Army and had forgotten how it felt to put on a freshly ironed suit. He traded in his camis for button-down shirts. His time in the military left nuanced marks on his character and would always quietly guide his footsteps. But at the end of the day, it was time for him to shed that part of his life and move forward.

He eased back into civilian life. He graciously accepted Uncle Nissim's continuous generosity and went back to work at the electronics store in Midtown. Raymond had a daily purpose in New York once again that came with an undeniable amount of joy and responsibility. It was exactly what he needed at the time, but with every train ride into the city, he knew New York could offer him more. He dusted off all the courage in his back pocket and checked the gold watch on his wrist. It was only a matter of waiting.

Time had a funny way of presenting itself. It leapt across weeks and months as Raymond picked up his life in New York but also moved in slow motion when it mattered the most. Raymond tried not to count the time since he had been with his family in Egypt, but, instead, counted down until they came to the United States. When the day finally came, and he'd stand in front of them again, he hoped they would be proud.

Raymond straightened his suit jacket in the mirror and wondered if it would be too warm outside. Springtime in Brooklyn was quickly heating up towards a warm summer. The brightness of the sun in his Bensonhurst window somehow reminded him of the Sahara's golden energy. He took off his jacket and placed it neatly on the back of a chair. He unbuttoned the top button of his shirt and shook off residual nerves. Years had gone by, and their lives had gone in wildly different directions, but all that mattered was that his family was all coming back together.

"*Yalla*, are you ready?" Uncle Nissim called from the living room.

Raymond walked out of his bedroom and met his uncle in the foyer.

"Are you familiar with the port?" Uncle Nissim asked.

"Familiar enough. I'm sure I can find the exact location. If not, I will ask someone for directions," Raymond assured him.

"I wish I could come with you to see their faces when they arrive." Uncle Nissim daydreamed. "But there isn't enough room in the car."

Uncle Nissim anticipated their arrival so much that he could hardly contain himself. Raymond shared the same sentiments and had hardly slept the night before. He slid on his glasses, and although it covered the remnants of a sleepless night, his subdued eagerness was obvious.

Raymond tucked a pack of cigarettes into his pocket and headed towards the door. "We will be back soon."

While Raymond occupied himself in the Army, life for his mother and sisters grew increasingly harder in Egypt. There were no

123

more prospects left in Cairo, and the Jews who once prospered in Egypt no longer had a home to call their own. One by one, his family and their whole community were exiled. Egypt plucked them out of the Sahara like a handful of sand and blew them away.

Raymond quietly made all the necessary preparations. He spent countless hours filling out the paperwork, coordinating their travels, and praying that all the happiness they could ever hope for waited for them in America. Eventually, his mother and sisters' time in Cairo settled behind a horizon ablaze with longing and a sky full of promise.

The first to arrive was Sylvia. She was his eldest sister, and as he embraced her for the first time in years, the torn fabrics of his life slowly came back together. Her perfectly applied red lipstick didn't mark the end of a long journey by boat across the world but the beginning of a new one on American soil. Together with her husband and their two young daughters, Raymond drove them back to Bensonhurst, to their new home.

His sister and her family lived with Raymond and Uncle Nissim until they got their footing in New York. Soon after his sister's family found an apartment in Bensonhurst, Raymond moved out of Uncle Nissim's house to his own apartment. His relatives were never far from one another. Raymond had spent too many years of his life away from his family to ever want to do that again.

One by one, they all came.

His sister Adele came next with her husband and their four children. Raymond picked them up from the dock, already familiar with where they would arrive. There was jubilation in the air when they reunited, and Raymond met some of his nieces and nephew for the first time.

His sister Rachel came with her husband, along with his sister Rose, her husband, and their two sons. Raymond took two trips to pick them up from the dock because now, with so many family members arriving in the United States, he didn't have enough room in his car. It was his privilege to be the man who welcomed them home.

His family had grown exponentially larger since he left Cairo. As his sisters slowly found their way to New York, they gathered at Adele's house every Friday night for dinner together. There was little more than Raymond wanted than the familiar aromas of home-cooked Egyptian food in the kitchen and the pitter-patter sounds of his nieces and nephews running through the house.

And piece by piece, so much of what he needed in the world came back to him.

Raymond never took credit that he was the sole person responsible for his whole family coming to the United States. He insisted that they stay with him as long as they needed to until they found their own apartments throughout Bensonhurst. It wasn't something Raymond boasted about, but it stood as his familial duty and true pleasure to help any way he could.

But the sweetest reunion of them all was when his mother came with his youngest sister, Olga.

The crowd opened up as Raymond's mother walked towards the entrance. Her smile tried to hide the few tears behind her eyes, and her outstretched arms tried to mask the void she'd felt for years without her only son.

"*Rohey*," she said as she cupped the palms of her hands onto Raymond's cheeks.

The warmth of her skin reminded him of tropical mornings in Haiti, when there wasn't a care in the world that could make his day go bad.

Raymond kissed his mother on each cheek and hugged her close. It had been years since they stood in front of one another. Her hair was shorter, but it still smelled of lavender. She seemed shorter, but her red lipstick still bounced off her fair skin in the same light. They hadn't seen each other since the night before he left Egypt for good, but she forgave him, just like a mother always would.

"My son, an American citizen," Raymond's mother said as she hugged him tight. He towered over her then, and since he'd last seen her, her hugs had become softer.

His mother and sister moved into his apartment. They soon settled into a routine in their new home together. Each morning, his mother made him a cup of coffee and a piece of toast with apricot preserves. Each evening, Raymond sat beside an open kitchen window and smoked a cigarette, thankful to be under the same roof as his family once more.

Raymond's mother and youngest sister arrived in New York in August, close to his birthday. His older sisters insisted that they have a party for him, and it was the first time in years that almost his whole family was together again.

Everyone except Albert.

It had been years since Raymond saw his family together, in one place. Even though he lived with Uncle Nissim before being drafted, his uncle was only a slice of the family, and nothing could ever replace the comfort in having his mother and five sisters near him again.

"Everyone is waiting," Uncle Nissim said as he opened the front door.

Behind the door was almost everyone Raymond loved. When he arrived at the party, the hugs didn't stop coming. Everywhere Raymond turned, one of his five sisters wanted to take a good look at him. They relished him with compliments and unconditional love. They reminded him of a time that was pure in his heart.

The party was held in Rose's backyard. His family learned the timeless American tradition of a backyard barbeque with ease. The Middle East's flavors mixed with the aroma of a summer barbeque just as seamlessly as clouds of cigarette smoke mixed with the Brooklyn air.

Bensonhurst backyards weren't necessarily spacious, but they always stood as the meeting point for summer family gatherings. They had traded in the hot desert sand for a concrete portion of Brooklyn and wouldn't have had it any other way. Most of the women spent a considerable amount of time inside preparing food, and Raymond's nieces and nephews ran inside to outside and back again.

All the men in the family sat around on plastic lawn chairs, each with a cigarette in hand and a mix of French, English, and Arabic on their tongues. Raymond lit a cigarette with a lighter he brought back from Germany and simply couldn't believe his eyes. His whole family found safety in New York. No one needed to run away anymore.

"Raymond is a military man now," Saleem said. Raymond's brother-in-law pulled out his lighter and lit a cigarette as he pulled a chair beside Raymond.

"Not anymore," Raymond said. He blew a puff of smoke into the air.

"Once a military man, always a military man," Saleem said. The white cigarette sat underneath a meticulously shaped mustache, something that would always remind him of Albert.

"How about you, Saleem?" Raymond asked. "I heard you are at the electronics store with Uncle Nissim."

"I am." Saleem was once a lawyer in Egypt, but his practice disappeared the moment he left Cairo. "Your uncle, he's a good man," Saleem said as he silently looked across the backyard for Uncle Nissim. "He's been such a good man to all of us since we moved to New York."

"He did the same for me when I came here, before the military," Raymond said.

"And he's had no word from Albert?" Saleem asked.

Raymond wasn't in the mood to get into the details with his brother-in-law. It was best to keep the details to a minimum.

"Nothing," Raymond said. "But I'm sure he's ok."

Saleem cocked his head to the side in confusion. "Why do you say that?"

"Just a hunch, I suppose."

Saleem's deep laugh filled up the backyard. "Raymond, we left Egypt already." Saleem laughed again as if he knew a joke that no one else did. "Maybe I should have said, once a spy, always a spy?"

Raymond's smile was coy. For the rest of his life, his family found ways to mention tidbits of his time as a spy in hopes of getting more details out of him, but he never budged. His nieces and nephews heard the stories, but it was more hearsay than anything else by the time it got to them. Raymond constantly brushed it aside, the only way he knew how, and changed the subject.

As the afternoon slowly faded into evening, a couple of his older nieces walked through the backdoor holding a birthday cake. A single candle was lit, and his family looked on and encouraged him to make a wish. Raymond took a quiet moment to himself and silently thought. He blew out the candle, knowing it had already come true.

He just regretted that Albert wasn't there to see it.

There was a time when all Raymond wanted was to focus his attention on finding his missing cousin, but as he eased back into his life in New York, his prospects changed. His job at the electronics store was stable, but it wasn't something that he wanted to sustain for the rest of his career. A small spark ignited under the base of his determination. It was only a matter of time before he set the world on fire.

If there was anything that the Army taught him, it was to be self-reliant and self-sufficient. Raymond played around with the idea of starting his own accounting business and saved enough money during his time in the military to give it a shot. Under Uncle Nissim's guidance, he tried to launch it, but it went flat.

It was a blessing in disguise because once his accounting business sank, Wall Street opened its doors.

Raymond's stint on Wall Street only lasted one year, but in that time, he learned how to keep up with New York City's pace. On the New York Stock Exchange floor, he truly felt the pulse of the city and understood the way it churned to keep itself one step ahead of everyone else. Wall Street wasn't necessarily the place he'd envisioned himself staying. The Stock Exchange could easily dispose of him in a New York minute, but Raymond always looked back at his time at the New York Stock Exchange with a certain kind of fondness, as if it was that job that completely solidified him as a New Yorker.

Raymond eventually turned to the computer industry, just as it was taking off. Every morning, he'd walk from his apartment in Bensonhurst, not too far from Uncle Nissim's house, and head towards the subway. Just like he had done before joining the military, Raymond got back into the flow of buying the newspaper every morning for the train ride to the city. He did so every morning until the day he retired.

Instead of taking the train to the New York Stock Exchange or to the small electronics store near Times Square, Raymond got off in Midtown. Irving Trust's headquarters sat on the forty-fifth floor of the Pan Am building, just above Grand Central Station. He flourished into one of the most respected information technology specialists in the banking industry. He learned the field just as the field was taking shape.

Banking and computers became Raymond's livelihood. In a time when computers were emerging, and their potential wasn't fully understood, Raymond had found his golden ticket. Even though he always had his sights set on becoming a successful accountant in Manhattan, the city had other plans for him.

Every morning, his mother continued to prepare him a cup of coffee and toast with apricot preserves, and every workday, for years, he climbed the corporate ladder. Haiti and Egypt never held such prospects for him. Only in the United States did he get the chances that he did. With the backbone and spirit that he had, he made his career look like a breeze.

When he wasn't working, his time was for his family. Having them in Brooklyn made him realize how the years he spent apart from them were ones that he'd never get back. His time with his family was irreplaceable, and it was a sentiment he continued to share when he had a family of his own. He watched his nieces and nephews grow, and as his sisters had more children, he wondered if a child would ever be in the cards for him.

The cards he were dealt were unexpected, and just like life had been since he was born, it uprooted itself time and time again. Irving Trust looked down Park Avenue and over the global horizon to what lay ahead for the company. Its office wasn't just in New York City; they were worldwide.

Raymond entered his boss' corner office. A backdrop of the most stunning Manhattan panorama draped George as if it were an oil painting at a museum.

"Raymond, have a seat," George said from behind his expensive mahogany desk. Before Raymond had settled in, George spoke again.

"Big things are happening here. I just got off a call with the CEO; the board wants to move forward with new openings." George clasped his hands before him, and a gold ring on his pinky finger caught the reflection of the sun.

"That is great news," Raymond said.

"We are opening two new locations in the next coming months. There will be one in the heart of London and another in Berlin."

"That's a big undertaking," Raymond said. "It should be great for the bank."

"We'd like you to be there for the openings, make sure all the new computer systems run smoothly."

Raymond's genuine surprise got tangled in his throat.

"In London and Berlin?"

"Yes, in both cities. London will open first, followed by Berlin. We will set you up with an apartment in each city, and all your expenses will be paid for while you live there. Furniture, food, transportation, you name it."

Raymond sat in a combination of silence and disbelief.

"You will mainly bounce back and forth between the two cities and occasionally come back to New York. But for the next few years, I want you to be focused on business in Europe."

Raymond couldn't find the words to express his amazement, but his silence said it all.

"There are talks to open more banks in North America too. We want one in Miami, eventually Toronto. We are also talking about having more in Europe, maybe even Asia. This is our first step towards becoming a widely known international bank. If we do well in London and Berlin, I see us moving forward with other locations soon enough."

"Wow, George, this is truly such a big opportunity."

"So, what will it be, Raymond? London and Berlin?"

Raymond followed the length of the city's skyscrapers as they reached for the clouds. He scanned the world before him as if looking for an answer when all the right answers were already within him.

"London and Berlin," Raymond agreed.

George offered out his hand, and Raymond shook it with gusto. The sky had never seemed so reachable.

Eleven

London, United Kingdom, 1970-1980

London came first.

Raymond's one-bedroom flat in Kensington was a stone's throw away from Hyde Park, and on days when London put a pause to rain-filled skies, the greenery at the center of the park became the backdrop of his living room. Raymond never thought it was possible to have a beautiful apartment with such a picturesque view. His natural humility never gave him enough credit for his accomplishments. Raymond found himself in the center of London with an apartment fully paid for by his company, not because he got lucky, but because he deserved it.

The flat was fully furnished but decorated in a way that Raymond would have never done himself. The living room housed a leather couch and matching armchairs that were perfect for conversations, and an elegant mahogany table anchored the dining room. Raymond's bedroom had a king-sized bed, the biggest bed he'd seen in his life, and he couldn't understand why one man would ever need such ample space to sleep. The simplicity in his upbringing never left him, not even when luxury knocked on his front door.

Nothing was overlooked, and it seemed like no cost was spared when Irving Trust furnished Raymond's new flat. Everything was thought out, from the silver utensils in the kitchen to the rounded nightstand beside his bed where he kept his glasses and handkerchief each evening. His ground-floor apartment in Brooklyn was shaded by well-established trees on 19th Avenue, but his new flat was airy and bright, with a posh air he'd only ever find in London.

In all sense of the word, Raymond had made it. His move to London as an international manager for Irving Trust represented a turning point in his career; New York City no longer served as the limit to his success. London catapulted him into decades' worth of international travels and adventures. But no matter how many first-class plane trips he took, a middle seat in economy was still perfectly comfortable to him. His company often paid for the many fancy steakhouse dinners, but Raymond tipped the wait staff with his own money. His pride was subtle, if not invisible, and was often overshadowed by his sincere goal to be an honest, hardworking man.

Work at Irving Trust was busy. Raymond was the senior manager of the bank's computer department for the new branch. He became the lone American in an office full of Brits. A gold placard with his name engraved into it sat at the front of his desk. It made Raymond feel more official than anything else in his corner office. Raymond never had to hide his true identity like he once did in Egypt. As he admired his office overlooking the River Thames, the gold letters of his name sat with purpose and dignity.

The workdays were long, and evening always seemed to settle in before he left the office. His colleagues looked to him for his expertise, and Raymond found a surprising level of fulfilment as he led his team. It was that kind of fuel that ignited his international career for decades to come.

But when there wasn't work, there was always London.

Raymond knew little to nothing about London before he touched down at Heathrow Airport. His knowledge of Europe had mostly been of France and Germany. He quickly understood how the United Kingdom simply couldn't be compared to the Continental countries. London breathed with an air of sophistication and royalty. It was steeped in tradition but pushed the boundaries of modernity. He appreciated its history in a way that surprised him. Raymond stepped foot in London for the first time, and by the way he was drawn to its magnetic energy, he knew it wouldn't be the last.

Raymond spent most of his weekends exploring the nooks and crannies of London. He experienced the changing of the guard at Buckingham Palace and downed a few pints at pubs in Islington. He found delectable snacks in Harrod's basement market hall when the luxury clothing upstairs seemed too far out of his reach. He let the quintessential British rain drizzle onto his shoulders as he walked around Notting Hill. He was a young man from a then British-ruled Egypt who finally made it to the land of the Queen herself.

When Raymond wanted a change of pace from the urban lifestyle of London, he ventured out. He took day trips to Bath, where he visited the Roman era mineral springs and stood in awe of Stonehenge's historical significance. Years later, he brought his wife and daughter to Bath and Stonehenge and saw it in a new wonderment through their eyes. The British countryside had a way of doing that.

Raymond was returning home from a Saturday spent on foot, walking through the West End. A man held the elevator door open for him.

"Going up?" the man asked.

"Yes, thank you," Raymond said as he hurried.

"No worries, what floor?"

"Seventh, please," Raymond answered.

The man pressed the button for seven, for them both.

"Looks like we are neighbors," the man said. His Cockney accent was jubilant and energetic.

Raymond looked in his direction as the man outstretched his hand.

"Jack," he said, with an honest man's smile.

Raymond shook his hand in return. "Nice to meet you, I'm Raymond."

"Sounds like you're not from this side of the pond," Jack said as the elevator made its way to their floor.

"Not quite," Raymond admitted.

"Via the States?" Jack asked.

In reality, it was via a lot of places. But Raymond nodded his head in agreement to make the explanation easier. "New York City."

For one reason or another, that took Jack by surprise. "New York City," he repeated. "My wife has been begging me to take her there one day. She wants to go shopping, as if we don't have enough shops on Oxford Street or in Knightsbridge."

"I'm sure she would like it there."

"I'm sure she would, but I'm sure my wallet won't."

Raymond joined Jack in a shared moment of laughter. He had a good point.

"Have you just moved here?" Jack asked.

"Recently enough, yes."

"Well then, it seems as if I am a horrible neighbor for never introducing myself sooner."

Raymond was used to the anonymity in New York City and expected more of it in London. The last thing he anticipated was a friendly neighbor in his apartment building.

"That's fine," Raymond said.

"Anyway, have a good evening, yeah? I better not tell my wife that our new neighbor is from New York. She will come banging down your door to hear all about it."

Jack ended up being the perfect neighbor to have in a city where Raymond knew no one. After a few more run-ins in the elevator and in front of the apartment building, Jack invited Raymond to a monthly poker night he hosted for a handful of his coworkers. Raymond was reluctant to join but found an eased comfort in smoking cigarettes around a felt-lined table, where he could gamble socially and make new acquaintances. Jack's friends were overwhelmingly sarcastic and witty, and each had their own very opinionated suggestion for where to find the best fish and chips in London.

But more than anything, poker nights at Jack's revealed a hidden truth that Raymond had buried for quite some time. Jack and his wife had three children, two boys, and one girl, which they adored with all the energy of the sun. Even in the middle of poker hands, Jack found time to sneak a kiss on his daughter's forehead or ruffle up the hair on his sons' heads as they ran by. It was something that Raymond watched wistfully. As he grew older, Raymond figured his time to start his own family was nearing expiration. Even years later, when Raymond invited Jack and his family to visit New York City for the first time, he still quietly wished to have what Jack had, a world of unconditional love.

What Raymond had instead was a solidly built career. He had a high-paying job, one that he would have never dreamed of as a child in Haiti or a teenager in Egypt. He was a man with an international job title and unique responsibilities. He'd forever be the shield for his mother and five sisters, even if they lived on two different continents. It was the life that unfolded before him, and even if Raymond wanted more, he'd always be grateful for all that he had. Raymond folded his hand and pushed the cards forward, face down. He lost the hand and thirty-five pounds to go along with it, distracted by his realization that having a family of his own just wasn't in the cards.

Over the years he worked abroad, Raymond saw his mother and sisters twice a year, once in the late spring when the New York heat hadn't become humid and relentless, and another at the edge of winter. Every time he visited New York, his family welcomed him with a huge gathering. His nieces and nephews were becoming young adults. His family was growing older, the laugh lines around his sisters' faces sat deeper, and his mother relished being a grandmother to so many. And like the dependable man Uncle Nissim was, he waited for Raymond's return and insisted on having a cigarette with him, even if opening the window to the cold of winter made his living room drafty.

Raymond never wanted to leave his family behind, but London was where he needed to be. Work was consistently busy. When he wasn't in the office, he spent many evenings at expensive company dinners in Chelsea or with his British coworkers sharing pints at the local pub during happy hour. Raymond found an undeniable fulfillment in his work, but he always came home to an empty flat at the end of the day.

After a company-paid dinner of lobster and oysters, nostalgia flipped through Raymond's Rolodex of memories. As he walked towards the tube station to go home, an unassuming shisha café caught his attention. Authenticity lived behind its door, and as Raymond was drawn into the café, he was transported from the heart of London to a golden era in Cairo. Before he realized it, he had a fresh apricot shisha in front of him, and billows of smoke clouded around his head. The flavors of the smoke covered his custom-made suit, and the air breathed of a time long gone. It was the first time in a long while that he ached for Albert. Albert loved apricots.

Once the shisha was put out, Raymond went back to his flat and pulled out a manila envelope from his desk. The flutter of old magazine clippings fell onto the desk's surface, each one individually clipped by Albert. He picked up the only clipping from London, a city that once held no value to him but was now at his fingertips. Raymond wondered if Albert had ever had the chance to see Big Ben for himself, if he ever blended into the crowds in Trafalgar Square, or if he felt the rain on the tip of his nose. It had been nearly twenty years since he saw his cousin, but when the wounds resurfaced, they stood as ongoing reminders that what was lost still had never been found.

Raymond slid the clippings back into the manila envelope, and it disappeared underneath a pile of papers in his desk, just what Albert would have wanted.

Raymond's time in London soon got split in half as he was tasked to open another branch in Berlin. The German city stood differently, with a sense of grit and history at every corner. The last time Raymond had breathed in German air was in Stuttgart, under the Army's regiment. But the second time around, he bounced back and forth from Germany to England on an almost biweekly basis, spending as much time in each city as he was in the airport. A rush of newfound adrenaline coursed through him as he was needed in many cities.

After Germany came Toronto. He landed in the Canadian city in the dead of winter. He quickly learned that almost the whole population of the city lived and breathed underground in Toronto's expansively connected network of businesses and shops. Raymond fell in love with Toronto almost immediately, even if it wasn't until spring was in full bloom when he could finally fall in love with it outdoors too.

When business boomed in North America and Europe, Irving Trust set its eyes on Asia. By the late 1970s, business trips took Raymond to the far corners of the world, to some locales that he never expected to visit. He dined at local sushi houses in Tokyo and walked the impeccably clean streets of Singapore. He found himself in throngs of congestion and traffic in Bangkok and tasted the bold flavors at hawker stalls in Malaysia. Asia was a walk of life so much unlike his own. It would forever be one of his most favored corners of the world.

Back stateside, Irving Trust set him up with an apartment in Miami. It had a wraparound balcony that seemed to touch the gates of the Caribbean. A hundred shades of aqua and blue drew a steady line across the horizon of his floor-to-ceiling glass windows, and the days never began as beautifully as they did with Miami sunrises. It was in Miami where Raymond's appreciation for coffee heightened with the taste of Cuban roasts, and it was where he got to kick up his feet a bit after years of nonstop international travels. Even though

Miami was just a couple of hours by plane from New York, he felt a world away in his apartment above the turquoise Atlantic Ocean.

Miami meant takeout dinners from Cuban restaurants. He occasionally ventured into the Little Haiti neighborhood for authentic dishes he recognized from his childhood. Every cashier always had the same look of astonishment when he spoke with them in fluent Creole, and they shared a little piece of their island nation.

He was in Miami when his mother passed away from a stroke. It was sudden and unexpected, something he nor his sisters were prepared for. The weight of a thousand regrets pushed on his shoulders because he wasn't there with her on her final days, but Raymond was thankful that he could easily get on a plane, and within a couple of hours, he could hold his five sisters in his arms as they each cried for a loss that time would never heal.

In the strangest of ways, Miami would always remind him of Albert. Even though neither of them had ever had their hearts set out on the tropical American city, it was where Raymond hosted a monthly domino night at his apartment, much like his former poker evenings in London with Jack. It was where he slapped down the bare tiles onto his dining room table with such confidence that he'd only ever seen in Albert when they played at shisha cafés across Cairo.

Raymond had found a new set of colleagues to socialize with from the Miami branch. He had come so far from those Cairo evenings with his cousin, and much of life happened without him by his side. Raymond was ashamed to admit that Albert wasn't always on his mind, if hardly ever, but he'd peek through during those games of dominoes like he had never left. Somewhere in between the slap of bones on the table and the crashing waves on the coast, Albert managed to do the impossible; be all around him and yet still nowhere to be found.

One day, Raymond would bring his wife and daughter to Miami, during a time when his career slowed down towards retirement, and extra time off meant walking along the tropical shoreline of Miami Beach. He'd show them his apartment building on the downtown side of MacArthur Causeway as if it were his just yesterday.

London was only supposed to be a couple of years. What started off as a company project with one international branch turned into a multi-country task that only Raymond could manage. His passport was slightly tattered and full of stamps, and his life was full of unforgettable memories. When seven-year-old Raymond picked fruit in the Haitian heat and sat underneath a sky full of stars with Albert by his side, he could have never written a wilder story than the one he ended up leading.

But even after all of that, home would always be waiting for him back in Brooklyn. Home stood at the doorsteps of his sisters' homes, in the contagious laughter of his nieces and nephews, and in the sweet taste of apricot preserves spread across freshly toasted bread. Home and family were interchangeable; home was with Uncle Nissim, and somewhere unknown, home still lived with Albert. Whenever Raymond had the chance, he always made his way back to Brooklyn.

"Raymond put on the record player for me." Uncle Nissim was never one to ask. Even as the last final moons of his story rose and fell in the sky, he still knew what he wanted.

Raymond found a record from Om Kalthoum. If there was anything that ran deeply through the walls of Uncle Nissim's Brooklyn house, it was nostalgia for a golden era where life was more aligned.

Uncle Nissim sat comfortably in his loveseat and closed his eyes. Age came across him like a steady wave that never receded. The music tickled his ears as if wailing in sorrow for a life that didn't exist anymore.

"Do you still have your apartment in London?" Uncle Nissim asked, still with his eyes closed. A place where once overly boisterous laughs escaped, valleyed lines ran down from the corners of his mouth.

"I officially moved out about two weeks ago," Raymond answered. "It was a beautiful apartment."

Uncle Nissim nodded in agreement as if he had seen its beauty firsthand.

"I can only imagine what Albert would think about all of this," Raymond said as he glanced at the faded photo of his cousin on Uncle Nissim's living room wall.

Uncle Nissim coughed and laughed at the same time. It was a combination of both the past and present living and breathing within him.

"He would have gotten a kick out of this." Uncle Nissim's laugh was much fainter these days. "His younger cousin, an international jet setter."

Raymond laughed at the absurdity of it all. That was exactly what he was, although he still thought of himself as that young man who looked up to his courageous older cousin for guidance through the world.

"He would have been proud of you, *Rohey*," Uncle Nissim said.

"I hope so."

Uncle Nissim cleared his throat. "Which of those cities do you think Albert would have liked the most?"

Raymond took a sip of his lemonade as the ice rattled against the sweating glass. Albert would have found endless thrills in Tokyo and lasting appreciation in the history of London. "Honestly, he would have liked it here the most."

Uncle Nissim's shoulders weakened. It was as if he had been trying to hold up the world for the past seventy years, and at that moment decided it was time to let it go.

"Can you replay that song for me, Raymond?"

Without saying a word, Raymond stood up. The sorrowful melodies filled the room when Albert couldn't. They sat together in silence as the Arabic words of misplaced love hit a little too close to home.

"Where is your next destination?"

"Irving Trust wants to send me to Hong Kong for a few years," Raymond said. He hadn't accepted the offer just yet.

"I'll be damned." Uncle Nissim's eyes held as much astonishment as his fragile body could muster.

Raymond smiled and leaned back into the chair opposite his uncle. He lit a cigarette and tapped its ashes into a clear glass ashtray on the side table.

"I haven't given them my answer yet."

"I don't see why not," Uncle Nissim said.

Raymond knew why not. It was because he had spent his whole life jumping from one house to the next, without ever truly knowing what it meant to stay still.

"Hong Kong," Uncle Nissim said, more to himself than anyone else. "And to think that I wanted you to spend your life working at the electronics store with me. Now you're off with apartments in London and Berlin and Miami and Hong Kong." Uncle Nissim's bellowing laugh seemed to shake the ashes over the edge of the ashtray.

Raymond never liked to boast of his work and was slightly shy about it, even around his uncle.

"You get on that plane and make yourself a home in Hong Kong," Uncle Nissim said.

"I don't know, I could also decline the offer and work from the Manhattan office. That way, I'd be able to stay in New York, at least for a few years, without so much traveling. Maybe try to settle down a bit."

"You have the rest of your life to settle down," Uncle Nissim said. "But you don't have your whole life to move to Hong Kong."

"But what about the family?"

"What about the family?" Uncle Nissim asked as if he were still fully capable of being the strong patriarch they needed.

"I've been away for too long," Raymond said.

Uncle Nissim took a sip of his coffee. "Raymond, do you even know what they say about you every time you leave?"

Raymond shook his head no. He had never even thought about it before.

"Your sisters tell every person who will listen in South Brooklyn that their only brother is out traveling the world. They make all their friends jealous when you send them scarves from London and brooches from Berlin. They wear them with this amazing amount of dignity. And your mother, you know she was a woman of many words, but Raymond, didn't you see how proud she was of you?"

Raymond finished his cigarette and twisted the butt into the ashtray until it went out.

"One day, when Albert comes home, we'll get the men together for a game of dominoes in the dining room, and you can tell him all about it."

At the end of the day, that was all Raymond wanted. He accepted the position for Hong Kong and flew out a couple of weeks later. He never saw Uncle Nissim again.

Twelve

Hong Kong, 1980

Raymond lost himself in the night market. Neon lights were mistaken for the stars, and left turns were not always the right way. Each stall came with a local who sold everything from hand-painted tea sets to jade jewelry or embroidered fabrics and porcelain antiques. Each vendor had lines on their faces and wrinkles on their hands that spoke of a lifetime's worth of honest hard work and memories. The maze of vendors blended one into another until both the market and the night seemed to stretch into tomorrow.

Nighttime in Hong Kong excavated dreams. In between the faces of strangers and the sharp aromas of regional cuisine cooking on outdoor grills and woks, Raymond found a renewed purpose. He was once a young boy who rode his bicycle through the Caribbean and a young adult who played a role in a social revolution. He was a man who would always find a home in New York, and after a series of steps and missteps, found himself on the doorstep of Asia. Raymond couldn't help but be humbled in a world so unlike his own.

Raymond was on a search for dinner. A colleague recommended that Raymond search the night market for some of the best wonton noodles in all of Hong Kong. Raymond never passed up a local recommendation wherever he lived or traveled. His colleague's meager directions didn't give Raymond a concrete roadmap to fill his appetite, but he was in no rush.

Friday evenings in Hong Kong were usually reserved for exploration. He had already been living in Hong Kong for nearly a year but hadn't even touched the surface of what it had to offer. The city had thousands of secrets, and Raymond wanted to know its details and intricacies. More than any other city he had ever lived in,

Raymond knew there would never be enough time to know it all, but he owed it to himself to try.

When it came down to it, Asia was another playing field. For most of his career, Raymond climbed his way up towards the top of his company in cities across Europe. It was what he was more familiar with. Besides New York, most of his time was spent in European cosmopolitan areas, and he blended in easily there. But in Hong Kong, there was no mistaking him for a foreigner. And at that moment, a foreigner who tried to mask how lost he was, just trying to find a bowl of noodles.

But that was the fun in it. There was something in Hong Kong that other places didn't offer, much more so than almost any other city he'd visited. Hong Kong gave him endless possibilities. Maybe he'd find the next best bowl of noodles or experience the most densely populated lifestyle he'd ever live in. Maybe he'd get so swept away with being halfway across the world that he'd become a true ex-pat in a country so different from his own. Or maybe he'd find someone to love for the rest of his life.

It was all possible, and all because he decided to take that leap of faith into Asia. It was then that Raymond realized that his whole life was designed as a series of leaps of faith, from one place into another, for one reason or another. Hong Kong was no different in that sense but unique in every other.

Raymond didn't know humidity until he lived in Hong Kong. It was the kind that rose with the sun, the kind that made the ground melt. One of the only times it dissipated, even remotely, was at night.

The pop-up stalls and the street vendors weaved in and out of side streets and alleyways. Restaurants extended their small storefronts, and just by placing a couple of tables and chairs on the sidewalk, each restaurant doubled its real estate.

After what seemed like half the evening spent, Raymond stumbled upon an older man in his seventies who cooked the famed wonton noodles. He ordered a bowl and sat down at one of the stall's handful of outdoor tables. The steam rose into his face, and the noodles tasted of decades of expertise and dedication. He wanted more than anything to share that bowl of noodles with Albert. He wanted to show him how far he'd come from the young boy in Haiti and the reserved teenager who became a man in Egypt. He pictured

142

Albert laughing wildly at the idea of Raymond as a powerful businessman with his own apartment in Hong Kong, but at the same time, he knew that Albert would have been proud.

But that was from another time and another place. Albert wasn't part of his life in Hong Kong, and it was something Raymond had to experience on his own.

Albert's jaw would have dropped at the sight of Raymond's three-bedroom apartment on the top floor of a Repulse Bay high-rise. It had views of the water that seemed to stretch across the earth. Every room opened up to windows with sweeping views of the crescent moon beach and the mountains that circled it.

The apartment was bigger than life. When Raymond held the keys of it in his hand, he finally understood that his life had become grander than he ever intended it to be.

Repulse Bay was what luxury was made of. High-rise condominiums were built to capture the views of the water from all angles. In terms of Hong Kong, living in the residential bayside community of Repulse Bay meant that you had "made it". And that's how Raymond felt, in a strange way, that he finally made it.

The only son of a textile merchant from the small island of Haiti somehow made a home high up in the sky where the South China Sea offered sweeping sunrises for anyone awake enough to appreciate it. Even though Raymond was undeniably humble at having the kind of life he did, he wished more than ever that he had a family to share it with.

Instead of pouring his love and energy into a family of his own, he steered all his energy into his work. His transfer to Hong Kong came with a promotion. The title etched on his gold placard read Assistant Vice President, and the door of his huge corner office said the same.

A knock rattled against the glass wall of Raymond's office. The door stood open, as it always did, and William, a fellow executive, leaned against the doorframe.

"Join us for dinner at our apartment tomorrow evening?" William asked.

Raymond put down his pen and leaned back in his leather chair.

"My wife is making this big American feast. She's getting a little homesick," William explained. "We'd love it if you can make it."

Raymond didn't have any other plans. "I'd love to."

William straightened his posture in the doorway and smiled. "Let's try out this new bottle of scotch I bought recently."

William was from northern New Jersey, and before moving to Hong Kong with his family, he lived in a typical American suburban neighborhood and commuted into the city. He had been living in Hong Kong for two years before Raymond ever stepped foot into Asia and took the time to help Raymond acclimatize. He became Raymond's closest confidant in the Hong Kong office. He was truly a stand-up man, one that Raymond was proud to call his friend. When William invited Raymond over for dinner with his family, he didn't hesitate.

Raymond held a nice bottle of wine as he rang the doorbell of William's apartment. He expected William's wife, Shirley, to greet him at the door but was instead welcomed by someone he'd get to know for the rest of his life.

"Hello, Mr. Blanco," a petite woman with shoulder-length hair the color of midnight opened the front door.

"Hello, how are you?" Raymond asked. "Please, call me Raymond. And you are?"

"I'm well, thank you." She had a thick Filipino accent. "My name is Maria." She opened the door wide and stepped aside. "Please, come in. William is waiting for you."

"Thank you," Raymond said as he walked into the apartment. A sweeping view of Repulse Bay at sunset illuminated the whole apartment.

"Raymond!" William said with his arms stretched out as he walked towards him.

"William," Raymond said and shook his hand. "This is a beautiful apartment."

"It's not too bad, isn't it?" William joked. "The company did a decent job finding us this place."

Raymond took one look around. It was twice the size of his own, which was already oversized for Hong Kong standards.

"I'll have to come by your place one day to see what they found for you," William said. "I hope they at least gave you a view this nice."

"They did," Raymond said. "That's something they didn't skimp out on."

"Raymond, this is my wife Shirley," William said as his wife walked into the living room. "And these goofy guys are Will and Jonathan."

Two boys ran into the living room, carrying toys with them.

Raymond greeted the kids with smiles and watched them run around in a circle throughout the living room and dining room.

"Maria! Maria! I bet you can't catch us!" Jonathan shouted.

Maria appeared in the middle of the living room and corralled the boys together.

"Come on, let's go have a little bit of dessert, and then it is time for bed," Maria said.

"Are we going to have some of the brownies you baked today?" Will asked.

"Yes, let's go have some. But only one, and then you'll brush your teeth."

Maria put each of her hands on the back of the boys' heads and lead them towards the kitchen.

"We never thought about getting a nanny," Shirley explained, "but the bank offered for us to have one, and Maria is the sweetest person you'll ever meet."

Raymond didn't quite know it then, but her words would ring true.

"Raymond, are you a scotch drinker?" William asked. "I just opened up a bottle of Glenlivet, have a glass?"

Raymond agreed, and they sat down in the living room. Another couple from the office joined them for the dinner party, and they got lost in conversations about private schools in Hong Kong for the children and what they missed most about the States. Even though the dinner was delicious, Raymond was more intrigued by Maria. By the end of the dinner party, he found a way to strike up a conversation with her as she cleaned up the kitchen.

"Dinner was absolutely delicious," Raymond said as he sipped his drink in the kitchen. Maria was positioned in front of the sink and was cleaning a few of the remaining dishes from the evening.

"Shirley is a great cook," Maria replied. "I helped her prepare the mashed potatoes and gravy, but she insisted on doing everything else on her own."

The scotch coated his mouth and soothed his throat. "It reminds me of back home. It makes me miss the States a bit," Raymond said.

"Are you from New Jersey also?" Maria asked. She began drying off the plates from the evening's meal.

"I'm from New York."

"Oh wow, New York," Maria repeated. "New York City?"

"Yes, well, I didn't grow up there. But I've lived there for some time now."

"I've never been to the States before," Maria said. "I hope I can see New York City for myself one day."

"William and Shirley want to bring you back to New Jersey with them when they leave Hong Kong, don't they?" Raymond asked.

"They do, to keep watching over the boys," Maria answered.

"New Jersey is right next to New York, maybe you will be able to see New York City then."

"Maybe one day," Maria said, as she stacked the plates away. "It's so far from home. We'll see."

"Where is home?" Raymond asked.

"I'm from the Philippines," Maria replied. "We don't have mashed potatoes and gravy the way you do in the States, so that was a new recipe for me to make today." Maria's laughter was contagious, and it always would be.

"Believe it or not, there are some decent restaurants in Central that have great American cuisine," Raymond said as he put his glass down on the counter. "Would you like to join me for dinner one evening? I can take you to one restaurant I know; that way, you can be prepared for what you'll eat when you make it to the States one day."

Maria's smile lit up the evening, and she nodded in agreement.

Raymond picked a fancy restaurant at the top of a hotel high-rise in Central, the heart of the business district of Hong Kong.

Maria had never been somewhere so fancy before, but she dressed for the occasion. Raymond later found out that Maria sewed all her own clothes, though everything she wore seemed to be plucked straight out of beautiful boutiques.

They ordered cocktails at the hotel bar. Raymond ordered a gimlet, and Maria had a glass of wine. She wasn't a big drinker, and a rosy look came to her otherwise tanned cheeks. Over a few drinks, Raymond learned she grew up as a farmer's daughter and how her family made a living off of selling coconuts. They were both the fourth born out of six children in their family, and while all his family lived across the world in New York, all of hers still lived across the South China Sea. Part of her family was in Manila, and the rest still resided in her home province of Southern Leyte.

Raymond ordered dinner for them both and suggested she try some of the most quintessential American dishes. Maria was genuinely excited, and even though her petite stature suggested she wouldn't be able to eat much, she ate it all with a deep appetite. Raymond always loved that about her.

Maria picked out dessert for them to share, a simple apple pie with a scoop of hand-churned vanilla ice cream on top. It was simple and understated, but it made her happy, and for Raymond, that was all that mattered.

Hong Kong became an entirely different city with Maria by his side. Work wasn't the center of his world anymore; she had become the only thing that grounded him. They shared stories of their childhoods and spoke about their siblings with the same love. He told her about his life as a spy in Egypt. He wanted her to know everything about him, including all the secrets he kept to himself for decades. They shared their dreams for the future but never took their time together for granted.

On an evening when the rain had just finished bursting from thunderstorm-packed clouds, Raymond and Maria took the centuries' old tram to the top of Victoria Peak. The rickety tram chugged its way up the steep climb of the Hong Kong mountain, which sat in the middle of the cosmopolitan city. Even though both of them had lived in Hong Kong for a number of years, neither of them had ever seen the city from the Peak. And once they found their bearings at the top, they'd never see the city in the same way again.

The countless skyscrapers and the endless lights of the skyline made the stars and the moon disappear.

"This is really something, isn't it?" Raymond asked. He leaned his forearms against the railing of the outdoor observation deck.

"I didn't know Hong Kong was so beautiful," Maria answered. The lights of Asia danced in her deep brown eyes, and the midnight sky never looked so promising.

They stood on the wide observation deck as it jutted out from the sloped mountain. Nothing about the terrain seemed natural, and everything about the world around him seemed unreal. Raymond didn't know why or how, but it was the first time he believed that there was a plan for the rest of his life. He knew he was the luckiest man on earth.

Love hadn't found him since his twenties, in a bakery in Marseille. Love had traveled down a myriad of other paths for countless other people, but for whatever reason, it had always bypassed him. Love wasn't ready for the kind of life it was about to embark on. Even though it had finally found him when he well into his fifties, and Maria was fifteen years younger, he knew it showed up for a reason. Love at that point in his life was meant to last.

Exploring the days and the nights of Hong Kong became brand new. Raymond never realized that he'd spent most of his life traveling the world without anyone by his side. It wasn't until Maria sat across from him at dinner tables or stood beside him at scenic overlooks facing the South China Sea when he finally understood what it meant not to have to walk the world alone.

He took every opportunity to take them places. They took ferry rides out to Macau and spent the day wandering through the old-world Portuguese-styled architecture. They hopped from one casino to another, and Raymond leisurely played his hand at blackjack tables while Maria tried her luck at slot machines. She had an uncanny way of somehow always making money on slot machines when every probability told her she couldn't.

Maria read through a local magazine about Lantau and the Tian Tan Buddha, and the next weekend they took a day trip out to the Big Buddha and walked up the steps to the statue. Raymond was far from his Jewish roots and Maria from her strict Catholic upbringing, but they both appreciated the Buddhist temple's undeniable beauty and landscape.

After a few months, Maria moved out of the apartment she shared with her cousin and into Raymond's oversized Repulse Bay apartment. Even though she grew up on the islands of the Philippines, the panoramic views of the water from every window of his new apartment still took her breath away.

They spent their mornings sharing home-cooked breakfast and freshly-ground coffee, where Maria often talked about her life in the Philippines as a farmer's daughter.

"My mother and father used to make us hold onto a rope inside of our house whenever a typhoon came. The winds would howl, and we'd hold on, but we thought it was fun. We used to collect the fruits from the trees every time a big typhoon hit our island," Maria said as she took a sip of her green tea.

Raymond took a bite of his fried eggs and hugged the mug of hot coffee with the palm of his hand. It had been decades since he even thought of it, but she helped him remember his childhood in Haiti, with Albert, collecting mangos after hurricanes.

Maria set up her sewing machine near a floor-to-ceiling window, facing Repulse Bay. In the evenings after work, she'd spend time quietly sewing dresses and skirts that she wore flawlessly.

Raymond loved to take her shopping in Kowloon. She admired the beauty of the clothing in the windows, and he always had to encourage her to go into the stores. She had never been able to afford anything in fancy boutiques, and Raymond had never had anyone to spend his acquired wealth on. Even if he gave her unlimited chances to buy anything she wanted, she still preferred to sew her own beautifully-made dresses. There was something more personal, she explained, to do things by hand.

Maria was there for him when news arrived of his sister Rachel's passing from a heart condition. She consoled him and took care of him while he sat on the other side of the world. The physical distance from his family was hard to stomach, but Maria helped the days heal. It happened once again when Sylvia passed away not too long after. Raymond would forever be grateful for the comfort in Maria's love and the compassion in Maria's heart.

One year after that fateful dinner party where their lives collided, Raymond suggested they go out for dinner at a high-end American restaurant in Central. He had a handful of expensive business lunches there with colleagues visiting from the New York office and knew Maria would love the salmon.

But before dinner, he had somewhere else he wanted to show her.

"Where are you taking me?" Maria asked. She walked beside Raymond through the steep streets of Central.

"There's something I'd like us to do together," Raymond said. He had never been so sure about anything else in his life as he was at that moment.

Maria's smile was quietly shy.

Raymond led the way until he eyed the jewelry store at the corner. He stopped in front of it and took Maria's hands in his.

"Let's get married," Raymond said as he saw the upcoming chapters of his life play out in her eyes.

"Married?" Maria asked, sincerely surprised.

"Yes, of course," Raymond said with confidence. "Let's get married, and let's go inside the jewelry store so you can pick out any ring you'd like."

Maria's smile was always contagious. She nodded her head in agreement, and they walked into the jewelry store together.

Maria was never the kind of woman who needed anything flashy. She didn't own much jewelry, and what she had was passed down from her mother. She had never stepped foot in a jewelry store as fancy as that one, and the number of jewels available was slightly overwhelming.

They browsed through the showcases of engagement rings, and Raymond insisted that she could pick anything that she wanted. His budget didn't have many limitations, and he was willing to do anything for Maria.

But Maria was never after riches. Her humble upbringing never tempted her to find a wealthy man to marry. She never expected many things in her life, including the beautiful apartment they lived in or the fact that she could easily go to that jewelry store and pick out whatever she wanted. She ultimately chose a simple ring with a single diamond in the center, with multiple smaller diamonds circling it. She wore that ring every day until arthritis in her hands made her knuckles larger, and the original band became too small to slip on.

They celebrated their engagement later that evening at a beautiful restaurant in Central. The waiter brought over a bottle of champagne and popped the cork tableside. The loud pop and bubbly liquid that spilled out made the other patrons clap and cheer with excitement. Raymond and Maria celebrated the start of the next part of their lives together, and it seemed like Hong Kong wanted to celebrate right along with them.

During the following week, Raymond tried to plan out a few details about their wedding and how they would ultimately move to New York once his contract in Hong Kong expired. Maria wasn't one of many words, and even though all she ever wanted was to find out if the United States was really closer to the clouds, the small doubts in her mind never made it to the surface. Raymond would have never guessed that she had started to get cold feet, and those feet just wanted to go home.

"I think this ring is too much," Maria said as they sat on their balcony that overlooked Repulse Bay.

"It's too much?" Raymond asked. He sipped his evening coffee as the sun melted away.

"I don't need a fancy ring like this. It's too much money," Maria said as she slid the ring off her finger. She grasped it in her palm and squeezed it with her fist.

"Maria, don't even think about the money," Raymond said, unable to realize what she truly meant.

"But you could have saved the money for something else instead."

"I work so I can do these things for you. I want you to enjoy it," Raymond answered.

"Are you sure?"

"Of course, I am sure."

"But are you sure that you want me to move to New York with you?" Maria asked.

Raymond suddenly realized that the only reason why she was asking was because she was the one who wasn't sure.

"Yes, yes, of course, I want you to move to New York with me. We can get married there and buy an apartment together, somewhere in Brooklyn."

Maria was quiet and gazed out onto the disappearing day before them.

"Brooklyn, New York," Maria said, more to herself than anyone else.

"You will love it there. I can't wait for you to see all the clothing boutiques in Manhattan. I know you will love all the dresses."

Maria fidgeted with the ring in her hand. The diamonds captured the fading lights of the evening. "It's so far from home."

And it was. It was not even a second thought for Raymond because for him, it was home. But for Maria, it was everything but home.

"Maria, you can go back and visit the Philippines anytime you want; that's not a problem."

"But that is expensive too. A flight from New York to the Philippines is long and costs a lot of money. Are you sure?"

"I am sure. You can visit your family whenever you want. We can try to have them visit us too."

Maria sat without words but filled with a thousand thoughts.

"I think I need to go back home," Maria finally said. She put the ring down on the small outdoor coffee table before them. The diamonds clinked against the glass with a sense of finality.

Raymond was taken aback by seeing the diamond ring on the table and not on her finger. He swallowed his initial fears.

"Of course, yes, go to the Philippines before we leave for New York."

Maria nodded in agreement, but her expression remained unsure.

"Would you like me to make a flight reservation for you next week at work? I can ask my secretary to arrange the trip for you."

"That's ok," Maria said. She stood up from her balcony chair and took his empty coffee cup and saucer in her hands but left the ring still on the table.

"Maria?" Raymond asked, just as she slid open the sliding glass doors to the interior of their apartment. "Does this mean you want to go home for good?"

Maria turned back towards him as the sunset finally sank behind the horizon line. "I'm not sure."

Raymond tried not to panic but was always one who needed definitive answers. "Do you still want to get married?"

"Maybe. We'll see."

And just like that, his day turned to night.

One week later, Maria left for the Philippines and never mentioned when she would be returning to Hong Kong. She explained that she wasn't sure if she would.

Raymond spent that first evening alone in their apartment and didn't sleep for more than a couple of hours without her.

He walked through the night markets and got a plate of noodles by himself. In every hand-sewn dress, he saw Maria sitting at her sewing machine. In every sunset, he saw another day gone by without her. There wasn't a single doubt in his mind of what he needed to do next.

If Raymond intended to make a home with Maria for the rest of his life, he had to go see what home truly meant to her. The next morning, he booked a one-way flight to the Philippines.

Thirteen

Manila, Philippines, 1983

The rain fell harder in Manila. It plummeted with more density and more complexity. It dropped from the sky like buckets of bullets and ricocheted off the asphalt and earth. Nothing could stop the skies from erupting and the lightning from sparking. Nothing could keep the typhoon from making landfall in the Philippines.

For the Philippines, it was routine. It was the way the world worked in the humid summers and how the seas churned that time of the year. It was late in the season and high time for explosive storms to traverse across the country. The residents knew it all too well. Maria had described the storms before, but it wasn't until Raymond felt the winds at the back of his neck that he truly understood what it meant to be in a Filipino typhoon.

But the worst of it hadn't made landfall yet. That was still a day to come, and Raymond was thankful that he made one of the last flights landing into Manila before the typhoon took the reigns. He stepped out of the taxi and onto the grand outdoor entrance of The Peninsula Manila Hotel in Makati just as thunder split the sky open.

Two cascading fountains rushed with water, and it was hard to tell if the gushing liquid came from the fountain or the sky. An overarching roof covered the few cars as they dropped off passengers, but the open-aired entrance became a wind tunnel for the gusts that grew in intensity. He caught a reflection of himself in the puddles and almost didn't recognize the man he was without Maria by his side.

Raymond only carried one bag with him from Hong Kong to Manila. He only packed essentials, even though he wasn't sure how long he'd stay in the Philippines. When it came down to it, he was willing to stay as long as he needed to. The plane ride from Hong

Kong to Manila was short, but the distance that stood between them was farther than he'd ever want to feel again in his lifetime.

He inhaled deeply as he walked towards the entrance of the hotel. Every minute he spent in the Philippines allowed him to breathe the same air Maria breathed, and he began to feel that much closer to her.

Raymond's secretary had made a reservation for him. He showed up to the Peninsula Manila Hotel's front doors without knowing it was one of the most exclusive hotels in Makati. International business people and wealthy travelers seemed to be its main clientele. Raymond blended in with all the foreigners in Manila's central business district. It was the first time in a long while that Raymond was traveling without business meetings, and it was slightly odd to him not to have a schedule to adhere to. Although he wanted to see the city, like he did anytime he traveled to a new place, more than anything he wanted to see Maria.

The hotel dripped in opulence and meticulous detail. A man played the piano at the lobby's bar, and Raymond couldn't help but imagine sitting with Maria and enjoying the songs. He made his way through the expansive lobby and checked into his room. He didn't know much about the Philippines but had a feeling that the hotel stood in stark contrast to what the rest of Manila was like.

His hotel room mirrored the beauty of the rest of the hotel. Everything in the room was perfectly designed, and no attention to detail was spared. He opened the floor-to-ceiling curtains and was greeted with the towering Manila skyline peeking through ominous storm clouds. At that point, it was only a matter of time before the world unleashed the brunt of the typhoon.

Raymond took out a folded piece of paper from his pocket. The only address and telephone number he had was for Catalina, Maria's sister, who lived in Pasay City. He picked up the hotel room's phone and dialed the number. He hoped that his plan would work because he didn't have any backup ideas.

"Hello?" a woman answered. Her accent was thicker than Maria's.

"Hello, is Maria there?" Raymond asked as he fidgeted with the telephone cord.

There was a slight pause on the other end of the line, and Raymond questioned if he dialed the wrong phone number. A shuffling noise filtered through the phone lines as the phone seemed to be passed from one person to another.

"Hello?" Maria's voice rooted him in place.

Raymond exhaled slowly and eased the tension from his burrowed brows. He had never been so relieved to hear Maria's voice.

"Maria, it's Raymond."

"Raymond?" Maria asked, and he couldn't help but notice that she sounded excited.

"I'm in Manila. I'm staying at a hotel in Makati."

Maria was speechless at first. "You came to the Philippines?"

Raymond sighed a breath of relief. "Yes, I did. I came to see you."

Maria laughed just a little bit, and Raymond felt more at ease.

"Can I see you after the typhoon dies down?" Raymond asked.

Maria took the phone away from her face, just enough to speak to her sister in Tagalog. Raymond didn't know one word of her native language but still tried to somehow decipher what they were saying.

"Do you have my sister's address?" Maria finally asked.

"Yes, I have the address you left with her telephone number."

"Ok," Maria said. "Come to that address. We'll have dinner with my sister and her family."

After their short conversation, Raymond had a renewed sense of purpose. He left Hong Kong without Maria and couldn't imagine leaving the Philippines without her too.

The typhoon hit the following day, and the high-rise hotel room's windows whistled with a loud intensity. Raymond watched the storm batter Manila below. Even though the eye of the storm spared the Metro Manila area, it still seemed like the whole world was going to drown in nature's fury. All Raymond could do was watch in the comfort of his expensive hotel room and wonder where Maria was braving the storm, somewhere else in Manila.

And just as quickly as the typhoon came, it went. By the following morning, the sun exploded into his hotel room and woke him up. As he got dressed and combed back his thick head of hair, he knew it would be a day that would turn the tides. It had to be the day that Maria would fall in love with him again.

Raymond found his way to Pasay City. He held two bouquets of flowers. One bouquet was in an unassuming small vase perfect for a table, for Maria's sister. The other bouquet was grander, a dozen of the reddest roses he could find, for Maria. Neighborhood gossipers leaned against the front of their houses as Raymond made his way through the narrow streets; they watched as he walked towards the love of his life.

He stuck out like a sore thumb. Unlike Makati, which was full of foreigners, he was surely the only white man who had walked through that part of Pasay City that day. Children played ball in the streets, and people walked to and from, holding shopping bags full of fresh fruits and *pan de sal*. It was the Manila Maria always spoke of when she talked about the Philippines. It was the backbone of the country, and the streets were the pathways to its lungs.

Raymond found the address and knocked on the front door. A dog's bark immediately sounded from within the house. Through the thin walls, Raymond could hear the chatter of people waiting for him.

Maria opened the door to her sister's house, and even though it had only been one week that they were apart, she seemed changed. She looked different there, standing in her homeland. She looked like she belonged there, and for a moment, he questioned if he was doing the right thing. He wasn't sure he could ever ask her to leave her home if she wasn't sure.

"Hi, Raymond." Maria's smile was always contagious.

Her smile bounced to Raymond as he gave her the bouquet of roses.

"These are for me?" Maria asked. She smelled them, and Raymond couldn't help but notice that she blushed. "You don't need to spend money on these nice flowers."

"It's nothing, really," Raymond insisted. "And these are for your sister." He held up the smaller vase of flowers.

Maria stepped back and opened the door widely. "Come in."

Raymond stepped into the modest home in the heart of Manila. A Filipino talk show played on the television in the small living room, and a rectangular table on the side of the kitchen was set for their dinner.

Maria introduced Raymond to some of her immediate family. She introduced him to her sister, Catalina, first, who was tenderly shy but excited about the flowers. She placed it in the middle of the coffee table and stepped back to admire it. He was also introduced to Catalina's husband and their three young sons. Maria then found her brother, his wife, and their two children, introducing them as well. None of them spoke English well enough to converse easily with Raymond, so Maria stood as the bridge between the life she had grown up in and the life she was about to join.

Maria's brother-in-law was the main cook for the night, and the recipes he used to prepare their dinner came from generations before him. Raymond tasted foods he had never even heard of before and began to understand where Maria really came from. A vinegar-based chicken adobo was the main dish, along with freshly fried lumpia and heaps of white rice. They just happened to be celebrating Maria's nephew's birthday that evening too.

"Have some of the *pancit*," Maria said as she put the traditional Filipino noodle dish on Raymond's plate. "It's the custom here to have *pancit* for birthdays. That way you will have a long life."

Maria shared stories of Hong Kong, and her whole family wanted to know everything about New York. No one let the language barrier stand in the way of a truly pleasant evening. Smiles and laughter would always be the universal way of communicating.

After dinner, Maria agreed to stay with Raymond in his upscale hotel in Makati. She packed her suitcase, and they took a taxi from the humble streets of Pasay City to the opposite side of town, where businesses and skyscrapers lit the night sky. Maria stood at the hotel room's floor-to-ceiling windows and kept a watchful eye on the expansive skyline of Metro Manila. No matter how extravagant or opulent, or how over the top and expensive anything was, Maria always remained the same. She was simple, humble, and she never took anything for granted. Every ounce of Raymond's heart knew he wanted to marry her.

The following few days were Maria's turn to show Raymond around the rest of Manila. Maria insisted they ride *jeepneys* around the city, and Raymond didn't hesitate to agree. The old American military vehicles, which resembled what would have happened if a Jeep stretched out into a limo, were all over Manila. Each one was elaborately decorated with a rainbow of colors and designs and packed with passengers. It reminded Raymond somewhat of driving vans when he was in the United States Army, except this was a thousand times more exhilarating. They hopped on *jeepneys* and swerved through the busy city streets, where traffic lanes didn't exist, and there seemed to be no rules. The air of the city was thick and mixed with humidity and smog. It was even more crowded than Hong Kong, and that was saying a lot.

They took a horse and carriage ride through the Spanish colonial area of Intramuros and walked through the park in Luneta. They wandered through the sprawling outdoor markets at Quiapo as a morning mass brought religious locals to a neighboring church. Older ladies sold strands of Sampaguita flowers, and an overflow of worshippers spilled out onto the sidewalk. Maria grew up a devout Catholic and Raymond a moderately religious Jew. He wondered how they could ever blend that together, but he knew he had to try.

Maria showed Raymond the ins and outs of Manila, but there was still one place only Raymond could show her. He had heard about an upscale casino from the hotel staff, and after dinner in one of the hotel's restaurants, they ventured out to press their luck. The casino was exclusive and only allowed entry to foreigners and whomever they brought with them. For Maria, it was something she would have never had access to without Raymond. For Raymond, he hit the jackpot by having her by his side.

Even with the thick humidity in the air, Maria convinced Raymond to go for a walk along Roxas Boulevard, right when the sun was about to switch with the moon. The pedestrian-friendly walkway along Manila Bay was crowded with couples and families. They found a spot to sit on the concrete ledge that ran the perimeter of the walkway, just as the sun began its nightly show of colors and textures in the sky.

"I haven't seen the sunset here in such a long time," Maria said. "It's nice to see it one more time."

"This area is beautiful," Raymond agreed. "Is that what it's like in your province too?"

Maria smiled at the thought of her hometown province of Southern Leyte. "Not at all," Maria explained. "We don't have any big boulevards like this one in my province. And the beaches there are calm, and not crowded. It's more peaceful there than in Manila."

159

Raymond sat quietly beside Maria as the sky turned into shades of purple and magenta.

"Do people do this in New York?" Maria asked. "Do they stop what they are doing to watch the sunset?"

Raymond shook his head. "Hardly ever," he said, which was unfortunate.

Maria turned her gaze towards the sky and water in front of her and breathed it all in. Despite the undeniable air pollution of Metro Manila, there was clarity along the shores of Manila Bay.

"I hope you can come with me to New York," Raymond said. "We'll find a spot to watch it there, somewhere in the city."

The deepening sunset paled in comparison to Maria's smile.

"Will you come with me, Maria?" Raymond asked.

Maria found his eyes and settled into their future.

"Will you marry me?"

Maria nodded in agreement as the sky burst into colors Raymond had never seen in New York. "Yes."

And that time, he knew she meant it.

It didn't take long for wedding arrangements to begin. They decided to get married while they were in the Philippines, which meant that all of Maria's family and friends could attend the wedding. But on the other hand, it also meant that none of Raymond's family could. It saddened him, but his newly found happiness quickly replaced that. Aside from his sisters, one of the only people he regretted not having at his wedding was Albert, but he was neither here nor there to attend.

They agreed on a simple courthouse wedding. Maria's sister and brother-in-law were the witnesses for the small ceremony. The remainder of her large family came to the dinner reception that followed. Maria sewed her own wedding dress, its simplicity shined with beauty. She also made a traditional Filipino barong for Raymond. That day in September became the absolute turning point in his life, even if he had waited more than fifty years for it.

Maria's brothers and sister-in-laws congratulated them with hugs and kisses. Newly met nieces and nephews ran to their sides for pictures and admired the beading of Maria's wedding dress. The private banquet room of the Aristocrat Restaurant filled up with Maria's loved ones, and it was then that Raymond realized how big her family was. He stepped into a world he knew little about but immediately felt welcomed. If there was anything he learned about the Philippines on his first trip it was that the people were some of the most warm-hearted he'd ever meet.

Maria's sister took charge, and even with such a short time frame to work with, she put together a simple and beautiful reception. Each table held a small vase of fresh flowers, each tablecloth was perfectly ironed, and each place setting was neatly set. To surprise them, Maria's sister arranged for a traditional Filipino dance company to perform.

The dance company performed *tinikling* at their wedding. Bamboo poles were tapped on the floor to the beat while dancers skillfully maneuvered their way around without getting their feet caught. Every step was calculated, and Raymond appreciated the traditional dance with his bride by his side.

The first time Maria stepped foot on American soil was for their honeymoon in Las Vegas, Nevada. It wasn't the part of the United States she always dreamed of, but she was still taken away by the unending glitz of Sin City. They stayed at Caesar's Palace, and Maria never thought she'd find her way through the fabricated streets of ancient Italy or walk beneath the dazzling lights of the Strip.

Raymond's game of choice was blackjack, and he taught Maria how to play. She joined him at the table on occasion but mostly liked to stand behind him and watch. Raymond wasn't a big gambler and always managed to go up and down steadily.

During a few hands where Maria didn't want to watch, she wandered off to a nearby section of slot machines and pressed her luck. After a couple of tugs at the handle, the machine's music and bells turned on, and a waterfall of quarters spilled out. Maria hit a little jackpot, and she was over-the-moon excited with her luck.

After a week of casual gambling and fine dining in Las Vegas, Raymond and Maria made their way home to New York. Raymond was eager to show her everything. He wanted her to fall in love with his apartment, and he hoped she'd be comfortable in his Brooklyn neighborhood. He couldn't wait to show her around the city and truly wished for her happiness.

"Now, keep in mind, the view from our apartment isn't exactly the same beautiful view we had in Repulse Bay," Raymond said as he led her from the elevator to his Brooklyn apartment.

"There's a view of the water from the living room, and in the corner, you can see the Verrazano Bridge going to Staten Island. But it's not the same as in Hong Kong."

Maria smiled. "I don't care about the views. I'm sure it'll be nice anyway."

Raymond took a deep breath and opened the door to the Bensonhurst apartment he kept while he lived in Hong Kong. One of his sisters had maintained the apartment for him while he was gone. It had been a long time since he had stepped foot in it himself, but it was still like returning home.

Maria walked into the foyer and then into the living room. Her small footsteps carried her from one room to another while Raymond followed behind. He originally was going to give her a little tour of their new home, but he stepped back and let her wander on her own. He hoped everything would be alright with her, that everything would be comfortable and that she'd think it was a beautiful apartment. Her footsteps against the wooden floor only slightly creaked as she walked to the bedroom and peered out the window. She turned towards Raymond as the sunlight caught the brown undertones in her hair.

"It's beautiful here," Maria said.

A certain amount of relief lifted off Raymond's chest as he sat down on the edge of the bed. It was all he ever wanted.

Raymond found a new rhythm as a married man. He picked up the newspaper at the corner store on his way to the subway every morning and went into the city with a purpose. He wasn't working anymore to climb the corporate ladder or make his way to the top. He was working to provide for his wife. He wanted to give her a world she could have never dreamed of, not even when she thought that New York sat closer to the clouds.

When Raymond wasn't working, he took Maria to the city, and they explored the ins and outs of Manhattan. Showing her around allowed him to be a tourist all over again, and he looked forward to the weekends when they could get lost in the sights of New York.

When Raymond was working, Maria found her rhythm in her newly adopted country. She set up her sewing machine in the spare bedroom and continued making beautiful garments. Raymond's sisters took her out shopping in Manhattan, and every evening,

Maria watched an episode of Wheel of Fortune until she became fluent in English.

Maria had only joined his family for a short amount of time before news broke that Adele had passed away. Raymond didn't depend on many people in his life, but Maria proved to be a quiet angel in the face of tough times. And in the way that life brought about surprises, less than one year after starting their lives together in New York, Maria was pregnant.

At his age, Raymond regretfully assumed he'd never have the chance to have a child. The news broke like an immensely powerful waterfall that shifted the edges of mountains. He was going to be a father, and even though he never would admit it to himself, he turned out to be the best father any little girl could have asked for.

Maria always loved to talk about the last trip they took together before their daughter was born. She was eight months pregnant, and they found themselves on a small plane ride to the Bahamas with a bunch of young Canadian students. Raymond and Maria spent a week in paradise and went for walks along the white sand beaches of the island. They only had a handful of weeks left until their vacations for two would turn into family vacations for three.

A few weeks after returning to Brooklyn from the Bahamas, Maria's water broke as they were having an early morning breakfast. Over plates of eggs and hash browns, Maria grasped at her moon-shaped belly.

"Raymond, we need to go to the hospital." There was a sense of urgency in her eyes but a larger-than-life smile on her face.

Raymond pushed his chair back abruptly and stood up from the kitchen table. A half-filled cup of coffee nearly spilled across the table. He helped Maria up from her chair. Before he could process how the momentum of his life was about to change forever, they arrived at the downtown Brooklyn hospital. Somewhere between all the excitement and nerves, Raymond forgot to grab the hospital bag Maria had packed, with clothes for their new child. It was something she would never let him forget and always joked about, even thirty-five years later.

In those moments, Raymond learned that everywhere he once lived meant next to nothing, compared to the home he was about to meet.

Raymond held a lot of titles in his life. He was a son, a brother, and a husband. He was a soldier, a veteran, and in the corporate world, an assistant vice president. He was a protector of many and a guiding light for others. And on a sunny Friday evening in July of 1985, as his daughter's first cries shook the entirety of his world, he transformed into the only title that mattered for the rest of his life.

He became a dad.

Fourteen

Izmir, Turkey, 1986

Home once meant four walls and a roof above his head. It meant Caribbean summers and the desert heat on the back of his ears. Home meant rooms full of sisters and international apartments alone. Home was with Maria, anywhere she laid her head to rest. But now, Raymond knew that the only home that mattered anymore had a beating heart of her own.

The April evening was a beautiful one, and Raymond knew it was more so because of the little girl he held in his arms rather than the warming of the season. He sat on the couch, still wearing the suit he wore to work earlier that day, his briefcase on the floor by his feet. He hugged Sadie close to his chest and he couldn't help but notice how tightly she hugged him back. After a moment of stillness, she wiggled in his arms, and the warmth of her hands around his fingers reminded him of all that was important in the world.

"Dinner is ready," Maria said as she approached the living room. "Do you want to change first?"

Raymond moved his head to the side as Sadie tried to pry the glasses off his face. Raymond smiled as he adjusted his glasses on his nose. He picked up his daughter from the couch and walked towards Maria. "Let's eat."

Maria situated Sadie in her highchair, and the three of them sat down at the kitchen table. It remained one of the only things in their Bensonhurst apartment that wasn't already packed. Boxes lined the walls of the living room and bedroom, and in some areas almost to the ceiling. Sadie loved to pull herself up by holding onto the boxes and took her first few steps before her parents were ready for it. Their crowded apartment became an oversized maze for her to explore with curiosity.

165

Sadie's first passport sat on Raymond's desk; her nine-month-old picture was one he always kept in his wallet. Their travel reservations were neatly folded into an envelope, and it was already arranged for a driver to pick them up from Izmir Adnan Menderes airport. Raymond ate dinner with the two most special ladies in his life and quietly hoped they were ready to embark on what came next.

What came next was Turkey. Irving Trust continued to grow internationally, and that only meant more opportunities for Raymond to move abroad. Just like he had done in the past, he packed up his belongings as his company arranged a fully furnished apartment, this time in Izmir, a coastal city so far away from anything he had ever experienced, but with hints of the Mediterranean lifestyle he had once known decades before. But this time, his wife and daughter would be by his side.

They traded their one-bedroom Brooklyn apartment overlooking the Verrazano Bridge for a three-bedroom apartment that overlooked the magical sunsets of the Aegean Sea. Every room had a view of the water, but the balcony became Raymond's favorite part of the apartment. It was where he sat with Sadie as the sun dipped behind the horizon, and the stars' light helped lull her to sleep.

Like all his apartments in the past, his company didn't spare a dime when it came to furnishings. Raymond and his family had everything they needed, down to the diapers Sadie used and the formula she drank. Raymond had a personal driver, and even though neither he nor Maria ever considered hiring a housekeeper, the company offered one. They agreed, more so for a bit of extra help in a foreign country where they didn't know the language. Her name was Selma. She knew just the right time to buy fresh bread from the Keremalti Market and taught Sadie how to say goodbye in Turkish.

Raymond quietly worried about his wife and daughter when he accepted the position in Turkey. It had only been a couple of years since Maria situated herself in New York City, and she had just gotten used to maneuvering through the city with an infant. But she was never one to get in the way of any plans; she insisted they would all be fine moving to Turkey.

Maria woke up each morning and prepared Raymond's breakfast with a sense of dedication he couldn't ignore. She spent each day nurturing their daughter with the kind of love only born from a mother and fell asleep each evening without a single complaint. Raymond kissed her on the cheek each time he left their apartment and knew without a shadow of a doubt that Maria was more resilient than he could ever be.

On weekdays, Maria and Sadie fell into a routine around the apartment and their seaside neighborhood. On the weekends, Raymond took Maria and Sadie around Izmir in a new car paid for by his company. They ate at Turkish restaurants in Alsancak and took walks along the Aegean Sea with Sadie leading the way. Sadie played with the neighborhood kids at the park as if they spoke the same language and came from the same part of the world. For Raymond, nothing in life compared to seeing Sadie flourish one baby step at a time.

Each morning before work, Raymond made sure to catch a few uninterrupted moments with his daughter. He held Sadie in his arms as they sat on the balcony; she loved to watch the boats bob on the sea, and the birds flutter in the sky. He kissed her on the forehead before leaving their apartment and could hardly wait to do it all over again when he came home for the evening.

A handful of months escaped them as they settled into their new lives. Somewhere in between almost-daily corporate meetings and stunning Turkish sunsets, Sadie turned one.

No expense was spared for Sadie's first birthday celebration. Raymond took the week off from work, and they spent it at a seaside vacation resort in Cesme, where the Aegean Sea turned aqua and turquoise underneath the midafternoon warmth. They woke up to room service each morning, and Sadie waddled in the kiddie pool each day. On the evening of her birthday, Raymond insisted they dine at the resort's most expensive restaurant. Raymond and Maria each had a steak dinner, and he placed a special order for a birthday cake for his daughter. A handful of waiters brought the cake to the table with a single candle lit for Sadie.

The three of them celebrated Sadie's first birthday together, while their extended families were scattered across the whole world. They sang the birthday song for Sadie and blew out the candle together. Even though the celebration was small, it was grand, and more importantly, it rose and fell with the breath of love.

"*Mabrouk*," Raymond said congratulations in Arabic. He kissed Sadie on the forehead as she sat on his lap.

"Happy birthday, Sadie," Maria said as she clapped at the end of the song.

The celebratory cake and song drew attention from a few tables nearby. All eyes were on Sadie as she smiled and tried to dip her hands in the cake's frosting.

"Happy birthday to the young lady," a blonde woman from a neighboring table said.

"Is it her first birthday?" her husband asked. His accent was thick and not from any country Raymond was familiar with.

"Yes, she is turning one today," Raymond answered. Sadie wriggled out of his arms and into Maria's lap.

"What a wonderful celebration," the woman said.

"Would you like to join us for some cake?" Raymond asked. Although he wasn't one to strike up conversations with strangers, an overwhelming sense of joy from his daughter's birthday changed him. "We have plenty."

The couple happily agreed and joined them at the table. In a random mash-up of overlapping lives, the family celebrated Sadie's first birthday in a Turkish resort with a friendly Norwegian couple. When Sadie got older, Raymond and Maria spoke of her first birthday party with such nostalgia and wonder that even the simplest of times seemed to be made of magic.

Sadie spent the first two years of her life in Turkey. Although she was born in New York, she didn't know it yet. She knew of mornings at a playground in Izmir and walks through outdoor markets. Sadie learned how to say a handful of Turkish words and knew which way the birds liked to fly over the Aegean Sea.

Irving Trust offered to cover the costs of two trips each year, intended on being vacations back home to New York. But New York could wait. When the first chance to travel rolled around, Raymond didn't hesitate to bring Maria and Sadie to the Philippines. It was the first time Maria had been back to her home country since they were married, and there was simply nothing that could parallel the amount of excitement that filled her as the plane landed at Ninoy Aquino International Airport.

They spent two weeks in the Philippines. Maria's family held Sadie in their arms for the first time. Underneath a Southeast Asian sun, Sadie played with her cousins and danced in the shade of coconut trees. It was one thing to see Maria hold their daughter in her arms, but it was another thing entirely for her to do it in the Philippines.

Raymond didn't realize it yet, but he had already planted the seed for Sadie's undeniable love for travel. Even before she could remember what taking off on a plane felt like, even before she understood what set places apart, Raymond brought his little family around the world with him. During their second year in Turkey, they flew to Paris instead of heading back to New York for an annual visit. Sadie played in a garden just outside of the Eiffel Tower. Raymond pushed his daughter's stroller down the European city's wide boulevards and past the bookstore full of Albert's secrets. He wondered if Albert ever knew the love of having a daughter.

By the time 1988 rolled around, it was time to leave Turkey and return home to New York for good. Traveling for business was something that Raymond knew wouldn't last forever, and as Sadie started to get bigger, he didn't want to be caught up in the office as much. He arranged to become a permanent fixture in the New York office, and just like that, they had their roots in New York again. His commute to and from work didn't require a plane ticket anymore, just a token for the subway.

The 7 train to Flushing was crowded like it almost always was during rush hour. Raymond stood on the platform as the train approached Grand Central Station and waited for the double doors to open in unison. Evening commuters held briefcases filled with paperwork to take home. Some held purses on their shoulders, and others had shopping bags sitting at their feet. Raymond was the only one who held a teddy bear.

During Raymond's lunch breaks, he liked to walk through the congested streets of Midtown. He enjoyed the sense of anonymity in a city that already knew him so well. He occasionally stopped at a deli for lunch, but Maria packed him a homecooked meal on most days. He sometimes window-shopped for his wife at jewelry stores, and if a gold necklace or a pair of ruby earrings caught his eye, he hardly ever hesitated to buy it for her. But now, he had another special lady to shop for.

Raymond walked by a boutique toy store on 42nd Street a few times a week and always peered in the window for something new, for Sadie. Her deep brown eyes lit up with excitement when he once brought home a doll. She loved to draw with crayons, and her little

169

fingers always fiddled with her toy piano. Watching her simple enjoyments gave him the greatest joy in life, more so than he could have prepared himself for. When he saw a row of oversized teddy bears in the toy store's window, he didn't think twice and bought one for her.

The toy store didn't have a shopping bag big enough for the teddy bear, which didn't bother Raymond one bit. In one hand, he held his chestnut-colored briefcase, and he tucked the teddy bear underneath his other arm. He carried the teddy bear onto the 7 train headed towards Flushing and knew without a doubt that he would forever be the happiest father in the world.

Sadie had a bench with pillows at the window, and like clockwork, she waited for him there as he walked up the street from the subway. It was always one of the highlights of his day, the moment when he'd catch her attention, and she'd wave with the pure thrill of spotting him. She would always be the most beautiful person he'd ever see in his lifetime.

"Daddy!" Sadie said as she ran to him in the doorway.

Raymond put down his briefcase on the floor and scooped up his daughter in a hug. She gave the type of hugs only a child could give, the kind made with unconditional love and innocence.

"Hi honey," Raymond said as he kissed her forehead.

"Daddy, what did you bring home?" Sadie peered behind his back. He picked her up with one arm as he tried to hide the bear with the other, but its arms and legs gave away its position.

Raymond revealed the hidden teddy bear, and Sadie hugged it tightly. Its oversized arms and legs almost matched her size. She jumped up and down with pure joy and insisted that the teddy bear sit with them at the dining room table during dinner. The teddy bear was simple and classic, but its meaning to her was powerful, well after Sadie became an adult. Raymond never knew it, but that teddy bear stayed with Sadie well after he couldn't even remember giving it to her.

Having Sadie made him young again. Even though he was nearing sixty when she was born, the youthfulness of having a child slowed down his aging process. Where people his age were focused on an upcoming retirement, Raymond only saw steady work ahead of him for years to come to make sure he provided for Sadie. His peers already had adult children off in college, but his own daughter headed to her first day of nursery school.

It was those moments of undeniable happiness that Raymond's heart beat for. He had never known love until he felt his daughter's hands squeeze his as they walked down the street to the playground. He had never understood how deep the valleys of his love could run until her eyes searched his for comfort and protection. He was made for loving her. He had never known home until his daughter lived in it.

Irving Trust kept Raymond busy in its New York office. In that first year back from Turkey, Raymond's company still managed to send him on short business trips to Europe, but each time it felt harder to leave home.

"Daddy, where are you going?" Sadie asked. She stood near the fireplace as Raymond brought his suitcase out of the bedroom.

"I'm going on a trip to London, honey," Raymond answered. He put his jacket on the back of the dining room chair like he always did when he prepared to go somewhere.

"London?" Sadie asked. She didn't know what London was, but one day she'd live there for a couple of months, just like her dad.

"It's a city all the way on the other side of the ocean," Raymond answered.

"Why are you going there?"

"I have to do some work there," Raymond said.

Sadie's rounded eyes looked into his with all the wonder in the world. He wondered what she was thinking.

"Ok, come back in five minutes!" Sadie declared as if it were that easy.

Raymond and Maria laughed at her innocence, but as Raymond traveled to the airport and boarded his international flight to London, all of his heart wished he could turn around and go back to his daughter in those five minutes. It was on that flight, as he sat in his first-class seat, where he knew that business trips and lavish apartments around the world didn't matter anymore. He scaled back his business trips after that trip to London because all he wanted was to be home with his family.

Home at that time was in Flushing, Queens. It was a stepping stone back into the United States, and they lived in a three-family house owned by a close family friend. That year in Queens gave them enough time to find a house of their own, and without any hesitation, Raymond knew that house would be in Brooklyn. After a career's worth of paychecks, he had saved enough money to buy an apartment for his family. By the time 1989 came around, he bought his first house, after all those years of living in different homes around the world.

Raymond and his family just spent the day looking for houses when they finally found the one to call home.

"Hold my hand, honey," Raymond said as he stretched his hand out to the side.

Sadie took it, and they crossed the street together. She released it as they walked onto the sidewalk and ran ahead of Raymond and Maria. She placed her hand on the top of each metal fence post in the grass and skipped from one post to the next on the way towards the front entrance. A grasshopper jumped on her hand, and she screamed and ran back to Raymond. He took her by the hand, and they walked towards their future home.

The six-story brick building on the corner of the block stood back from the street, with a communal park and sitting area in front of it. In terms of New York real estate, the outdoor space was hard to come by.

"Do you like it here?" Raymond asked Sadie as they sat on the bench in front of the building.

"Yeah, I do, dad," Sadie answered. Her four-year-old legs dangled from the edge of the bench, not long enough yet to reach the ground.

"The elementary school is only two blocks from here," Maria said as she pointed in its direction. "Did you hear the realtor mention that?"

"I did," Raymond said. "That would be very convenient if you can walk Sadie to school."

"And there's lots of shopping in the area too," Maria continued.

"Can I have the room with the crayon wallpaper?" Sadie asked.

Raymond kissed his daughter on the forehead. "Of course, honey."

"And you and mom will have the big room?" Sadie asked with curiosity.

"Yes, that would become our room."

"What do you think, Raymond? It's a good price, isn't it?" Maria asked. She looked down at the paper in her hands and reread the apartment's features.

"It is a good price."

"And we can afford it?" Maria asked. She was always conscious of their spending.

"We can afford it. This is what we've been saving up for all these years," Raymond answered. "What do you think, Sadie, should we move here?"

Sadie's smile was as wide as the Atlantic Ocean. "We should move here!"

"I think we have our decision, Maria," Raymond said with a smile that mirrored his daughter's.

After all the papers were signed, and the keys were in their hands, Raymond and his family moved to Brooklyn. Raymond finally found a place where he could set down roots, in a way he had been waiting his whole life to do. Maria made pancakes for breakfast on the first morning they woke up in their new apartment. They sat together at the kitchen table. Sadie poured too much syrup on her pancakes, but Raymond didn't stop her because she looked so happy. He sipped his coffee and listened to his daughter talk about how she wanted to decorate her bedroom. There was nothing more that he wanted than to hear the happiness in her voice.

Raymond's birthday approached as the middle of August neared, and the boxes slowly began to get unpacked. While Maria was determined to make their house a home as quickly and efficiently as possible, Raymond wanted her to take a break. He took them to Atlantic City for a long weekend and celebrated his birthday by the sea.

The sun of the Jersey Shore turned Raymond's fair skin a bit pink, while Maria and Sadie's naturally tanned complexion came back golden. They spent their days walking the boardwalk and playing on the beach. Raymond had never been much of a beach person, but he was always content while watching the steady tides come and go. The ocean contained some of the clearer memories he still had of Haiti. When it was time to leave, there was nothing that could make Raymond happier than knowing they returned to a home they owned.

After dropping off their suitcases in the house, Sadie disappeared to play with her toys, and Maria found her way into the kitchen. Raymond gathered a fresh pile of mail and brought it to the living room coffee table. He sat down on his corner spot on the couch and began going through all the envelopes they acquired during their long weekend away.

Raymond made organized piles on the coffee table. There was one for the junk mail, one for bills, and another for a few magazines. Organization and punctuality never left him, not since his days in the Army, and even well into his later years when he couldn't remember why.

"We were only gone for a few days; that seems like a lot of mail," Maria said as she appeared with a cup of coffee and a single pastry for him. She always took care of him, and he was forever grateful for that.

"It's mostly junk.," Raymond said. "Your sewing catalog came in the mail."

Maria picked up the catalog and began to thumb through it.

Raymond picked up a plain, white envelope. His name was written in a handwriting that was strange but also familiar. He searched the corner for a return address and then flipped to the back flap, but there was none.

"What is that?" Maria asked.

"I'm not sure," Raymond said as he opened it.

There was no letter inside. Instead, Raymond took out a single magazine clipping. It was a short article about Atlantic City. The weathered boardwalk was the same one they had just walked on earlier that day.

A lifetime's worth of heartbeats accelerated within his chest. Raymond clutched the clipping close to his heart and rested his back against the couch. He didn't need to read the clipping or look at its photos of the Jersey Shore. He didn't need to know what magazine it came from or when the envelope had been postmarked. In that single magazine clipping sat fifty years' worth of missteps, fifty years' worth of truths, and fifty years' worth of all he had been searching for.

Maria stopped looking through her sewing catalog at the sight of Raymond's immediate reaction to the clipping. He didn't

174

have the focus to notice his wife's concern and didn't realize Sadie had walked into the living room.

"Dad?" Sadie asked. "Are you ok?"

Raymond looked up from the couch with the clipping still pressed tightly against his chest.

"I'm ok, honey," Raymond answered.

"What is that?" Sadie asked.

Raymond took the clipping in his hand and gave it a good look.

And just like that, Raymond knew his cousin was ok. He knew that his cousin had been ok since the day they separated on the ship en route to France. He finally understood that no matter what happened in the lifetime they had lived apart, everything settled back into place. Even though the heat of the summer sun and the drive back to New York had tired him, Raymond had a hard time sleeping that night. Not because of all the questions that remained unanswered, but because of the overwhelming contentment he felt, knowing that after all those years wondering, his cousin had been alright.

"It's Albert."

Fifteen

Brooklyn, New York, 1995

Albert came back years after the dust had settled on their missed connections. He came back when they had more days gone by than they had in front of them. Raymond had learned to live what he thought was a complete life without his cousin until he quickly remembered how much better it was to have him near. Albert found his way back into Raymond's life when no one expected it. Raymond found comfort in knowing that Albert still wanted to be by his side after all that time.

Raymond spent most of his life not knowing where his cousin was but always wondered if Albert would come back when the time was right. He and his family were settled in their Brooklyn home, he had stability in his career, and in the moments in between, Raymond's heart opened for his cousin's return. Albert came back, and every bit of Raymond was ready.

The magazine clippings first came sporadically. Raymond desperately tried to search for a pattern, but he couldn't pick up on any. Every time Raymond spotted a plain envelope in his mailbox, he knew Albert sat on the inside of it. Each clipping read of an international destination, anywhere from Spain to Israel, Morocco to Mexico. He wondered if Albert had traveled to all those countries, if he had finally become the adventurer he was destined to be as a young boy. He hoped Albert saw the world.

But one thing that Albert didn't send was any other clues. There was never a return address. There was never a note attached to the clippings. Even though Albert had found him, the communication remained one-sided. In years past, Raymond would have wished to have conversations with his cousin and ultimately get disappointed when he couldn't. But as he settled into older age, he let it be. Albert had cut the paper's edges with a steady hand and licked the envelope's adhesive himself. And at the end of the day, that's all that mattered.

After reading through each article and admiring its beautiful photography, Raymond slipped them into a manila envelope and stored them in a cabinet with all his family photo albums. Raymond secretly hoped that one day he'd be able to share stories of his own travels with his cousin, but life had to move on until that day ever came.

He wanted his cousin to see the Brooklyn apartment he bought with his own money and how much sunlight poured into the windows of his fifth-floor home. He wanted Albert to hear the wooden floors creak on the way to the bathroom and have lunch with him in the large eat-in kitchen.

But the time for that hadn't come yet, and Raymond had to find contentment in knowing that even though Albert was all around him, he was still nowhere to be found.

Life went on in Raymond's Brooklyn apartment and in the best way possible. Sadie had a bedroom all to herself where she listened to music and created pieces of art. Maria sewed curtains for each window and made a table runner for the dining room table. She neatly made the beds each morning and dusted the lampshades once a week.

They slowly decorated their home with pictures from around the world. An authentic screen divider from Hong Kong hung perfectly on the dining room wall, and traditional Turkish plates lined the hallway towards the bedrooms. There were photos from Egypt in the living room and a tropical envelope holder hanging in the kitchen from the Philippines. Raymond's home had touches of every place he'd ever been, all in the only country he ever truly called home.

Mailings from Albert continued, and although it was once something that would garner all of Raymond's attention, it didn't receive the same amount of spotlight it once would have. In between giving Sadie piggyback rides from the couch to her room and family dinners around the dining room table, Raymond received the sporadic envelope from Albert. In between coffee and desserts on the living room coffee table and board games on Friday nights, Raymond tucked away Albert's clippings into the manila envelope. Albert was with him and all around him, and at that time, it was enough. Raymond's life went on with a renewed sense of comfort, just knowing that his cousin was somehow part of his world again.

He hoped that one day, Albert would hear the beautiful music Sadie was learning. She was five years old when she began piano lessons. A richly dark brown Wurlitzer upright piano quickly found its permanent place in the corner of the living room. There was nothing Raymond enjoyed more than when he got out of the elevator each evening and heard Sadie's musical notes twinkling down the hall. Her feet dangled from the bench, and she couldn't touch the pedals yet, but it was her favorite seat in the house.

Raymond took his camcorder to each of Sadie's annual piano recitals, and in the back of his mind, he hoped that one day Albert would see the videos. After each piano recital, for as long as Sadie would allow him, Raymond took her out for ice cream with a few of her closest friends. They always went to their favorite ice cream parlor on Emmons Avenue, just steps away from where a dozen swans glided across Sheepshead Bay. Sadie's youthful innocence sat behind a vanilla ice cream cone, and it was something Raymond never wanted to forget.

They blew out birthday candles and celebrated anniversaries in their Brooklyn apartment. Each autumn, they decorated for Halloween and each winter, they lit a menorah on the living room windowsill. It was in that apartment where Raymond quit smoking, something that would have shocked Albert. He decided to stop cold turkey when Sadie put a pretzel stick in her mouth and pretended it was a cigarette; he knew it was no good for either of them. It was in their Brooklyn apartment where life proved itself to be nothing but beautiful, and in Raymond's eyes, every day was cause for celebration.

"Happy Father's Day, dad!" Sadie exclaimed. Sleep was still painted across her face but excitement for the day emerged as she handed him a homemade card and a small gift bag.

Raymond sat at the corner of his couch and pretended not to know it was Father's Day. "Is that today?"

"Yes!" Sadie said as she sat down next to him. "I made the card in my art class."

Raymond opened the card to see a painting of a small turtle holding balloons as confetti streamed down from the sky. It was the most perfect Father's Day painting from a seven-year-old that he could have ever imagined receiving.

Maria joined them in the living room, and his family showered Raymond with simple presents. He took his time opening each one as if the process of unwrapping the present was half of the pleasurable experience on its own. He received a bottle of cologne from Maria and a wallet that Sadie picked out herself. When he transferred his belongings from his old wallet to the new one, he made sure to slip a new photo of his daughter into it too.

Raymond spent many special days with his family. If the weather was nice, they'd go for walks in Marine Park or along the water near Shore Parkway, where the coastline curved around the south end of Brooklyn and dipped underneath the Verrazano Bridge. And at the end of every Father's Day and every birthday, Raymond, Maria, and Sadie sat in the living room and shared slices of apple pie at the coffee table. There was nowhere else he was supposed to be.

If there was one thing Raymond was proud of, it was the idea that Sadie grew up with New York City as her backyard. Raymond once had a home on the edge of the Sahara Desert and stayed a stone's throw away from the Eiffel Tower. He lived in high-rise apartments in Miami and Toronto and fell asleep underneath a sky of London fog. But nothing compared to living in New York, and nothing ever would.

When the flowers emerged from under a warming bed of grass in the months of spring, Raymond took his daughter to Marine Park, where she rode her bicycle or spun around on her rollerblades. They played at the playground at P.S. 52 and watched cartoons together on Saturday mornings.

Summers in Brooklyn meant weekdays at Manhattan Beach and early evening walks along Emmons Avenue, where more often than not, Raymond and Maria treated Sadie to ice cream and fed the swans on the bay. Fireworks above Coney Island sparkled like the fireflies they caught in front of their building, and sunsets sank behind the Brooklyn horizon until the magenta and violet undertones of the sky dimmed for the night.

Autumn in New York City held the promise of a new school year, and with that came the bittersweet excitement that Sadie grew one year older. Raymond and Maria never had to worry about Sadie's performance in school and found unparalleled joy in watching her learn. She became friends with a family of four boys who lived in their building, and she emerged with an artist's soul. She painted her way into art exhibits, played instruments in music performances, but most importantly, found her way with words.

Winters meant the falling of temperatures, and as low-bearing clouds opened up to snowstorms, Sadie built snowmen in front of their building. Raymond took her ice skating in Prospect Park and, on special occasions, watched her twirl around the rink at Rockefeller Center with rows or international flags fluttering all around her.

On Sundays, they drove to the city when parking on the street was free and threw pennies into the waterfall at Midtown's Greenacre Park. They walked through summertime street fairs and watched tour boats glide underneath the Brooklyn Bridge from South Street Seaport. Each moment he spent with Sadie added up to a life he never thought was possible and questioned what he ever did to deserve it all.

New York City would always be the epicenter of Raymond's world, but it came to life differently with Sadie in it. Each corner held a new sense of promise, each day a new hope for the future. Raymond wanted nothing more than to witness the sense of adventure Sadie exuded while exploring the city.

Raymond spent as much time as he could seeing the city through Sadie's eyes, but once a year, he got the chance to show it to her through his own. "Take your daughter to work day" had become one of his favorite times of the year, even if he kept his smile subdued and professional.

"Are you ready?" Raymond asked as he slipped on his suit jacket.

"I'm ready, Dad," Sadie said.

"Have fun in the city today," Maria said as she straightened the back of Sadie's skirt. "Are you sure you don't want to bring any lunch?"

"We are sure," Raymond said. "We will have lunch in my building."

"Can we have some hamburgers?" Ten-year-old Sadie asked.

Raymond smiled, knowing she would ask for that. "We can have some hamburgers."

Raymond kissed Maria on the cheek as he left the apartment with Sadie by his side. They walked to the bus stop and took it to the train station, where he gave Sadie a token for the turnstile. They sat together on the Manhattan-bound B train as it made its way towards the city. There was nothing like seeing Sadie's face in wonderment as the train emerged from a tunnel onto the Manhattan Bridge; the skyline of Lower Manhattan would always be her favorite.

Raymond didn't plan on doing much work on those days, as the pure excitement of showing his daughter his office was all that consumed him. He introduced her to his coworkers, taught her how to use a computer, and she always marveled at the room where the larger-than-life printers were housed. He took her out to lunch in the dining hall of Grand Central and took a half-day off from work so they could spend the rest of the day wandering through the streets of Midtown.

While most of the year was spent in New York City, summers between each grade in school meant weeks of traveling. More than anything, Raymond wanted to show Sadie the world. He wanted her to taste the aromatic flavors of the food in Europe and feel the sand between her toes in the Caribbean. He wanted her to have the sun of Southeast Asia tickle the back of her neck and the stars of America to sparkle until she fell asleep. He wanted her to grow up in a world where she could travel and see the ins and outs of other countries and places but always come back to the one place that made her feel at home.

They took a road trip down to Florida and stopped along the way. They stood together in front of the White House, not knowing that one day, Sadie would live in Washington D.C. herself. They stayed a few days on the coast of Virginia Beach and took a trolley tour around downtown Savannah, where the willow trees hung low in the shade, and park benches were made for lingering. Raymond and his family made their way to Orlando, where they spent a week at the theme parks, and finished their trip in Miami, where the aqua-colored waves blended in with translucent skies.

They visited the Philippines, where South East Asia's heat hadn't changed a bit since Raymond had visited last. Maria's extended family had grown in size. It was as the furthest Sadie had traveled from home, but it also felt the closest to it.

They took a guided vacation up and down the coast of California. After all of Raymond's international travels around the world, it was the first time he ever stepped foot in Los Angeles or tasted the flavors of San Francisco's Chinatown. No one knew at the time that Sadie, who was only twelve, would one day call California home as well.

In between the years of making memories in their Brooklyn apartment, Albert continued to send clippings. It was a comfort at that point for Raymond, and nothing more than that, to have the occasional envelope from Albert, to know that he was still thinking of Raymond. Each time, Raymond read the article and appreciated its photography, then slipped it into the manila envelope where the rest of the clippings lived.

Sadie eventually ventured off to high school. Even though he knew all the great things that New York City had to offer, Raymond always made sure she was home before it got dark because New York City at night was a whole other beast.

It was in all the nuanced moments where Raymond's life happened. More so than the homes he built across the world, it was in that living room in his Brooklyn apartment where he learned how to live. With every after-school conversation at the dining room table or slices of apple pie at the coffee table, the years that moved and breathed with Sadie by his side were the ones that mattered to him the most.

Raymond started to slow down at work. He accepted a consulting position at the National Bank of Australia's New York City location, which gave him more flexibility to stay home and relax when he wanted to; it was well deserved. Even though he could make his own schedule and take days off when he wanted to, he put on his suit on the morning of September 11, 2001, and took the train to the city. In his office, which stood atop Park Avenue, Raymond had an unobstructed view to lower Manhattan as the second plane crashed into the World Trade Center. Raymond had left countries and escaped near-capture, he went through boot camp and military training, but none of that could have prepared him for the ball of fire that rose into the cloudless New York sky.

He walked down forty flights of stairs to get to street level. He still carried the brown-bagged lunch Maria packed for him earlier that morning as he walked downtown. Panic and mayhem grew around him in every direction as he made his way towards the Brooklyn Bridge. At seventy-four years old, Raymond walked from Midtown Manhattan to Brooklyn, a journey that took him most of the day.

Burnt papers from the World Trade Center landed on the grass in front of his apartment building in Sheepshead Bay. It took him a moment to understand the scope of it, that thousands of sheets of paper flew from lower Manhattan to the far corners of his Brooklyn neighborhood. He hugged Maria and Sadie the moment he walked through the door, their heartbeats pressed against his own.

Raymond was a man who found hope in hopeless situations, a man who could carve the right path in a series of wrong turns. But on the evening of September 11, it was hard to find comfort in a world set ablaze; it was almost impossible to stay calm as an era of uncertainty began. He sat on the couch and fiddled with the handkerchief in his pocket. He watched the news long after Maria and Sadie fell asleep for the night, and he quietly prayed for their protection and safety as ashes fell from the sky.

Sixteen

Brooklyn, New York, 2003

    Raymond blinked, and his daughter turned eighteen years old. Sadie wore a white cap and gown. Midwood High School's emblem, a blue silhouette of the Brooklyn Bridge, sat atop her heart. She straightened her graduation cap, and the tassel swayed against her midnight-black hair. She held on to her high school diploma as if it contained all her greatest achievements on a single piece of paper. Raymond was overwhelmingly proud, not just because his daughter had graduated high school as an honor student but more so because he knew all her greatest achievements were yet to come.

    "Stand here, with mom," Raymond said as he pointed to a sun-filled area of grass.

    Sadie and Maria positioned themselves together, and their smiles shone brighter than the flash. Raymond snapped a photo of his family and wondered where all the time had gone.

    "Now switch," Maria said, as she reached for the camera.

    Raymond stood next to his daughter and bent his arm at his side for her to link her arm through it. The wrinkles around his mouth and in the corners of his eyes etched a little deeper into his skin when he smiled. It was proof of a life well-lived.

    After Maria took a few photos of them, Raymond pulled out an envelope from his suit jacket's breast pocket.

    "We have something for you," Raymond said, "for your graduation."

    "You do?" Sadie asked curiously.

    Raymond handed her the envelope. The surprise was more than a month in the making, and he could hardly wait for it to be revealed. "Take a photo, Maria," he said softly.

Maria took a few photos as Sadie opened the envelope and unfolded the few sheets of paper within. Her dark eyes scanned it for more information, and there was a quiet moment of anticipation before Sadie realized what she was reading.

"A hotel reservation?" Sadie asked as she continued to search for its location.

"Yes," Raymond answered.

"In London? And Paris?" Sadie screeched. A mix of disbelief and excitement sat in her eyes as she hugged her parents tightly at the same time.

"*Mabrouk*, Sadie," Raymond congratulated his daughter in Arabic.

"We are very proud of you, honey," Maria added.

"We want to take you on one more vacation this summer before you go off to college. This is our graduation present to you."

Sadie had never been to London and had only been to Paris once when she was too young to remember. There were pictures of her standing at the base of the Eiffel Tower with Maria, with rows of fresh flowers blooming behind them. Europe had always been a place Raymond wanted to share with his daughter, and now that she was old enough to appreciate it, he was over the moon to take her.

They would leave in a few weeks, just in time to spend Sadie's birthday in London and Maria's birthday in Paris. Summer vacations almost always fell on one, or both, of their July birthdays, and it gave Raymond an extra excuse to plan something special. Nothing matched his happiness when the two most important women in his life were happy too.

London and Paris were places of the past for Raymond. They held stories and secrets that neither his wife nor his daughter knew much about. They were cities that Raymond knew well before he had a family of his own. Bringing them to places he once called home would be different that time around. The London and Paris he knew in the past would be experienced through a new filter.

On a weekend afternoon after Sadie's graduation, she asked to see pictures of those past cities in a way to prepare herself for their upcoming trip.

"I think the pictures are in that green photo album," Raymond said, pointing to it from the couch.

Sadie sat on the living room floor. A cabinet at the base of the television stand sat open. A stack of neatly-organized photo albums was housed within the cabinet and, with it, a lifetime's worth of memories. Raymond didn't look at the old photos often, and he didn't know that one day it would be one of the only things that could help him remember his life.

Sadie pulled out the evergreen-colored album and began flipping through its glossy pages. There were old photos of Raymond in front of Buckingham Palace and in the middle of Trafalgar Square. Raymond stood prominently behind his desk; a gold name placard sat in front of him, back when he was the Assistant Vice President at his company. There were photos of rainy London streets, followed by a series of pages of Parisian cafés and the Eiffel Tower.

"Did we go to the top of the Eiffel Tower when I was little?" Sadie asked as she looked at a twilight photo of it.

"Did we?" Raymond asked Maria for more confirmation.

"We did," Maria answered. "There should be a picture in that album from when we went to the top. It was so windy that day your dress flew up almost over your head, and your diaper and belly were showing."

Raymond and Maria laughed in unison as the memory came back to them, clear as day.

"I remember that now," Raymond said, his genuine smile lit up the room.

"Do you remember my hair?" Maria asked, still caught in mid laughter. "I could barely see because it was flying in front of my face."

Sadie smiled from where she sat on the floor. "It's in here?"

"It should be," Maria answered.

Sadie continued to look through the photo album.

"Where is this?" Sadie asked as she tilted the photo album towards Raymond's viewpoint.

"That's the Palace of Versailles."

"Wow," Sadie said as she marveled at the perfectly maintained gardens.

"We can go there too," Raymond said. "It's less than an hour outside of Paris; we can go there for a day."

Sadie continued to look through a photo album of Paris, while Raymond and Maria sat on the couch and looked through another London album. It had been a while, probably too long, since Raymond looked back at his time in both of those cities, but each picture seemed like they were just snapshots of yesterday. He pointed out a photo of his favorite restaurant in London, the way Big Ben overlooked the River Thames and remembered how London was the first international city that catapulted his career.

Sadie made her way towards the end of the Paris album and closed it. She took out a manila envelope from the stack of albums in the cabinet, the only oddly-placed item in there. She opened it before Raymond noticed what she was doing, and at that point, it was too late.

Sadie took out a copy of a National Geographic Magazine from the manila envelope. The old copy of the magazine was still in fair condition, considering how far it had traveled and how many years had gone by since. Sadie began flipping through its pages to a mixture of days gone by and travel destinations that would always remain classic. Raymond hadn't looked at that magazine since Albert threw it onto his lap decades ago, the night before they left Egypt for good.

"Why do you have this in here?" Sadie asked.

Raymond stared at the magazine, and it was as if he were looking directly into Albert's eyes. A thousand memories returned of Albert sitting on his bed in Egypt, thumbing through National Geographic Magazines with his single bedside lamp, a cigarette hanging from his lips.

"My cousin Albert gave that to me," Raymond said. It wasn't much of an explanation, but to explain everything would have taken another lifetime.

"What year was this even published?" Sadie asked, more to herself than anyone else. As she looked through its outdated pages and nostalgic photography, it was clear that it was from another era.

"Long before you, that's for sure," Raymond answered.

Up until then, Sadie had been quickly glancing over each page of the magazine, but she stopped at an article that caught her attention. With the magazine fully opened on her lap, her head tilted toward the left-hand page as she read a small column.

"What are you reading?" Raymond asked curiously.

Sadie finished up the short section before responding. "There's a bookstore here in Paris," she said as she lifted the magazine and turned it towards Raymond. "It's mentioned as one of the best family-run bookstores in Paris, at least at the time. Dad, why did you circle it?"

"Circle it?" Raymond asked. His eyes rounded with surprise. "I didn't circle anything."

"Yeah," Sadie said as she brought the magazine closer to him. "This whole little section, it's circled." She passed the magazine to him on the couch.

Raymond took the magazine and put on his glasses to get a clearer look. Sure enough, the small article was circled in red ink. The circle went around it a few times and the ink pressed hard into the page with urgency. He had never noticed it before, and when he finally did, it took his breath away.

The photo of the small, family-run bookstore in Paris was unassuming. Its glass storefront window showcased a row of new books for the time, and a single bell sat at the corner of its front door. The blood in his veins nearly froze as Raymond connected the dots. He had been to that bookstore before; he had once opened that front door to a jingling bell and to a world where Albert once stood. The address at the bottom of the article was one that he knew well: 818 Rue de Juliette.

"Sadie, can I have that envelope?" Raymond asked as he motioned to the manila envelope.

Sadie handed him the envelope, and Raymond gently took out a stack of magazine clippings, all the ones Albert sent to him since they moved to their Brooklyn apartment. He placed them on the coffee table in front of him and desperately searched for more clues, something else in any of the clippings that could help pinpoint a missing link that he hadn't already noticed.

Raymond picked up a clipping of Marseille and read it over to himself again. He read through clippings about London and Israel, articles about New York and Beirut. He reread a clipping on Brooklyn, and then right there, underneath the title, he noticed the author's name.

Max Labaton.

Raymond picked up another clipping, followed by another. He took the stack of clippings into his weathered hands and, one by one went through almost all of them in search for the author's name. Each one was written by Max Labaton; it was the name given to Albert in their spy ring.

Albert had been writing to him all along.

Finally, Raymond picked up one last clipping. It was written in 2016, and even though it had a more modern photograph of a storefront window, it seemed to stand still in time. A row of books was showcased behind the glass façade, and a single bell sat in the corner of its front door. It was located on 818 Rue de Juliette, and the title of the piece was "*A Safe Haven in Paris.*"

Without letting go of any of the clippings in his hands, Raymond leaned back against the couch. His heart thumped the same way it had on the eve of his departure from Egypt, the same way it did when he saw Albert jump over the railings of the ship. With more certainty than he had ever felt in his whole life, Raymond knew at that moment that Albert had found his own safe haven in Paris, and he'd been trying to get Raymond to meet him there all along.

Two weeks later, Raymond and his family boarded a plane for Heathrow Airport.

Even though Maria had always been the one to pack for the both of them on any vacation they went on, Raymond secretly packed a bit for himself that time. He slipped the manila envelope into his carry-on bag and made sure that all of Albert's clippings were inside. It was all he could think about on the flight to London. He was traveling back to Europe one more time, and underneath the circumstances of another life entirely, he felt that he had to give it one more shot.

Their first stop though was London. They spent nearly a week walking through its streets, visiting famed places like Big Ben and Buckingham Palace, all while Raymond had his mindset on Paris. Sadie snapped photos in Trafalgar Square and insisted on having proper afternoon tea in their hotel as Raymond's mind raced around the anticipation of France.

London became an afterthought. He was glad that Maria and Sadie were enjoying their time in the United Kingdom, and for the most part, he was too. Even though he was often distracted by what waited for him during the next leg of their trip, he stopped himself in moments when Sadie seemed to sit at the edge of the world, in awe of where they traveled to, and he couldn't help but realize that she was on the brink of her own adventures like he once was decades before.

When the time came, Raymond and his family packed up their bags and crossed the English Channel to France. The hovercraft ride was quick and smooth, and with every nautical mile covered, Raymond wondered if it was bringing him one step closer to a cousin he lost such a long time ago.

Raymond and his family checked into a luxurious boutique hotel just steps from Champs-Elysees. They walked the famed Parisian boulevard to the base of the Arc de Triomphe and meandered down smaller back streets lined with French cafés and bistros. As Raymond stepped back onto French soil for the first time in over fifteen years, something about the way the boulevards coursed through the city set him at ease.

He treated his wife and daughter to a quintessential French dinner at a restaurant with a stunning view of the Eiffel Tower that evening. The landmark lit up in a dazzling spectacle of lights; Raymond loved to watch its reflection in Sadie's eyes. He wanted a glass of wine, something he rarely drank, and when the waiter suggested a Merlot from the vineyard in Marseille he once worked at, he undoubtedly knew that the wheels of the universe were finding alignment once more.

Raymond slept well that night with a glass of wine in his belly and a grateful heart ready for whatever manifested next.

The following day, Raymond sat with his wife and daughter at the hotel's main restaurant, a full French breakfast before them.

"How about you two do a little bit of shopping this morning if you want?" he suggested.

"Do you want to see Galeries Lafayette, Mom?" Sadie asked.

"Sure, we can go there," Maria agreed.

"You two go ahead and do that after breakfast, and let's meet back here at noon?" Raymond asked.

"You don't want to come with us?" Sadie asked as she took a bite of a fresh croissant.

"Not this time," Raymond said. "I'd like to go to the bookstore we read about in the National Geographic Magazine."

Sadie and Maria nodded in agreement. They both knew it meant something to him, but Raymond kept its magnitude a secret.

After finishing up their breakfast, Sadie and Maria left for a morning of Parisian shopping. Raymond drank the last few sips of his strong coffee and found himself walking down Rue de Juliette; it remained the same even if a lifetime had gone by. The limestone buildings of the street still stood with the same elegance, and the history of the architecture traced the stories of the lives lived within. He had been a different person, almost another person entirely, the last time he walked the streets of that arrondissement.

The bookstore stood right in the middle of the block, sandwiched between two residential buildings. Its wide, wooden doors still had the same long brass handles, and its façade was weathered with time. His hand fiddled with a handkerchief in his pocket before he pulled open its old door. He hadn't been there in decades, but he knew it all too well.

Raymond walked into the bookstore as a single bell jangled against its glass door. A young woman welcomed him into the shop from behind the cash register. Raymond had only stepped foot in the bookstore once in his whole life, but something about it made it feel like home. It smelled of old stories and new adventures. Each book seemed to hold its own place in the shop; each story meant to be there. He walked down its narrow aisles to the back of the shop, where, like it once had done before, it opened up to a quiet reading area.

The communal area felt just how he remembered it, even though it seemed to have been slightly remodeled over the years since Raymond had been in Paris. The couches were updated but still felt worn in. The reading tables and chairs that anchored the room were weathered by hundreds and thousands of readers. But it still felt like he had been there just yesterday.

Raymond wasn't sure where to look first. His attention rested on a rack of magazines, as its colors and fonts looked similar to the clippings that he received from Albert. Raymond picked up the magazine and began looking through it. There in the palm of his hands was an article by Max Labaton. It was about New York.

Raymond took the magazine to a table and began to read the article. It was almost like a love letter to a place Albert had once lived but would never visit again. It was beautiful, and it was heartbreaking, and everything about it sounded like Albert.

Raymond questioned if he should ask the woman at the front for information, perhaps if she knew if the author had ever come into the store before or maybe was a frequent customer. Raymond had arrived, but didn't know where else to go. He looked around at the people in the aisles and didn't know what his next step should be.

Raymond had been so busy looking around the whole bookshop that he hadn't noticed the man who sat across from him at the communal table. His thick head of hair was neatly parted to the side, and he held an olive complexion that could only be a product of the Mediterranean sun. An opened book blocked the rest of the man's face from sight.

"Excuse me," Raymond said just loud enough for the man but quiet enough for the rest of the bookstore. The man lowered the book to reveal a handful of wrinkles on his forehead, followed by his thick salt and pepper eyebrows, a mustache, and a pair of moon-shaped eyes that reminded Raymond of home. Two worlds that had run parallel for the past fifty years had finally crossed.

Raymond took a deep breath and pointed his face towards the ceiling, for one last moment by himself. The bookstore's ceiling was painted a midnight blue; it was the kind of sky he remembered from clear nights on his front porch in Haiti. Gold flecks of constellations dotted the ceiling as if all the stars in the universe had come together to watch the moment unfold. The man before him sat where he promised he'd be, and when everything in the world seemed to have worked against them, they had finally found their meeting point.

Underneath a sky full of stars was Albert.

Seventeen

Raymond's finger shook slightly as he rang the doorbell with a combination of apprehension and old age. The doorbell chimed with the bells of Paris. Raymond straightened the sides of his sport jacket and fiddled with the handkerchief in his pocket. He stood at the grand double-door entrance and knew that somewhere along the way, Albert had done well for himself.

Raymond put his hand on Maria's shoulder as if to give her reassurance, although he was the one who needed it the most. Footsteps on the other side of the thick doors shuffled towards them, and with a couple of clicks, the door unlocked.

Albert opened the door and stood in the doorframe, and it was as if they were on the ship from Cairo to Marseille once more. He had remained slender, and his mustache was neatly trimmed. He was just the way Raymond remembered him as a young man in Egypt.

"Raymond." Albert cupped Raymond's face in his hands as if embracing a discovered treasure and kissed him on both cheeks. "*Yalla*, come in, come in."

Albert led Raymond and his family into a round foyer where a single table with an oversized bouquet of tulips sat. A crystal chandelier hung above them and made the Parisian apartment come to life. "Welcome. *Comment ça va*, Raymond?"

"*Ça va bien, Alhamdullah*," Raymond said that he was doing well, thank God, in a mixture of French and Arabic. It was like nothing had ever changed. "Albert, this is my wife, Maria," Raymond said as he put his hand on her back.

"Lovely to meet you, Maria," Albert said and kissed her on both cheeks. His English was coated with a thick French accent, something Raymond wasn't used to hearing.

"It's very nice to meet you, as well," Maria said.

"And this is my daughter, Sadie." Raymond presented his daughter as if showing off his whole world.

"Sadie," Albert said her name as if they had known one another all along. He kissed her on both cheeks and gave her a big hug. "Never in my wildest dreams did I think you would have a daughter," Albert teased Raymond. "Sadie, your father is one hell of a man."

Sadie's smile bounced between Albert and Raymond.

"Raymond, this young lady is beautiful," Albert said about Sadie. "Sadie, does your father still tuck a handkerchief in his pocket?"

"Every morning." Sadie laughed.

"Just like I remember him," Albert said and teasingly slapped Raymond on the back of his shoulder. "Please, please, come in. Why are we standing in the foyer? Come in and meet my family."

Albert ushered them out of the grand foyer, and the rest of his Parisian apartment opened up to a European dreamscape. From the outside, Raymond had assumed that Albert's apartment was located on one of the building's four floors, but he soon realized that Albert's house took up the whole building itself.

Albert's home was beautiful. It stood unapologetically French with its classic décor and historic architecture. The high ceilings gave way to elaborate moldings, and a herringbone design on the hardwood floors stretched from one room to the next. Each of the expansive windows were lined with elegant drapes, and wrought-iron balconies gave way to one stunning view of Paris after another.

Raymond could hardly believe what he saw. This sophisticated Parisian house was his cousin's, the same cousin with whom he once shared a bedroom in Cairo, the same cousin who could never be contained indoors for too long because his innate need to explore the world always called him outside. It was almost unbelievable to realize that Albert's house was as grand as befitting a prince, and its refinement could not be understated.

After taking in the French opulence of his cousin's home, Raymond quickly came back to what mattered the most. He stood with his cousin by his side, and no sense of grandiose or extravagance could take that moment from him.

"These are my children: Joseph, Victor, and Margaret," Albert said as he introduced them. They were in their late twenties and early thirties, much older than Sadie.

"Victor, is your mother in the kitchen?" Albert asked his youngest son.

"She is. Let me go get her."

"Thank you, *Rohey*," Albert said.

A thin woman with hair the color of Egyptian kohl emerged from the kitchen. An apron covered most of her dress, and a string of pearls sat delicately atop her collarbone. There was something about the way she smiled that immediately reminded Raymond of Sami's parties. He knew her in a previous life.

"Raymond, this is my wife, Lily."

"Lily," Raymond said and kissed her on both cheeks.

The group of them found their way into the formal living room.

"Raymond, it has been a lifetime," Lily said as she sat down on the edge of the sofa.

Raymond sat opposite her and studied the lines and edges of her face. He had met her before, he was sure of it, but the details were blurry. Her name had floated around Albert's for his whole disappearance, but her face stood in a combination of familiarity and newness.

"At some of Sami's parties," Lily continued, trying to refresh his memory.

"Yes, yes, of course," Raymond said with certainty.

Lily had been involved with Albert that whole time. It was something that Raymond had always considered, but with not enough substantial evidence to back it up, it was just another theory that eventually dwindled away. Uncle Nissim had been right all along.

"This is truly remarkable," Raymond said. He couldn't contain his disbelief that two people from a life he sometimes forgot he led were sitting right before him.

"No, what's more remarkable is that my cousin is right here," Albert said. He got up from the couch and gave Raymond a bear hug as if making up for a lifetime's worth of lost embraces.

"It's very nice to see you again, Raymond," Lily said respectfully. "And you have a beautiful family. Do you live in New York?"

"Yes, in Brooklyn," Raymond answered.

"Brooklyn, New York," Albert said, more to himself than anyone else. It was as if just the mention of his favorite borough immediately brought him back to another time when things were much more innocent. "Raymond and his family are visiting Paris on vacation. I hear it is for Sadie's graduation."

Albert beamed his love onto Sadie as if she were his own, and at that moment, all of Raymond's apprehension disappeared in thin air.

"Yes, Sadie graduated from high school recently," Raymond answered.

"Brava," Lily said as she clapped her hands together.

"And what is next for you, Sadie?" Albert asked her.

Sadie smiled with pride. "I'll be going to college in Miami in the fall."

"Miami," Albert repeated. "Have your dad show you where he lived."

Raymond caught Albert's attention, and their eyes locked in a way they hadn't since the day they left Egypt. Up until that point, Raymond hadn't mentioned anything about previously living in Miami. There was so much more that Albert knew about him that Raymond hadn't yet realized.

"Well, let me get back to the kitchen for a moment," Lily said as she excused herself from the living room. "I hope you all have a great appetite; dinner will be ready in just a few more minutes."

Albert poured them each a glass of wine. He raised his glass in the air and made a toast to Sadie's upcoming adventures in college. He sat back against the couch with nonchalance as if they had only been apart for a few weeks. Over a small spread of hors d'oeuvres in the living room, more than fifty years of explanations began to surface. He didn't take his time because too much had already been wasted.

He had fallen in love with Lily on the first night he met her at one of Sami's parties. They kept their love secret; not even Raymond knew the extent of their relationship while they were in Cairo. Their love was something he didn't want the outside world to taint, so he treated it with the most precious care he had ever treated anything in his life. Although some people who attended Sami's parties were part of the Egyptian spy rings, not all of them were, and he wanted to protect Lily from that part of his life as much as he could.

But in reality, she was more embedded into espionage than he was.

When the day came that Raymond and Albert were to leave Egypt, Albert wasn't scared of the Egyptian authorities catching him on the ship to Marseille because his worries had nothing against fate. He wasn't worried about leaving their whole family behind because he knew one day they could eventually be reunited, but he did fear one thing. The worry that cracked his heart and spine in two was the idea that he'd have to leave Lily behind.

He boarded the ship to France with a smile on his face and a cigarette in his mouth, not knowing that Lily was already on board, waiting for him. She hid from him the whole trip and heard from other passengers that there was an altercation between the Egyptian authorities and a small group of young Jews, the ones thought to be spies. She stayed out of sight until the ship finally reached the shores of Marseille.

"And that's when I saw her, Raymond," Albert said as if he was just seeing her again for the first time in his life.

"She found you at the dock?" Raymond asked.

"I don't know how she did it, but she managed to be one of the first people who departed from the ship. She waited for me at the dock; it was her plan all along."

Raymond took a sip of his wine and placed it down on the coffee table. He could hardly wrap his mind around it.

"She asked me to come with her," Albert explained in a way that harbored a lifetime's worth of regrets but, also, a lifetime's worth of memories. "And so I did."

In a series of quick decisions, Albert and Lily disappeared from Marseille's port before the majority of the ship disembarked, Raymond included. She left a note for her brother Henry to give to Raymond. On one side was an address in Marseille, and on the other was an address in Paris.

"I wanted you to come with us to Paris," Albert admitted as if apologizing for the way things panned out. "Things didn't go as planned."

"It didn't," Raymond answered. "But we are here now." He always had a way to see the light when things got too dark.

"But we are here now," Albert repeated.

"*Yalla*," Lily said as she appeared in the living room once more. "Dinner is ready."

Raymond snapped out of the past and realized that his wife and daughter had been sitting on the couch, listening to their whole story in silence. He wasn't sure if it were too much for them to take in and was glad that dinner would serve to lighten the mood. As he stood up from the couch, he caught a comforting glance from Albert, the way it used to be from the opposite side of their shared bedroom.

"There is more, *Habibi*," Albert said as he placed his hand on Raymond's shoulder, guiding him towards the dining room. "After dinner, I'll explain the rest." Dinner that evening was coq au vin which was prepared with perfection by Lily. Together with Albert and Raymond's families, they shared a meal that was a lifetime in the making. Wine was poured, and laughter was shared as an old set of cousins reunited with an expanding family neither knew existed. Albert's sons and daughter spoke English well, but when the conversation naturally fell into the comforts of French, Raymond translated for Maria and Sadie.

"Your father was always a gentleman," Albert explained to Sadie as he placed down his utensils on the table. "Never in my whole life did I meet another person who was as much of a gentleman as him."

Sadie smiled from her seat at the compliments to her dad.

"Raymond, I'm not sure if you remember this, but you would always get up from your seat at Sami's parties and give it to me," Lily reminisced.

It wasn't something Raymond particularly remembered, but he smiled in confirmation anyway.

"If anyone tells you that nonsense that chivalry is dead, have them meet your father," Albert said to Sadie.

As dinner wound down and Lily served coffee and French pastries for dessert, Raymond and Albert found their way out of the living room and onto one of the handfuls of balconies that adorned the Parisian house. The Eiffel Tower shimmered in the distance and stood as a reminder to both of them of how far they had gone to find one another again.

They sat down on the balcony's table and breathed in the same air. It reminded Raymond of that night in Haiti, where underneath a sky full of stars, they promised each other they would meet again if they were ever separated. The wistful thoughts of young children finally came to fruition, and it seemed like the twinkling lights of Paris danced around them for their reunion.

"If this isn't fate, *Habibi*, I don't know what it is," Albert said. He took a bite of the Roquefort cheese from the cheese plate before him.

Raymond took a sip of coffee. "If this isn't fate," he repeated in agreement.

Albert stood up and leaned against the balcony railing. The lights of Parisian street lamps bounced off the top of his head.

"I had to stay away," Albert admitted.

"Stay away?"

"Yes, *Habibi*. I had to stay away from you. For you."

Raymond was caught dumbstruck. "What do you mean by that?"

"Because I was responsible for everything."

"Responsible for what?"

"If I had never introduced you to Sami, we would have never left Egypt the way we did. We would have never been split up the way we had."

"That's not something you know for sure," Raymond said.

"Of course I do," Albert said. Even sixty years later, he was still always completely sure of himself.

"And anyway, everyone eventually had to leave Egypt," Raymond replied.

"Not the way we did."

"What happened to you on the ship?" Raymond asked.

Albert took a deep sip of his wine. "One of the crew members saw me jump over the railing from the top deck to the deck just below. He was a Jewish man himself, from Marseille. He took me with him to a storage closet in the crew cabin. He knew the police were searching for us, so he let me stay there until we reached France."

"Wow," Raymond said. It was eerily similar to his own journey to France, on the same ship as Albert, but already lifetimes away.

"Raymond, when I saw Lily standing at the dock, I couldn't leave her," Albert said with his whole heart in his hands. "I hope you understand."

Raymond had never understood before, but at that moment, he did.

"The address on that paper, the one in Marseille, did you go there? Did Henry tell you to go there?" Albert asked.

"He told me, yes. And I did go there. I waited there for hours, I wasn't sure what to look for, but I waited there for any kind of clue."

"And nothing came," Albert admitted, a part of him defeated.

"No, nothing came," Raymond said.

"I was supposed to meet you there, Raymond; I need you to understand that," Albert said carefully. "I was supposed to find you and take you with us to Paris. But Henry needed us to leave sooner, there was someone we needed to meet in Paris, and we ended up leaving almost immediately from the port of Marseille."

"That other address, the one for Paris—" Raymond continued.

"Henry took us to that bookstore," Albert said. "It was our safe haven in Paris for a few days. Lily's mother's family are from Paris. I am not sure if you knew that before; you might have heard stories about her family when we lived in Egypt."

"It sounds familiar."

"Her mother's family is well known in the haute couture jewelry business here in France," Albert explained. "Her grandfather owned that bookstore; collecting literature was a sort of hobby for him aside from dealing with jewels."

Raymond finally understood where all the wealth came from.

"Henry took us to the bookstore and to the apartment they owned above it. That's where he recruited me to join Mossad."

"Mossad," Raymond replied in almost disbelief.

"I became an agent for Mossad, Raymond. For years. And that also meant I had to leave Lily behind."

Raymond tried desperately to wrap his mind around the new information. His cousin had left the ranks of being a spy in Egypt to become a spy for Israel.

"So then from France, you moved to Israel?" Raymond asked.

"Yes," Albert answered. "I stayed in Israel for almost ten years as an agent. No one knew anything. I couldn't let anyone in the family know where I was or who I had become."

"Your father," Raymond began, "he knew."

For the first time in his life, Albert was immediately speechless. "He knew?"

"He never got the concrete evidence he needed, but he knew," Raymond said. "He searched for you. Every single day of his life, he looked for you. And he figured it out, he knew deep down inside, that you had joined Mossad."

Albert stroked his mustache and covered his mouth with his hand as if to hold back a lifetime's worth of regrets.

"What happened after you left Mossad?" Raymond asked.

"I had to come back to Paris. I had to find Lily," Albert answered. "I had to find her and apologize and beg for her back. But can you believe what happened?" Albert broke out into a spurt of laughter, something that Raymond found a complete surprise.

"I thought she would have been married by then, that she would have given up on me. I had been gone for so long, Raymond. There is no way a woman as beautiful as Lily should have waited for me to return. When I came back and asked for her forgiveness, she just smiled and told me that it had been her plan all along."

"What do you mean, her plan?"

"It wasn't Henry who got me recruited into Mossad. It was Lily."

Lily, the secret agent no one knew of.

"And when I returned, she was waiting, and it was like we never missed a beat," Albert said in delight.

It was the same, between Raymond and Albert. It was like they never missed a beat. Raymond finished his cup of coffee and set it down on the table before them.

"I knew you'd come looking for me," Albert said with an air of regret. "That's why I had to disappear for your own good. Our job in Egypt was one thing, but getting involved with Mossad was something else entirely."

Raymond sat in silence.

"Did you ever receive the mail I sent?" Albert asked.

Raymond nodded in agreement. "I did."

"Did you know who it was from?"

"I had my suspicions it was you," Raymond said. "But then it stopped, for a long time. I had to give up hope."

Albert sat down next to Raymond once more. "That's where you went wrong, Raymond. You can never give up hope."

Raymond finally understood that to be true.

"It stopped for a long time, honestly, because I lost track of you. It must have been when you were busy traveling the world. But when it was time, I started sending you clippings again to let you know that things were ok. I knew, eventually, if you wanted to, you'd find me."

Albert went inside and brought back an envelope of magazine clippings, a huge pile of the places he'd been. It told a lifetime's worth of stories: places Albert traveled to during his time with Mossad, vacations he took once he settled down in Paris, and the places he wished he had experienced with Raymond. Albert saved each clipping for Raymond if they were ever to meet again.

"Twenty years of writing," Albert said. He looked at his magazine columns as fondly as if they were his children. "After I settled down in Paris, I took up a position of a travel writer. You already know this, *Habibi*; it's what I've always been destined to do."

"Under the name of Max Labaton," Raymond confirmed.

"Clever, wasn't it?" Albert laughed. "And I've been writing to you ever since."

Raymond finished his coffee and took one more bite of cheese. The strength of the flavors settled in his mouth as clouds covered a portion of the moon.

"Things could have panned out so differently for us," Albert said, as the twinkling lights of the Eiffel Tower danced in the near distance.

"But here we are," Raymond said with hope.

Albert raised his glass and toasted in the air. "Here we are."

"Next time we meet, let it be underneath a sky full of stars," Raymond said as he remembered Albert's wish for them on his porch in Haiti.

Albert smiled upon realizing that Raymond had never forgotten about that night. *"Inshallah."* God willing.

Raymond left Paris two days later, on a flight back to New York with Maria and Sadie. Even though Albert wasn't physically with them on the plane, it was the first time in nearly sixty years that Raymond knew with certainty that wherever he went, Albert was right there with him. Raymond left Paris with a piece of his heart that he thought he'd had lost forever; it was the greatest souvenir he could have brought back from France. He would never have to be without Albert again.

Raymond and Albert fell back into a routine as if they hadn't been apart for the majority of their lives. Every Friday afternoon, just like clockwork, Raymond sat down at his bedroom desk when Albert called. The letters they once wrote to each other as young boys were replaced with weekly bouts of laughter and conversation as old men, something Raymond looked forward to with all of his heart.

And for both of them, life continued.

During those phone calls, Raymond talked about how well Sadie was doing in college in Miami. When Raymond eased into retirement, he and Maria decided to spend winters in Florida, both to get out of the cold New York weather and to be near their daughter. They spent early mornings walking along the beach, and once a week, Raymond sat on their rented apartment's balcony to call Albert, where he told him about the sunshine and the smell of the ocean's breeze.

Albert became a grandfather for the first time when his eldest son had twin girls, and Raymond was the first person he called. They celebrated together over the phone. Despite the Atlantic Ocean standing between them, Raymond could feel his cousin's overwhelming pleasure when he talked about holding his granddaughters for the first time. Maria sewed the twins a pair of matching hats and booties while Raymond relished in his older cousin's pure joy.

Sadie transitioned from a college graduate to a young professional in New York City, where she tried her hand at travel journalism.

"She's inspired by you," Raymond said to Albert on the phone.

Albert laughed, and Raymond could only imagine the excitement in his eyes.

"I'm concerned for her," Raymond admitted.

"Of course, you're concerned for her; you are her father." Albert laughed. When it dissipated, he added, "Is she really inspired by me? That's why she's going into the field?"

"That's what she says," Raymond acknowledged.

"You don't sound all too confident in her choices," Albert said.

"I just hoped she'd choose something more stable."

"Raymond, look at you," Albert said. "I'm sure your mother hoped that you'd choose something more stable for yourself when you were Sadie's age. But you figured it out, and everything ended up being fine."

Raymond sat for a moment and knew Albert was right.

"Let her explore the way you did."

The following week, Raymond took Sadie and Maria out to the ice cream parlor on Emmons Avenue in celebration; Sadie had landed her first position as a journalist and photographer for a travel magazine. The last time they had been there as a family was after Sadie's last piano recital. Raymond's daughter had found her footing in a career she loved. Raymond called Albert a bit early that Friday afternoon to tell him the good news, but by the way Albert laughed and joked, it was as if he already knew.

In between all the phone calls, Raymond read all the articles Albert ever wrote. He read them as if he were reading Albert's journal since the day they left Egypt. Albert stopped sending clippings, but instead, they talked about their favorite destinations on the phone. And only once did Albert send Raymond a small package: an empty toothpaste tube similar to the one Raymond left Egypt with and a rolled-up piece of paper with all the memories that came along with it.

Years went by, and life went on, but Raymond and Albert never missed a weekly phone call. They shared worries when Lily was diagnosed with breast cancer, when the pain in Albert's voice struggled to contain optimism, when Albert knew it was too early to lose the love of his life. They struggled together through cycles of chemotherapy and radiation until she went into remission, and even though Albert never admitted it, their weekly phone calls helped the nights turn to day until the cancer was gone.

Albert was only a phone call away when Rose passed away, and then a handful of years later when Olga passed away. Raymond found solace in his cousin's voice during those darker days, when he was left the sole sibling, all his five sisters gone. Raymond buried each of them as if it were always his plan to protect them until their very last days.

Raymond had Albert right by his side as they shared climbs and reached summits. They maneuvered through the pains of what life had to bring and celebrated lives well lived. In those years of reconnection, it was as if Raymond and Albert had never skipped out on sixty years apart. They grew older together, and they found a familiar comfort within one another that never truly left that porch in Haiti. Every Friday afternoon, the sound of Albert's voice helped Raymond remember that in his life, it was the people he loved and the memories they shared that made his heart beat.

Until he had a hard time remembering Albert at all.

Eighteen

Hong Kong, 2014

Just like it did every Friday afternoon, the phone rang.

Maria put down a wooden spoon on the counter beside the stove and answered the phone that hung on the kitchen wall.

"Hello?" Maria asked as she leaned against the door frame. She already knew whose robust voice would be on the other end.

"*Comment ça va*, Maria?" Albert asked in French, even though Maria didn't speak it. Over the years since they met in Paris, Albert got into the custom of asking her how she was doing in French. He promised her, as a joke, to teach her French since Raymond never did, but it never amounted to anything tangible.

"I'm doing well, Albert," Maria answered in English like she always did. "How are you?"

"Could be doing better if my doctor would let me eat a steak," Albert teased about his declining health. A heart attack had set him back, and he no longer functioned at the speed he used, but that never slowed down his humor.

Albert always made Maria laugh. "You better take care of yourself, Albert. I'm sure Lily doesn't let you eat steak against your doctor's orders."

"That's half of the problem."

Maria laughed again and pulled the phone away from her face. "Raymond, it is Albert."

Raymond got up from the couch and began walking towards the hallway. "I will pick it up in the bedroom."

Raymond turned on the light in his bedroom and sat down at his meticulously organized desk. Albert once lived only in letters and magazine clippings, but all of that was replaced by a weekly phone call with his cousin. Although they were separated by decades apart and now lived across two different continents, Raymond looked forward to his scheduled phone calls with Albert. He couldn't wait to tell him the good news.

"Raymond, *comment ça va?*"

"*Ça va bien, Alhamdullah,*" Raymond answered that he was fine in a combination of Arabic and French. Certain things from his past were as innate as breathing. "We have some big news to share," Raymond said, almost unable to contain the joy from spilling out.

"You have decided to move to Paris, finally?" Albert joked.

Raymond's thin lips curved into a smile, and from it came a genuine laugh.

"Sadie is engaged," Raymond said; the words sat the way pride did on elevated shoulders.

"Is that right? Engaged?" Albert asked with genuine excitement.

"Yes, my girl is going to get married."

"*Mabrouk,*" Albert congratulated him in Arabic.

Sadie showed him the diamond ring on her finger just days earlier. Sadie and Scott announced their promising news when they came over for dinner, and the whole apartment shook with jubilation as the gemstone sparkled underneath the kitchen lights.

"That is wonderful news, Raymond," Albert continued. "How long have Sadie and Scott been dating?"

Raymond paused in thought and tried to answer truthfully, but the correct answer escaped him. "It's been about two years," he said, unsure if that was the right amount of time.

In reality, it had been almost three years of Sadie and Scott dating before he proposed. Their chance encounter in a city of millions turned into a destined love that Raymond knew was pure.

"Beautiful, beautiful," Albert said, and Raymond could almost envision his cousin clapping his hands together in approval.

"We are going to take them on a trip to Tokyo instead of having an engagement party," Raymond said. "They don't want to do everything traditionally."

"Why Tokyo?" Albert asked.

"Because that is where Maria and I met; Sadie wants to see it herself."

Albert laughed, ready to correct Raymond's comment. "I thought you met in Hong Kong."

"Yes, that is where we met. Did I say Hong Kong?" Raymond asked, unable to admit his flaws.

"No, you mentioned Tokyo," Albert said.

"Oh, well, I meant we are going to Hong Kong," Raymond said assuredly.

A stagnant moment of silence sat between them as Raymond hurried to clarify it for himself in his mind. It was something he caught himself doing from time to time but put a pin in it before it had the chance to become something bigger. He covered up how confused he became at times, as he needed everyone to know that he was fine.

Raymond knew how to stand his ground even against the strongest of winds.

"Anyway, how are things with you? How is Lily?" Raymond always changed the subject when things got uncomfortable.

Raymond listened intently as Albert talked about his last doctor's appointment and how Lily forced him to eat more vegetables. They joked and laughed; every time Raymond spent an afternoon on the phone with Albert, it was as if they were still those young boys on the porch of his house in Haiti.

"Send me a clipping from Hong Kong," Albert joked as their weekly phone call came to an end.

"How about I give you a call from there instead?" Raymond suggested.

"Much better, *Habibi*," Albert said.

Time seemed to fast forward after Sadie and Scott got engaged. Raymond tried to hold onto it, but his weathered hands were slowly losing their firm grip on what was then and what was now. His daughter's happiness was the only element in his life that anchored him when other parts of his world seemed to float about. Before he knew it, Maria had packed their bags for their Hong Kong vacation.

It didn't matter what time it was in Hong Kong; it was always humid.

Raymond stepped out of the airport, and as he walked towards the taxi stand, the humidity of Asia swept him up into a nearly suffocating bubble. He adjusted his lungs to the climate as sweat stuck to the back of his shirt. It was just as he remembered it.

Maria walked beside him. She pulled a single suitcase with enough clothes for a week. The last time they had been in Hong Kong, they had enough to keep them there for a lifetime. But that was another part of their lives, a part that only existed in memories. It was a past before Sadie was born and before she was about to get married.

Sadie and Scott walked ahead of them in a bubble of anticipation, their suitcases in tow. The last time Raymond was in Hong Kong was when he met his wife, and now his daughter stood before him with her own fiancé. It was hard for Raymond to see the full circle of his life drawn right before him, but an undeniable pull at his heartstrings reminded him how much the vacation meant to all of them.

The airport was relatively quiet at 6:30 in the morning. With the long flight from New York and the considerable time difference, Raymond wasn't sure if day felt like night or the other way around. He hadn't traveled that far in so long, and it would be the last time he'd ever feel such a drastic shift in time.

The line at the taxi stand consisted mostly of passengers from their nonstop flight from JFK. He recognized a couple that sat in front of them on the plane. A line of eager taxi cabs waited to swoop people away into the heart of the city. They piled into a car with the destination of Kowloon. The last time Raymond had been in Hong Kong, Kowloon hadn't been the popular vacation spot it had become today. When Sadie encouraged him to book a hotel there, he was surprised but intrigued to see how much the city had changed.

The taxi dropped them off at the Marco Polo Harbor Hotel in the heart of Kowloon. Hong Kong looked entirely different, and almost nothing about the area stood the same way it did over thirty years prior. Canton Road was full of designer clothing stores that weren't open yet for the day. Raymond could envision the throngs of people walking up and down the busy thoroughfare, and its energetic promise reminded him why he loved Hong Kong as much as he did.

After learning that their hotel rooms weren't ready to check into yet, they left their bags in the hotel's luggage room and walked the short distance to the harbor. Hong Kong might have transformed into a new entity over the past thirty years, but one thing that remained the same was its beautiful waterfront skyline.

"Do you remember it here?" Maria asked Raymond as they leaned against the railing. A green ferry docked at the Kowloon side of the pier, and a crowd of early morning commuters deboarded.

"I do, but so much has changed, hasn't it?" Raymond asked.

"It really has," Maria answered. "I don't recognize much."

"Where did you used to work?" Sadie interrupted their side conversation as she easily got caught in Hong Kong's trance.

"Oh, I don't remember it now," Raymond said. He scanned the skyline as if one of the buildings would miraculously jump out at him. "I worked in Central. I think it's that general region over there." Raymond pointed to a section of the skyline he believed was Hong Kong's main business district.

"And you never came to this side of the harbor much?" Scott asked. "It seems pretty lively over here."

"It wasn't like this before," Raymond said. "It's changed a lot."

"This area used to be where you go to discount shops," Maria explained. "Now it's full of designer boutiques."

"I guess that's what happens when you're away for more than thirty years," Sadie said. "It's beautiful, though, don't you think?"

Raymond couldn't help but agree with his daughter. Sadie and Scott didn't waste any time taking photos with the harbor and the skyline behind them. Even after a nearly sixteen-hour flight and a considerable amount of jet lag, Maria and Raymond stood in photos with them. When the day came that Raymond had a hard time remembering his trip to Hong Kong with his family, Sadie would always show him the picture of the four of them, Hong Kong standing bright in the background.

Raymond and Maria found an empty bench and sat down while Sadie and Scott searched for a quick breakfast to bring back to them. As they walked down the promenade together, Raymond couldn't help but love and miss his daughter at the same time. In just a few more months, she would be married, and because of Scott being active duty in the United States Marine Corps, they would be moving to San Diego. Raymond wasn't nearly ready to be apart from his daughter, but it was another part of his life that he couldn't prepare for.

Raymond had waited nearly thirty years to bring Sadie to Hong Kong. There was something unparalleled with seeing Sadie walk the streets of Kowloon or climb the steep hills of Central, knowing that the last time Raymond was there, Sadie was just a hope and a dream. Raymond didn't want to hold back on anything that vacation, because if anything, it would become the most important vacation they'd ever take together.

The Marco Polo Hotel was a surprising epitome of luxury at the edge of the harbor. After their rooms were ready, Sadie and Scott spent the rest of the afternoon exploring Kowloon on foot while Raymond and Maria relaxed in the comforts of their luxurious junior suite. It took Raymond and Maria decades to come back to Hong Kong, but now that they were there, Raymond intended on enjoying every moment of it.

The next day, Raymond took his family on a tour of the whole city. They sat on an open-aired double-decker bus as it curved through the streets of Hong Kong; the skyscrapers stood as seemingly never-ending buildings of steel pointed straight at the sky. Raymond sat next to Maria, and they took turns pointing out places they remembered from their time living together in Hong Kong, but more often than not, they pointed towards a brand new city and way of life that didn't exist thirty years prior.

The first place they visited as a family was Victoria Peak. It was still a show stopper and would probably always take people's breaths away. The expansive views from the top of the Hong Kong mountain gave way to hundreds of skyscrapers below, and everything about the scenic overlook made their hearts skip a beat. Sadie and Scott stood in awe of Hong Kong as it sat below them, and it gave nothing but pure happiness for Raymond to watch his daughter marvel at a part of the world that was, in a sense, responsible for bringing her to him.

The Tian Tan Buddha was on the top of Sadie and Scott's list of places to see during their vacation, so Raymond and Maria didn't hesitate to join them. The four of them boarded a cable car high above Lantau Island and, as a family, made their way to the famed Buddha monument. A steep set of stairs seemed to endlessly climb up the mountain until it reached the Buddha statue perched at the top, and although everything in Raymond wanted to climb it with them, his body and age said otherwise.

"You go ahead," Raymond said to Sadie and Scott as they approached the tips of the stairs. "I'll wait for you down here."

"We'll take some nice photos for you," Scott assured him as he held his camera in his hand.

"Maria, you go too, if you want." Raymond encouraged her.

"No, that's ok," Maria said. She could easily climb the stairs to the top, but she preferred to stay by her husband's side so he wouldn't feel alone. "Let's go find somewhere to sit."

A small shopping village sat at the base of the Tian Tan Buddha's stairs. Maria browsed a handful of souvenir shops while Raymond sat on a bench in its garden area. His chest tightened from a sense of overexertion that he'd never willingly admit to, and the air in his nose made his lungs sting. He took a few deep breaths to calm down. It wasn't the first time it happened, and it wouldn't be the last. Raymond was slowly getting used to his new reality but silently fought with his whole existence for the strength he once had. Maria came back with a small bag of souvenirs and sat down next to Raymond on the bench, both of them silent, but in those shared moments, they knew how time was changing things.

Raymond was still sad that he hadn't been able to join Sadie and Scott at the top of the Tian Tan Buddha and that he had limited Maria from enjoying it too. He suggested that they have lunch at the Jumbo Kingdom, a huge floating restaurant in the middle of Aberdeen. They took a boat to the restaurant and snapped a family photo together in front of it before having one of the most delicious meals they had on that whole trip.

After looking through dozens of sightseeing suggestions online, Sadie suggested they see the Chi Lin Nunnery. Raymond and Maria had never heard of Kowloon's outdoor garden despite living in Hong Kong for a few years. Hong Kong had secrets kept in hidden corners, and even the most seasoned local couldn't know them all.

Raymond walked the perimeter of the garden as the Hong Kong sun warmed the back of his neck. It was a beautiful garden, something that came as such a surprise amid the city's constant buzz. He walked alone, his steps slower than they had been the last time he had been to Hong Kong, but each step was purposeful and determined. It was remarkable how quiet the garden was once he was inside, it was as if he could hear the quiet reverberations of Hong Kong's pulse within its lungs.

A row of high-rise condominiums stood as the Chi Lin Nunnery's backdrop, a clear juxtaposition from the ancient Tang Dynasty-style temples within the garden. Meticulous trees were shaped and groomed to perfection, and every path around the garden was spotless. Raymond found a single bench in a shaded area and breathed in a rare fresh breath of air in the congested city. He wondered where his family was and hoped they appreciated nature's beauty as much as he did.

He checked the time on his gold watch; it was just past one o'clock, and he could have sworn that they were supposed to meet by then. He scanned the scattered faces of people who walked by him, but none looked like his family. He fiddled with the handkerchief in his pocket as he continued to look for them. He wasn't worried; they probably took a few extra photos before meeting back up with him. He didn't blame them for being a few minutes late.

But in reality, they had been searching for him for the past half an hour. While Raymond thought they were supposed to meet at one o'clock., their actual agreed-upon plan was to meet at twelve-thirty, at the entrance gates. Sadie was frantic as she approached Raymond on the bench; her cheeks were rosy and flushed from the heat and constant movement.

"Dad, where have you been? Are you ok?" Sadie asked as she sat down beside him on the bench. Her shoulders fell as if an invisible weight disappeared.

"Hi honey," Raymond said, as he kissed her on the forehead like he used to do when she was younger.

"Have you been sitting here this whole time?" Sadie asked.

"No, I just sat down a few minutes ago waiting for you all," Raymond answered. "I was walking around the garden."

"We've been looking for you everywhere," Sadie said. "We got worried when you didn't show up to the gates at twelve-thirty."

Raymond's current train of thought was replaced by confusion. What she said sounded familiar, but it wasn't their original plan.

"The gates?" Raymond asked.

"Yeah, in the front," Sadie said as she pointed to the entrance. "That's where you were supposed to meet us."

Raymond stretched out his wrist and glanced at his watch one more time. He wasn't sure why Sadie was saying that. "Where is your mom?"

"She's waiting with Scott at the gate, just in case you went there. I've been walking around looking for you."

Raymond smiled at his daughter and knew she would always be there to look for him. "I must have gotten the time mixed up." He got up from the bench and stood in the direction of the entrance. "Come on. I don't want to keep them waiting."

And just like that, the conversation ended. Within a couple of minutes, it was like the conversation had never happened.

Raymond had a way of erasing what he didn't want to be true. He'd never know the rising panic that filled Maria and Sadie's throat when they couldn't find him. He would never truly understand that things were slipping from his mind and that his once firm grasp on his surroundings was slowly melting into something else altogether.

In reality, things were starting to change and would continue to change for the next few years. He'd forget. He'd repeat. He was still the same person, but his exterior shell was beginning to crack.

Sadie and Scott decided to wander Hong Kong's streets while Raymond and Maria retired back to their hotel room for the afternoon. The rising heat and strong humidity left both of them tired, and even more importantly, it was Friday afternoon. Raymond checked his watch and knew it was time to call Albert for their weekly call.

"*Comment ça va*, Raymond?" Albert asked from Paris.

"*Ça va bien, Alhamdullah*," Raymond answered as usual. He would always make everyone believe he was doing fine, even when he wasn't.

"How is Hong Kong?" Albert asked.

"Hong Kong is wonderful," Raymond said. "But it is a different city than what I remembered."

"That's bound to happen after being away for thirty years."

"I can't imagine what it must be like in Cairo after us being gone for so long."

"Cairo is a different world entirely," Albert said. "And honestly, I don't want to know."

There was a brief moment of silence between the two of them.

"Anyway, tell me more," Albert said with anticipation. He always wanted to hear more about destinations, especially ones that he never went to himself. "Where did you go today?"

"Where did we go today?" Raymond asked, buying himself some time. He flipped through a Rolodex of memories in his mind, but each card came up blank.

Albert waited quietly.

"Today?" Raymond asked.

Maria caught a glance of Raymond faltering on the phone. "We went to the temple garden," she said.

"Oh yes, that's right," Raymond said, as the memory came rushing back towards him with the force of a tsunami. "We went to a temple garden in the middle of Hong Kong; it was really beautiful."

Raymond and Albert continued their weekly talk as Raymond sat at the desk in his hotel room, looking out at Kowloon Bay and Hong Kong's skyline. Memories of the distant past mingled with memories of the past few days, and it became a bit of a struggle to distinguish between them. Raymond would never admit that to himself, even when it was clearly visible to everyone else.

It would never stop him from going forward.

They took a day trip to Macau where Raymond and Scott played a few hands of blackjack together in casinos that almost mimicked those of Las Vegas in grandiosity and decor. They walked the Portuguese streets and felt like they were in Europe more than in the middle of Asia. The colorful buildings and mosaic designs on the sidewalks gave the city its own flair that he had never seen anywhere else in China.

More than any other place, bringing Sadie to Repulse Bay was the highlight for Raymond. The affluent area just outside of downtown Hong Kong stood almost exactly how he remembered it. The crescent moon beach was still lined with expensive condominiums, and the one where he and Maria used to live still stood. Sadie seemed to stand there in awe as she understood the weight of how far they had traveled to come right back where it all started.

215

That evening was their last in Hong Kong. Sadie and Scott were going to meet up with a friend who moved to Hong Kong from New York years prior and opened up a Malaysian restaurant.

"Where is Kris' restaurant?" Raymond asked. He sat on a loveseat in his hotel room's adjoining living room as night fell in behind him.

"It's in Central," Scott answered. He adjusted his tie clip onto his shirt. It had been a long time since Raymond wore a tie himself.

"We will take a cab there," Sadie said. "And then probably meet him once his shift is done."

"You two have fun and tell Kris we say hi," Maria said.

"Sadie, come here," Raymond said.

Sadie fastened a necklace on and walked towards him. Raymond shifted in his seat and pulled out his wallet. He opened it and took out a few bills.

"Dessert is on me tonight," Raymond said. He gave the money to his daughter; it was enough to cover their whole dinner.

Sadie looked down at the money in her hand and then back up at Raymond. "Thanks, Dad." She leaned down and kissed him on his cheek.

The Malaysian restaurant was in the same area of Hong Kong where Raymond used to take Maria out for expensive dinners and drinks. It was where he fell in love with her. Thirty years later, his heart swelled with happiness to see Sadie do the same.

"Maria, what time is it?" Raymond asked as he squinted towards the digital clock on the nightstand. "I don't have my glasses with me."

"It's only seven o'clock," Maria said.

"Do you want to go for a walk?" Raymond asked.

"Let's go," Maria said with a smile on her face, and it was as if time rewound thirty years.

Raymond and Maria walked out of the Kowloon hotel and, within minutes, were at the edge of the Tsim Sha Tsui Promenade. Raymond's strides were shorter than they once were the last time they'd walked the streets of Hong Kong. Maria slowed down for him, and they fell into a unified pace as the rest of Hong Kong seemed to zip by them. Even though Raymond didn't have the same physical stamina he once did decades prior, he cherished every moment and made himself believe that he was still as strong as he once was. Even when his chest hurt from walking too fast or too far. Even when it took longer to get to where they were going, he was still happy he got there.

Hong Kong by day was fast-paced and energetic, but Hong Kong by night was something else entirely. Where Kowloon Bay ended, the steel and skyscrapers began. Where the moon and stars twinkled in the sky above, the lights and lasers of the buildings continued. Hong Kong was different from the time they fell in love there, but as Raymond walked alongside Maria, their pace slowed but steady; he knew their love hadn't changed one bit.

The lights danced across the Hong Kong skyline like confetti in a nighttime sky. Raymond was caught by its beauty almost as much as he was caught by Maria's. Thirty years later and she still had saved reserves of energy and excitement. It was something that always made Raymond laugh. Her natural sense of humor balanced his seriousness in the same way the laser lights of Hong Kong lit up the dark night. It was the first time they ever watched the light show together, but he could have sworn he'd seen it before.

It was their last night together in Hong Kong, and as they slowly walked back to their hotel and went to bed, the city that welcomed them and gave them life knew they had to leave. By the time the next morning rose and all of their bags were packed, Raymond and his family left Kowloon behind for the airport.

"Will the Blanco and Murphy party please see an agent at gate fifty-two," the voice on the loudspeaker boomed over the mingling conversations in the waiting area.

"Did they just call our names?" Sadie asked Raymond.

"Did they?" Raymond asked. "I wasn't paying attention to it."

"It sounded like it," Scott assured her.

"Will the Blanco and Murphy party please see an agent at gate fifty-two," the announcement repeated.

They were requested at the front gate, and none of them knew why.

"We'll go," Sadie offered herself and Scott up to the task.

Sadie and Scott left their carry-on bags on their seats and walked through crowds of people towards the gate. Raymond's curiosity piqued as he watched from afar. It didn't look like they were in an argument with the agents, so Raymond assumed that there weren't any hiccups with their flight back to New York. Sadie seemed to do the majority of the talking, and after a few moments of back and forth, along with an airline agent typing away at a computer, the agent handed Sadie a short stack of papers. Sadie turned around and immediately began talking to Scott; both had smiles on their faces as they looked down at the boarding papers.

"What happened?" Raymond asked as Sadie and Scott returned to their seats.

They had returned with undeniable energy.

Sadie handed a boarding pass to Raymond and then one to Maria. They both looked down at it in unison, unsure of what they were reading.

"The airline upgraded us to business class," Sadie said with pure excitement.

Raymond looked up from the newly printed boarding pass. "Business class?"

"Why?" Maria asked. She was always a bit apprehensive.

"The agent said they just had extra seats available in business class and chose people at random to fill them."

Raymond looked down at his newly-printed plane ticket with a bit of disbelief but, instead, laughed at their luck.

"And we don't have to pay extra for this?" Maria asked.

"No, it's a free upgrade," Sadie said.

The four of them sat with anticipation and excitement as they waited to board the plane. The sixteen-hour non-stop flight from Hong Kong to New York transformed from one that none of them were particularly looking forward to into a surprising bonus at the end of their family vacation.

A line of flight attendants greeted them by name as if they knew each other in another life. Raymond and his family walked into business class, and it brought back snippets of times when he flew first class on international business trips. He held onto those days gone by when his home away from home was up in the sky. It had been years since then, but its familiarity was like seeing an old friend who had never truly left.

They were shown to their seats, which were more like personal pods. The area was backlit with soft purple lights, and a welcome bag of gifts and toiletries waited on each seat. Sadie and

Scott had never flown in business or first class before, and they both spoke in hurried excitement as they settled into their areas.

"Mr. Blanco, can I offer you something to drink?" a young flight attendant asked as Raymond fastened his seat belt.

"Yes, please," Raymond said. "Can I have a cup of coffee?"

"Of course. Any cream or sugar?"

"Just black coffee will be fine, thank you."

The flight attendant nodded in a silent agreement and disappeared to prepare Raymond's cup of coffee. It was just like he remembered, where service was meticulous, and no attention to detail was spared. Even though he hadn't arranged it himself, he was quietly overjoyed that he could share the experience with his family.

The plane took off as Raymond adjusted the pillow behind his head. The peaks of the mountains and the tips of Hong Kong skyscrapers disappeared under a thin sheet of clouds. Raymond gently turned the pages of his menu and took a sip of his coffee. He stretched his legs in front of him and decided on the filet mignon for dinner. A flight attendant with the most courteous smile brought him a hot towel on a silver platter, and Raymond steamed his hands clean with it. It was as if the universe wanted to spoil him one more time because it knew it would be his last international flight for the rest of his life.

Nineteen

Raymond found his spot on the couch like he did every day after breakfast. Cinnamon apple oatmeal was his preferred choice. Maria prepared it for him every morning, and it had become a routine. There were no more mornings of room service in international hotel rooms and no more expensive steakhouse dinners in the city with colleagues. Breakfast, lunch, and dinner were all served at the round wooden kitchen table in their Brooklyn apartment, complete with a fifth-floor view of a fire escape and a neighboring outdoor parking lot.

Breakfast took longer than it used to. Old age brought about a string of new ways of living, and swallowing had become a bit more difficult. Raymond took it in stride, the only way he ever lived his life. The shake in his hands never seemed to keep the spoon steady, but at the end of the day, that was the least of his worries. His once-refined palette dwindled to only foods he could physically consume without choking. The flavors of Egypt were a taste of another lifetime.

The morning sun had already shifted high in the December sky by the time Raymond finished breakfast. Like clockwork, he pushed himself away from the kitchen table, clutched onto his cane, and walked his way to the living room. The living room was painted white, the kind of white that could bleach a life away. It was lined with framed artwork and photos of his family. Maria made sure that the living room was always bright and welcoming. After all, it was where Raymond spent the majority of his time.

Raymond walked towards the couch and sat down at its far right corner. It was the spot that was always designated for him, long before he had become homebound. Each fiber and thread of the cushion conformed to the shape of his body, even as he seemed to slowly shrink in size. He sat down on the couch and leaned his head back against a pillow. He'd been enough places, and now it was time to rest.

The man who had made it a point to get out of the house every single day hadn't felt the world's fresh air on his bare arms in months. The last time he went to the supermarket, he bought a jar of peanut butter, not knowing that he'd never step into a grocery store again. The final time he visited the post office, he purchased a book of stamps with the American flag on it, not knowing it was the last time he'd ever fold the wax paper envelope into his pocket. The final time he sat in the park, he watched the leaves flutter off the branches and fall onto newly mowed grass, not knowing that he'd never have another afternoon on that bench again. But none of those memories stuck, and to him, he had just left the house yesterday.

What was left for him to see came from his living room's view. Five floors up in his Brooklyn building, the fallen leaves of winter left empty branches and a dusting of snow.

He rested his cane against the armrest, and its crimson color stood in sharp contrast to the beige couch. Thin lines of sunshine peeked through the semi-closed blinds and mimicked the wrinkles on his forehead. It had been a while since the sun-kissed his skin, and the breeze danced through his hair. He thought it had been just a handful of days, but everyone else knew it had been months.

Maria walked into the living room and pulled up the blinds. Their Brooklyn street sat down below. Double parked cars dotted the street, and even though it was still early in the morning, there was a restlessness in the air.

"It's too bright," Raymond said as she slowly closed his eyes.

"It's good for you," Maria insisted and made no motion to close the blinds. "You need some sunshine."

Raymond didn't agree or disagree but let his heavy eyelids shield him from the outside world.

"What time is it?" Raymond asked. It was the third time he asked in the past twenty minutes.

"It's almost ten," Maria answered.

"What time will Sadie be here?" Raymond asked.

"She will be here at noon," Maria said as she took a seat on the opposite end of the couch. "And you'll meet Gabriel."

"Gabriel," Raymond repeated.

"He's really something else," Maria said. "I can't believe we have him now." Maria leaned back on the couch and smiled, even if Raymond didn't notice it.

"Why Gabriel?" Raymond asked.

"What do you mean?" Maria asked.

"Why did they name him Gabriel? Does it mean something? Is it a name in the family?" Raymond opened his eyes to both hear and see Maria's answer.

Maria shook her head. "They liked the name; it's not something from the family." Maria wasn't sure what family Raymond was speaking of, but it wasn't his own.

"Gilbert," Raymond said as he closed his eyes again. It wasn't the first time he'd repeated the wrong name, and it wouldn't be the last.

"It's not Gilbert," Maria corrected him like she often had to do at that point. "His name is Gabriel."

Raymond didn't answer and continued to sit with his eyes closed on the couch. Bits of his mind were everywhere but also nowhere to be found.

"Can you iron my suit?" Raymond asked. "The dark gray suit."

Maria couldn't help but smile. It was a smile mixed with hope and relief; she still allowed herself to believe that even a small part of him was still there.

"Of course," Maria said. She got up from the couch and walked to their shared closet. Ironing his finest suit was the least she could do for him.

The last time Raymond wore a proper suit was for Sadie's wedding, nearly four years prior. He was once a man who wore a suit almost every day and owned some of the finest money could buy. At the height of his career in Hong Kong and New York, Raymond often had suits custom-made and tailored to his liking. He wore suits to elegant dinners around the world and on the dusty streets of Old Cairo. He tucked a handkerchief in his pocket, just like his father did, and all the gentlemen that came before him.

Even though Raymond asked to wear his gray suit, it took some persuasion on Maria's part to get him dressed. It was often like that, at that point, where days and nights blended into each other so effortlessly that changing out of pajamas and into slacks was much more complicated than it should have been. Maria had to remind Raymond a handful of times that Sadie was coming over, and it was only at the sound of her name that Raymond found a few ounces of extra strength to put on the suit he asked for.

Maria wanted to help Raymond comb his hair, but he insisted on doing it himself. He found a half-used bottle of styling cream and squeezed a quarter-sized amount into his nearly translucent palm. He still had an almost-full head of hair, but each strand was as white as a full moon. Raymond's hand shook with old age as he combed his hair back neatly. He stroked the stubble on his cheeks and chin. He never used to go a day without a clean shave, but now his short mustache and beard would only get bigger in time.

Sadie arrived at noon, just as she promised. She was always punctual, and there was a time in his life when Raymond liked to attribute that trait as something she had learned from him. Maria opened the door just as Sadie came out of the elevator, pushing a stroller before her.

"Hi sweetie," Maria said as she kissed her daughter on the cheek. Even as they embraced, Maria only had eyes for her new grandson. "There he is," Maria said with a widening smile on her face.

"He just woke up," Sadie said as they walked into the foyer of their apartment.

"Perfect timing," Maria said. She was eager to unbuckle Gabriel from the infant car seat and hold him in her arms, the way she did just four days before, on the day he was born.

Sadie took off her jacket and picked up Gabriel from his seat. "Welcome home," she said as she nuzzled his small face with kisses.

"Come into the living room," Maria said.

Sadie held her newborn son in her arms as they walked towards Raymond, who sat patiently on his spot on the couch, waiting for his whole family to come in.

"Hi, Dad," Sadie said. She could hardly contain herself when she saw him dressed up for the occasion of meeting his only grandchild for the first time.

All the aches and pains, all the worries and missteps, and all the lost memories seemed to disappear in the single moment Raymond met his grandson. His only daughter, the shining force in his life, had a child of her own. On most days, Raymond had difficulty comprehending even the simplest of tasks, but there sat an undeniable understanding between them; he was already madly in love with Gabriel.

"Meet Gabriel," Sadie said. She sat down next to Raymond on the couch and positioned Gabriel towards him.

Raymond stretched out his hand, and Gabriel's miniature fingers instantly grabbed Raymond's pointer finger. Gabriel's whole hand grasped at his grandfather's finger as if it was his lifeline to the past, as if everything in his existence depended on that of his grandfather's.

"Gabriel," Raymond repeated his name correctly. "Look at all of his hair," Raymond said in amazement.

Gabriel was born with a full head of hair the identical shade of midnight as Sadie's.

"*Mabrouk*," Raymond said. "*Mabrouk*, Sadie." Raymond congratulated his daughter on the birth of her son in Arabic.

"Do you want to hold him?" Sadie asked.

Raymond nodded in agreement, and even though he couldn't articulate the correct words fast enough, the excitement in his aging eyes said yes.

Sadie placed Gabriel into Raymond's arms. No longer was that spot on the couch only reserved for Raymond. Love was easy, and it melted into Raymond's arms as he held Gabriel for the first time. Since he had Sadie at an older age, he never thought it would be possible to hold a grandchild in his arms. Even though most of his memories in life had faded away, he'd always remember what it felt like to hold a piece of his soul right there, before him.

There he was, sitting in a full suit on his living room couch, holding his only grandchild. Raymond didn't have the energy to go to the hospital on the day Gabriel was born but waited patiently for the news of his birth. It took a few days for Sadie to bring Gabriel to his house, but when she did, it was as if all that ailed him drifted away.

For three years after their marriage, Sadie and Scott lived in San Diego while Scott was stationed at Marine Corps Air Station Miramar. Their move came with a mixed bag of feelings. Raymond was proud of his daughter in her new marriage but missed the young girl who always sat by his side. He lived to see her grow into adulthood and adventure off to the other side of the country but missed the times when she'd come home and tell him about her day. It was in those three years where Raymond's mind started to wander, where everyday tasks he once did without thinking took him double the time and effort. During that time, age finally started to catch up to him, and his body couldn't keep up the way it once could.

Sadie and Scott moved back to New York right when it mattered the most. After three years in California, Scott was stationed in Long Island, where Sadie was just a stone's throw away. Raymond often got confused on whether Sadie still lived on the west coast or if she had come back to the east. He asked for her constantly, and his mind sometimes did acrobatic movements as he tried to grasp onto anything real.

Raymond's weekly phone calls with Albert became both a lifeline and a nuisance. On some weeks, Raymond looked forward to his calls with Albert, and in a way, the nostalgia of his voice brought him back to simpler times. During those calls, glimpses of Raymond flickered underneath his deskside lamp, just as he was.

But other times, Raymond had very little to say to Albert, if anything at all. Confusion and tiredness often blanketed him like the weight of a blizzard's fresh covering of snow. On those nights, Raymond didn't want to talk on the phone and declined the calls, leaving Maria to apologize for him and spend a few moments catching up with Albert on her own.

But when Sadie moved back to New York, Raymond tried to hold onto some sort of stability for as long as he could. He never disregarded her the way he sometimes did with Albert. He pushed himself to be her protector, even at an age when it was hard to stand up on his own. Raymond's determination never ceased, not even at the end.

After Sadie and Gabriel left for the day, Albert called. It was the first time in a while where Raymond was genuinely excited to talk to him on the phone. It would be the last time it would ever happen.

"Raymond," Albert said. "*Comment ça va?*"

"*Ça va bien, Alhamdullah.*" Raymond had the same answer. He always said he was fine, thank God, even when he wasn't. But on that day, he had just a little more enthusiasm than usual, and Albert picked up on it immediately.

"You sound stronger," Albert said. His voice wrapped around the phone line and stretched between Paris to Brooklyn as if he were just in the other room.

"Sadie came over today," Raymond explained.

"Oh, that's why you sound cheerful," Albert said.

"She had her baby a few days ago," Raymond said. "A boy." Raymond's mouth opened up into a wide grin that was felt from one side of the Atlantic Ocean to the other.

"*Mabrouk*, Raymond, *Mabrouk*." Albert congratulated him in Arabic. "What is his name?"

Raymond sat at his desk for a short moment; the single lamp at the left corner illuminated the veins in his hands. "His name is Gabriel."

"Gabriel," Albert repeated with a French accent. "*Mabrouk*," he said again.

"Can you believe it? In this old age of mine, I finally made it to grandfather."

Albert chuckled his heavy laugh, and Raymond smiled, thinking of his grandson.

In one of Raymond's last conversations as truly himself, he beamed at the reality that he finally had a grandchild. It was never something on his radar. It was never something that Raymond thought would come true during his lifetime. But when the stars and skies aligned at the end of 2018, Raymond felt an emergence of love in places his heart never knew existed.

But soon after meeting his grandson for the first time, his shell started to crack.

The shield that protected Raymond from Alzheimer's disease had been slowly eroding for years. It was delicate and had an expiration date. It was nearly weightless but held the weight of the world in its hands. It waited for the right time to finally give out, to surrender to the strength of time and fate.

Alzheimer's disease took over with the brunt of gale force winds, but at the speed of sand slowly falling through an hourglass. No amount of love from Maria and no amount of hugs from Sadie could stop what fate had planned. There was no amount of resiliency or determination that could bring the disease to its knees.

And so, beautiful parts of Raymond disappeared behind the clouds of dementia.

A combination of his natural independence and stubbornness made it hard for him to let Maria become his caretaker, but there was no other way. Where he once was the sole provider for his family, Maria had become the single lifeline that kept him afloat.

"Maria," Raymond said, still half asleep.

Maria was asleep to his left, in an identical twin-size bed separated by a single nightstand. It had been years since they slept in the same bed together.

"Maria," Raymond repeated. A renewed sense of urgency sat in the depths of his voice; it had become his new way of talking.

Maria stirred underneath her blankets at the sound of his calls.

"Maria, Maria," Raymond urged.

"What?" Maria asked as his voice startled her awake. It was nearly two in the morning. The room around them remained dark, but Raymond's heightened need snapped her into place.

Raymond sat up in bed. The pinstripes of his matching pajama set stood as a patterned reminder of his fragility.

"What's wrong?" Maria asked. She put on her slippers, already used to what usually came next.

"It's tight," Raymond said as he put his thinning hand up to his chest.

"It's ok, just relax," Maria reminded him. It was already the second time that night that she had to do so and probably wouldn't be the last.

"My chest, it's tight," Raymond repeated as if he needed to hear it again for himself.

"Just relax," Maria said again. It was the only thing that would comfort him at night when he became increasingly restless and unable to sleep.

"What am I going to do?" Raymond asked.

"There's nothing wrong," Maria assured him like she did every time he complained of his chest hurting. She wasn't sure if it was a phantom complaint or if he did feel a tightening sensation over his lungs, but it was something he'd been doing for more than a year, several times a night, and nothing ever changed.

"It hurts; it's tight," Raymond said. He closed his eyes as if it would help make it disappear.

"Do you want me to call for help?"

"Call an ambulance?" Raymond asked as his eyes widened.

"Yes, do you want me to call an ambulance if it hurts?"

"No."

And it was as if that was the end of the episode. The threat of calling an ambulance always settled him back into place.

"Try to lay down," Maria suggested.

Raymond sat with his eyes closed, unable to move or speak.

"Come on, just lay down," Maria tried to coerce him.

"One more minute," Raymond said as he clutched his chest again. "Just give me a few more minutes."

And so it went, almost every single night. The moment eventually passed, like it always did, and Maria helped Raymond lay back down underneath his comforting blankets. He fell back asleep almost instantly as if it had all been a dream. He'd never know how much sleep Maria was robbed of. Almost every night, she lay awake, unable to fall back asleep as seamlessly as he did.

There were times when aggression got the best of him, when the utter confusion of his new reality frustrated him more than anyone would ever know. A man who once never raised his voice about anything became a person who yelled for everything. Each day and each night, Maria carried on caring for him, and Sadie visited him with laughter and smiles because they both knew that the gentleman they loved was still inside.

Where the days seemed long, time seemed short. Gabriel sprouted before Raymond's eyes like a little beanstalk. Sadie made sure to come over at least once a week, always with Gabriel, and if Scott were available, he would come by too. There was nothing brighter underneath the sun-filled sky than a day he shared with his grandson.

It was in his Brooklyn apartment where Gabriel learned how to crawl for the first time. Gabriel's eyes lit up as he tried to reach for the remote control on the floor, and Raymond sat on his corner of the couch as he watched Gabriel's miniature arms and legs propel him forward. Sadie and Maria gasped and cheered Gabriel on with encouragement, but Raymond found a silent stillness in his happiness, somewhere deep within.

Gabriel mastered the art of walking in his Brooklyn apartment as well. It happened four months after he started to crawl, but it seemed like four days to Raymond. He held a strange sense of time and wasn't ever sure how fast or slow things were moving but measured the days by the length of Gabriel's growing hair and how it always reminded him of a midnight sky. He wasn't sure when Gabriel progressed from walking to running until his one-year-old excitement carried throughout the whole apartment. Raymond wasn't sure when Gabriel figured out how to climb onto furniture until Gabriel found his favorite spot on the couch, right beside him.

But there were days when Raymond couldn't take it. When the shrieks and cries of a toddler became too much for his aging ears and mind to handle. When the shouts and discipline became overwhelming, all Raymond wanted to do was tune out the world that left him with more confusion than clarity. On those days, Gabriel orbited around him, much like a growing moon that always filled the earth with light, but Raymond had to shut him out. His mind had too much information to absorb, too many sights and sounds to process, and not enough capacity to do so. He closed his eyes as his grandson fervently explored the world around him with the same passion and curiosity Raymond once had for most of his life.

Raymond continued to shrink into a quieter person; he became more of a spectator than an active participant. He had moments of animations, where he engaged with Gabriel the way a grandfather and a grandson should, the way it was meant to be. In those moments, Maria and Sadie were allowed a glimpse back at the man they loved, the one who didn't have an aggressive bone in his body, the gentleman who opened doors for others and cherished moments with family more than anything else he ever accumulated in his life. Those moments became rare, but it didn't make it any less magical.

Sadie set up a video chat with Albert and his family in Paris so that they could all have a small celebration for Gabriel's first birthday. Even though he was older than Raymond, Albert's mind and manners were as sharp as they were decades prior. Raymond and Albert smiled at each other through the computer screen as everyone sang happy birthday to Gabriel, a mixture of New York and Parisian accents in the conversation.

Raymond had a hard time following some of the conversation with so many people around, yet in that shared smile with his cousin, he felt at peace knowing that Albert finally got to see Gabriel. Even if they weren't together in New York or Paris, even if a computer screen and the stretch of the Atlantic Ocean sat between them, Raymond had his whole family around him. At the end of the day, that was all that mattered.

Raymond fell asleep like a baby that night, his mind clear, his heart full.

Two weeks later, the phone rang, and not even the abrupt shrill tone made Raymond flinch. He sat on the couch with his eyes closed and only peeled them open because he had the sense that Maria moved. It took him a moment to register where he was, and by the darkness of the living room window, he knew night had fallen.

Maria walked to the kitchen wall and answered the phone after a few quick rings. Aside from Sadie, not many people called them anymore, and Raymond became alert enough to know that Maria wasn't talking to their daughter. Her conversation was short and stoic; her voice was low and almost muted.

After a few moments, Maria hung up the phone on the wall delicately, as if not to disturb whoever was on the other end of the line. The pattering of her slippers against the wood floor broke the silence between them as she walked back to the living room with a heart heavier than it was just a couple of minutes before.

"Who was that?" Raymond asked with his eyes closed.

Raymond felt the weight of Maria's petite body as she sat down on her side of the couch. There was a short hesitation before she answered. He would never know how hard it was for Maria to find the right words to say. "That was Lily, in Paris."

"Lily," Raymond repeated as if the syllables of her name were something he should have known.

"Albert's wife," Maria had to remind him.

"Oh yes," Raymond said, more as a reassurance to himself than anyone else. "What was she calling for?" He opened his eyes and looked for answers from his wife.

"Raymond, Albert passed away this morning," Maria said as if saying the words out loud finally made them real to herself as well. She didn't cry often, but when she did, her eyes turned red almost instantly.

Raymond's usually soft eyes turned to stone. They retreated into his face and searched for a deeper meaning, for something to hold on to.

"Who?" he asked.

"Albert," Maria repeated. "Your cousin Albert, in Paris."

"Albert," Raymond said once more, with more finality.

"Yes," Maria said. "He had pneumonia. He passed away in his sleep."

Raymond pulled out the handkerchief from his shirt pocket, and his opaque fingers fidgeted with its corners. His right hand trembled with a combination of old age and nerves. The hands that once held his family together with solidarity, the same hands that carved their way, inch by inch, into a world that wasn't supposed to be meant for him, shook without control.

"Albert," he repeated. He repeated himself in an attempt at memorization, but ultimately he still forgot he ever did. "Albert passed away."

Raymond's voice was vulnerable while his mind made endless acrobatic moves around his daily life. He so desperately tried to find a soft place to land in a reality that had none. He dabbed the handkerchief against the corners of his eyes until the cloth soaked up the few tears he had reserved for that moment in time.

"Help me up," Raymond said.

Maria stood up from the couch and walked towards her husband's side. She held on tightly to his thinning arm and anchored him until he was steady enough to stand. Like she had done so for months, she began walking alongside him, wherever he needed to go.

"It's ok," Raymond said as he tried to release himself from her assistance. Even when all the memories were gone, his innate determination would never disappear.

Maria was reluctant but let go of his arm. He clutched at his cane and took a moment to find his center of gravity before his footsteps started for their bedroom. He walked to their espresso-colored dresser and opened the top right drawer. It was where he kept his wallet, an organized console of loose change, his wedding ring, a single comb, and the one item he walked there for.

The toothpaste tube Albert had mailed him.

Raymond slowly made his way back towards the couch with one hand on his cane and the other wrapped around the toothpaste tube. It took half a day's energy to get him around his three-bedroom apartment. His breaths were deep, and his steps were shallow, but his grip on the toothpaste tube was tight.

It had been a while since Raymond walked anywhere without assistance. His back curved like a thinning crescent moon and his line of vision faced the floor, more than straight in front of him. In a moment of relief for both Raymond and Maria, he sat down on the couch without any hiccups along the way. He hooked the cane on the armrest of the couch, and as if nothing else mattered, he leaned his head back on a pillow to rest.

It was only a matter of time until confusion set in like it always did. It often hid there in plain sight. Any type of conversation could trigger it, and any news of change could heighten it to its peak. Raymond's eyes deepened every time it happened as if another entity shined through his once understanding eyes. He searched for something to hold on to, anything that could provide him comfort, something that was real.

And on that day, the only thing he held onto was the toothpaste tube.

The sudden clarity of Albert's death washed over him like a year's worth of rain. Not even half a lifetime apart from each other could stop the pain from hurting. Raymond would no longer hear his cousin's thunderous voice over the phone, he'd never feel the weight of his laughter behind his ears, and he'd never know another day with Albert by his side.

The edges of the toothpaste cap made indents on his thin skin, like tally marks that counted the decades he spent apart from his cousin. Raymond's hand shook as he held it, and with what little strength he had left, he grasped it tightly in his hand. It held a lifetime's worth of moments, and it always held the promise that maybe tomorrow, things would be better.

Raymond twisted the toothpaste cap open. He tipped the tube into the palm of his hand until a thinly rolled piece of paper poked out of it. He tucked the toothpaste tube in the pocket of his shirt and closed his eyes for a moment. When he was ready, with delicately trembling fingers, he grasped at the paper and opened it. He unrolled the paper and flattened it out on his lap.

Staring back at him was a photo of a sky full of stars. It was hard for him to be sure of much, but he knew that one day they'd meet again.

Inshallah.

About the Author

Sarah Dayan Mueller is a native of Brooklyn, New York. She is the author of two novels, including *Home in a Hundred Places* and *Greater than the Still*. Aside from writing her next novel, Sarah enjoys playing piano, ukulele, photography, and traveling the world. She lives in the suburbs of Chicago with her husband, son, and mother.

Made in the USA
Middletown, DE
05 November 2021